Eurydice dipped a foot into the sun-warm spring.

"Sweet ladies of the water," she called. "Would you like to dance at my wedding? Silver-tongued Orpheus will play and sing for his esteemed guests."

"Or-phe-us," the water sighed, its surface rippling. The silt at the bottom bubbled. A pale arm emerged, as strong and slender as a young tree.

"Yes, Orpheus! He will be my husband!" Eurydice dove eagerly into the water and took hold of the hand, helping the Naiad out of the sucking sand.

The nymph clasped the offered hand and crawled up Eurydice, her skin cold and slippery. She darted between Eurydice's legs, her moss-green hair tickling her thighs. She wrapped her arms around the young woman's stomach and surged up to break the surface, her pebbled nipples scraping Eurydice's.

Eurydice gasped, her lungs suddenly tight.

"The wife of Orpheus," the Naiad purred. "We have heard him sing. Is his tongue worth the silver of its sound?" She winked. A clever hand darted between Eurydice's legs, parted her folds.

—from *The Snake and the Lyre* by Annabeth Leong

If you enjoy this collection, you can sign up for a free membership at ForbiddenFiction and discuss it with other readers
and the authors at the *Bi Magic* story page.
at http://forbiddenfiction.com/library/collection/SPC-1.100005
We do our best to proof all our work, but if you spot a text error we missed, please let us know via our website Contact Form
at http://forbiddenfiction.com/contact.

Also recommended...

You may also enjoy these other ForbiddenFiction works:

Wicked Fairy Tales

An anthology of bedtime stories for adults!

Just what kind of happy goes into "happily ever after?" As children, it was enough that Pinocchio got to be a real boy and that Red wasn't eaten by the wolf. As adults, we have a slightly different perspective. Being a real boy means having boy parts, and being eaten by someone big and bad doesn't mean quite the same thing it once did.

What if your fairy godmother wasn't circumspect in what wishes could be granted, or if that dainty little fairy had a much bigger appetite than you might guess?

http://forbiddenfiction.com/library/story/SPC-1.100002

Held in Dreams by Ava Burquette

Elaine is an ordinary human with ordinary dreams, maybe a little shy. At least that's what she tells herself, until she is kidnapped off of a city bus by a strange and charismatic man named Ghalib who has come looking specifically for her. Ghalib definitely isn't ordinary. He isn't even human. He's a Dream Architect, one of the beings who create dreams for humanity. His world is the realm of passion, imagination and nightmares, where humans may be kept as pets, or personal slaves. Elaine will have to do more than let go of her shy, inhibited waking manner. She will have to realize her own dreams. (F/M, F/F, M/M)

http://forbiddenfiction.com/library/story/AB1-1.000093

Bi Magic

Best Bisexual Fantasy Anthology

edited by D.M. Atkins

ForbiddenFiction
www.forbiddenfiction.com

an imprint of

Fantastic Fiction Publishing
www.fantasticfictionpub.com

BI MAGIC
A Forbidden Fiction book

Fantastic Fiction Publishing
Hayward, California

© D.M. Atkins, 2014

CREDITS
Editors: D.M. Atkins, Rylan Hunter, Lon Sarver
Cover Design and Art: Siolnatine
Internal cover art: Siolnatine; Ekhphoto, Marcinski and Curaphotography, Macmoss, Mocker and SpinningAngel, Mimagephotography at Dreamstime
Internal cover design: D.M. Atkins and Siolnatine
Production Editor: Erika L Firanc
Proofreading: Kailin Morgan, XochitLina, Jae Knight, Todd Michaels

SKU: SPC-100005-02 FFP
ISBN: 978-1-62234-178-8

Published in the United States of America

DISCLAIMER

This book is a work of fiction which contains explicit erotic content; it is intended for mature readers. Do not read this if it's not legal for you.

All the characters, locations and events herein are fictional. While elements of existing locations or historical characters or events may be used fictitiously, any resemblance to actual people, places or events is coincidental.

Some stories in this book depict depicts fictional BDSM; it is not intended to be used as an instruction manual. It contains descriptions of erotic acts that may be immoral, illegal, or unsafe. The characters are not models for the Safe, Sane and Consensual forms embraced by most current practitioners of BDSM. The authors take license with the use of BDSM for dramatic effect. Do not take the events in this story as proof of the plausibility or safety of any particular practice.

For everyone who could never decide if they wanted the hot warrior dude or the sexy elf babe.

Contents

Sacrifices to Ecstasy

James L. Wolf

James L. Wolf hails from the busy corner of sex and gender. In other words, he is a Radical Faerie with a degree in Women Studies. He has written hormone and surgery letters to help people transition from one gender to another, and has letters of his own. James lives in the SF Bay Area.

Chapter 1
Not Quite Virginal

When Boci and Seria were chosen to be the virginal sacrifices for Beatitude Solstice, it was quite the scandal in the village of Schoondack Brood. Indeed, there were objections in the rectory itself. After all, neither chosen sacrifice was a virgin. While God was forgiving—he'd committed plenty of mistakes in the creation of the Castora, and so did not judge others harshly—the priests were less willing to make allowances. It was their night of indulgence at risk. Or as Brother Cohose muttered, "If I'm to dip my wick only once a year, then I want an unshorn ram and ewe beneath me."

The debate on whether to accept Boci was lengthy and strictly confined to the parish of Schoondack Brood as an internal matter. That day the priests almost missed the milking and Brother Anik's chickens were left longer in the deepening twilight than usual, inviting a fox dog to harry them for sport, if not actual killing. Brother Yaan summed up the quandary in the first hour of debate. "Boci's case is no mystery," he noted with a sigh. "None of the facts are in dispute. It is our own definition of purity that's at stake."

It was true: Boci's defacement had impacted them all. Boci had been a typical Beatitude Solstice birth: supported by the church until his ascension at thirteen, after which he'd served the parish at need, doing odd jobs around the rectory after laboring in the fields. They'd overseen his soul with discipline and love as was the will of God. And yet a priest—one of their own—had mounted Boci against his will. The incident had shocked and dismayed the village. Even after five years the recollection was sickening. God was love and he was pain, yet according to sacred texts he clearly preferred love... and lawfulness. While priests righteously enjoyed the sweet gifts of both women and men, by church regulation they limited their enjoyment to only one day a year — the Beatitude Solstice itself.

The violation and flaunting of church law had resulted in a disciplinary counsel. A mid-rank inquisitor had been sent from the capital city of Saint Quin Du Mane in the grim aftermath. The culpable priest had been publicly defrocked and tattooed with a criminal mark, though he'd been allowed to keep his sacred organs before banishment. The inquisitor had looked kindly upon Boci, who was found lacking in guilt. The bloody evidence of his assault had been locked in a trunk pending the inquisitor's arrival, and Boci had cried guilelessly when it was presented before him in private council. The inquisitor himself had been quite moved. Why else would he have ceded church funds to settle the matter? It was well done: no one in Schoondack Brood had wanted Boci to end up in the capital, earning a besotted livelihood as a brothel meretrice. Yet despite pity and kindness, Boci was no longer pure by any standard. Or as Brother Cohose grumbled, "He is broken meat, not befitting for us. We should break our fast with the purest and most worthy in the village, not a petulant, pitiful victim without place in the Castora."

"I believe you do Boci great disservice," Brother Tabel argued. "From the moment the inquisition ended, he voluntarily sought purification rituals in every church south of the Zinnwaldite Sea. He's even traveled to remote shrines outside our boundaries to pay tribute. He's attended every service when he's home, praying deep into the night after others abandon the altar..."

"Your point?" Cohose growled, arms crossed.

Brother Tabel glared in return. "Boci's ritualistic purity is unquestionable. As is his demonstrated faith in God. He is pure enough for us. After all, have not each of us felt some measure of sorrow upon the breach of his trust? A measure of responsibility? Of shared guilt?"

The rectory erupted in protest and even High Priest Aldrich had difficulty obtaining order. Yet even after the debate simmered down between opposing factions, none could deny the simple economy of choosing Boci as their male sacrifice. Indeed, since he was already affiliated with the church as a Solstice birth, he might have already served if not for the scandalous violation. Last year's drought and hard winter had taken its toll on the parish purse. They simply did not have excess funds to pay the landowner for a qualified, fully-ascended man from the fields. Boci would serve his place. His ersatz purity was good enough for Schoondack Brood, at least this year. And despite grumbling in the parish and amongst the congregation, that was final.

The objections regarding Seria were intense and well documented on parchment. "She was married!" High Priest Aldrich cried out when the Hierophant sent on his verdict. To further punctuate his point, Aldrich wrote upon three feet of calf skin, mixing his own ink long after moonset.

The return letter from the Hierophant's secretary was brisk in tone and bureaucratic in structure, sharing nothing the high priest had not already known. She bore no child, the Hierophant's secretary wrote in a fine, copperplate hand. Her husband died in His Majesty's service during the Crusade. She was bedded young enough that she was not fertile when he left. She should be fertile now.

"You couldn't possibly know that," Aldrich grumbled when he reached this part of the letter. He turned to his eunuch secretary, Isaiah, and tossed the parchment with less reverence than it would normally deserve. "File that in the hot coals, as please you."

High Priest Aldrich well knew the truth behind the placement—it was obvious. Seria was the bastard daughter of a neighboring duke, a landowner of some acclaim. She had been brought up in Schoondack Brood by her insistent mother, a woman who knew her due. Out of sight but not out of mind—or pocketbook. Her mother had died last year and the duke wished Seria off his hands. He couldn't marry her off to nobility again, after all. Foisting her on the church was a common ploy, but the duke—a notorious spendthrift—refused to pay the common tithing. Sacrificing her to the Beatitude Solstice would earn him coin rather than debt. Yet the priests couldn't help but feel cheated at the idea. The girl had been married.

"I wonder how many favors have been expended to kindle such support in the bureaucracy," Brother Yaan whispered when the official decision was announced to the parish.

"That will be enough. The Hierophant of Saint Quin Du Mane has spoken and his word is final," High Priest Aldrich said as if he agreed with the decision. Doubt and disappointment broiled amongst the brethren. The gossipmongers in Schoondack Brood could speak of nothing else. It was scintillating news.

So when Seria approached the parish gates five days before the Beatitude Solstice, she was hesitant. Isaiah met her and escorted her to the tower. "I don't feel I should be here," she confided to him, her voice quivering. She had known Isaiah since before she could remember: the eunuch was stabbed each week with porcupine quills during church services. As a child, Seria had considered this the most interesting part of the ceremony. She'd always loved how patiently he bled during the Opening Rite.

Isaiah cast her a measured look. "They may wag their tongues now, but the brethren will enjoy your gifts regardless."

Seria bowed her head, breath quickening in her tight throat. Her late husband had showered her with cruel words. He'd pinched her under-ripe flesh until she was bruised from shoulder to knee. Then there was the matter of the perfectly oblong burn marks upon her back, created with a fiery poker. And when she had been beneath him in bed... Seria bit her lip. Her father, whom she had never met in person, had thought the marriage perfect and promised her hand long before she had blossomed into womanhood. It had hurt. Every part of it had hurt. Seria expected this too would hurt. She would be scorned once again for her lacks.

The eunuch escorted her into the tower and up the stairs. They emerged into the upper room where two men stood waiting. Seria recognized both of them: High Priest Aldrich, of course, a familiar face to every churchgoer in the village (in other words, everyone). Beside him stood Boci. They had played together as children before her marriage had separated them, confining her to the landowner's big house. She smiled tentatively at him, uncertain of her reception. He smiled back, his expression quivering with nervous excitement.

The high priest cleared his throat. "Welcome. You are the thirty-first pair that I have personally ushered into this very tower. There have been twenty-nine babies born out of Schoondack Brood parish during that time, nine months after the Beatitude Solstice. Of which you, Boci, were one." He smiled with pride upon Boci, who grinned in response, bouncing on his heels. "Over the next five days we must prepare you with sacred oil and scripture. You may now remove your clothing."

Seria's hands shook as she removed her layered kirtles, linen shirt and finally, breathing shallow with fear, her undergarments. It felt aberrant to do so in front of men. Her husband had never actually asked her to remove her clothes. He'd preferred to rip them off her as she'd screamed. She had learned that if she was to save woven cloth (and hours of backbreaking labor upon the house loom) then she should be naked under the bedclothes to await his stinking, sweating arrival.

Boci, too, gulped as his undergarments pooled around his ankles. He kicked the garments away decisively. He had worked so hard for this privilege; he should be jubilant with fortune. Indeed, he was. He had been recognized as pure, as faithful, as worthy. He'd showed everyone in Schoondack Brood. But now... his bare skin prickled, sensitive to the summer breeze that puffed through the open windows. Boci had been fooled into his own violation, screaming as the priest's hands bruised him. He'd been held down as the bloody pike rammed through his being. The violation had not taken place in a bright, sacred space such as this. But still, Boci shivered.

Aldrich knew it, too. His eye missed nothing as he regarded pair with a sigh. "This Solstice will be special, for purity is not just about virginity but the reclaiming of lost potential. We may translate the word of God but often do not fully understand its meaning. I shall make a point of this when I write my sermon, so that the congregation may contemplate the sacredness of what we do here."

Seria curled her shoulders and stared down, willing herself not to cry. Her late husband had not liked tears. She was not pure, and Aldrich had just stabbed at what little confidence she had. Still, she would go through with this. Where else could she go? The village landowner had little interest in her plight. Women in the fields gossiped that her father would dispose of her in a more thorough fashion if she remained his chattel. Seria shivered. High Priest Aldrich offered her a smile: not a chilly smile, to be certain, but not nearly as warm as the one Boci had received. "Please take your places on the beds."

They turned to face the rest of the room, its function simple. Two beds faced one another, each arrayed with carmine cushions. The intense color would not stand up to washing. Beets and elderberries were grown and harvested every year for the dye. Indeed, everything but the bed frames was new: gathered, threshed, cured and woven by the priests over autumn and the long winter. Boci bit his lip as he settled upon the purified cloth, feeling its softness under his bare buttocks. Seria, her hands hovering over her small breasts, settled on the edge of the opposite bed. She wished she were not the only woman in the room, that she had not been forced upon the parish as an imposition.

Aldrich started with Boci, the clear favorite. He intoned scripture as Isaiah washed him with holy water. At the appropriate moment they gestured for him to roll over. Boci spread his legs, his breath shaking, anticipating the finger. He nearly leapt through the tower roof when the eunuch placed a flat palm on his buttocks. Then, at the correct place in the scripture ("...and Meistro entered Saint Quin in the grove, as God had filled his first prophet with his sacred organ. And thus Meistro and Saint Quin were brothers, as the stallion mounts stallion and as the ram seeks not ewe in the pasture...") an oily finger found his rectum, pushing inside with gentle insistence, then held still. It didn't hurt nearly as much as Boci remembered, but then, it was just a finger, and a blessed one at that. Not a whole penis. Not in the night.

Seria shuddered when they turned to her, leaking an errant tear. She felt numb. Memories of her husband seemed to envelope her whole being, as if he were alive instead of her, rendering her into a ghost-like shadow. The high priest did not break his place in the scripture, though he did pat her shoulder in an awkward manner, as if trying to convey that everything would be fine. Seria shivered in waves as the eunuch washed her. Her quavering grew fierce when it was motioned that she should lie upon her back and spread her legs.

Isaiah leaned over and pressed his mouth upon her font, then brushed it with his tongue.

She gasped in shock, startled out of memory. The tower room was real again, carmine cushions soft beneath her, the smell of incense tickling her nose. Seria stared downward as Isaiah released her and stroked her with oil, opening her like a flower. Oh. She was safe. How astonishing. Seria moaned low in her throat, her eyes upon Isaiah as he continued his work.

"That's enough for today," High Priest Aldrich murmured, eyes bright though his expression was solemn as ever. "Tomorrow we shall open each of you a little bit more."

Newly clad in white robes, the sacrifices joined the remaining thirteen priests for supper in the rectory. Despite underlying apprehension, the priests went out of their way to make the pair feel welcome. Boci joked and laughed with them, enjoying their attention. Feeling more than ever the outsider, Seria picked at boiled mutton and fresh turnip greens from the garden, her appetite absent. Soon each of these men would be atop her. Inside her. It made her stomach curl. Yet... they were so kind. The two serving women—both former sacrifices who had not yet married—certainly seemed to think so. Their Solstice babes were passed from lap to lap after supper. Brother Farragon even attempted to draw Seria out with stories of runaway chickens and the foibles of Solstice children now living in the village. Seria almost forgot herself and laughed out loud, though she swiftly clamped her hand over her mouth. Farragon smiled peaceably at her, his gaze temperate.

Seria relaxed further as Solstice approached. No one mentioned her benighted marriage. No one commented on her slim frame, shy smile, scars or lack of breasts. Either she had blossomed in the last few years or the priests did not think in those terms. She liked to think it was the latter.

Oddly enough, the five day wait was worse for Boci. The tower absolutions had grown intense for him, and he couldn't help but flinch whenever Isaiah penetrated his rectum with fingers and tongue. At those times Boci grew inarguably aroused to the touch, squirming against his erection upon the pure, woven sheets. His reaction was shameful. Boci had lived through his disgrace by believing that nothing about the experience had been pleasurable. Now that he was on the brink of proving his purity—his innocence, even—beyond the shadow of a doubt, and he was... excited.

On the final day of preparation, as High Priest Aldrich droned away in the background, Isaiah leaned over to lick Boci's ear. He whispered, "If I were not clipped, I would enjoy you myself tomorrow."

Boci shuddered. "I'm afraid," he confessed. The eunuch had two fingers inside him, wriggling them in slow arcs. The sensations were overwhelming, making him squirm.

"Mmm. I'm ensuring that you'll be open. It shouldn't hurt too much."

"But... that means I'll enjoy it, too. This ceremony should be about the priests enjoying me."

Isaiah chuckled in his ear. "Boy, when the sun goes down, your purity is to be sacrificed. Don't you understand? The priests will plunge and hammer and make you do things you've always dreamed." He demonstrated with his fingers, plunging deeper into Boci's rectum. Boci gasped and went rigid, his stalk quivering beneath him, his whole body attuned to the touch. Isaiah grinned at this response. "Why do you think I'm opening you, if you are not meant to take pleasure in it, too?"

High Priest Aldrich cleared his throat. "Please attend, gentlemen. The scripture is not just meant for me, you know."

Isaiah cleared his throat, his fingers letting up pressure. "Sorry, Father." Boci continued panting as they finished up, his seed stoppered within him, eyes closed tight. Tomorrow could not come soon enough for him.

Seria, lying upon her bed, witnessed this interplay with a slight frown. She had been listening to the scripture. It had always bothered her — somewhere in the back of her mind — that God did not seem to care for women. God enjoyed the gifts of his male prophet but not his female one (clearly respecting her choice, but still). Seria nibbled on her lip as Isaiah finished up with Boci, trying not to feel envious of him. The priests clearly held affection for Boci. They were sympathetic to his plight and even seemed to respect him. Was it because God's preferences or their own? She expected the Solstice to bring her a child and sever her from her father's patronage... but was there anything else here for her? Or was she a beast of burden, ugly and unloved as she had always been?

The Beatitude Solstice dawned at last, yet the day dawdled by, lackadaisical as grazing sheep. The congregation wasn't even to assemble until mid afternoon, and of course the ritual wouldn't commence until after sunset. Boci chopped wood while Seria weeded the vegetable beds, each lost in their own thoughts while priests disappeared indoors, one by one, to prepare.

Finally, Boci stuck the ax into a stump and collapsed beside Seria. He eyed her curiously as he chewed on a blade of sweet grass. "I always thought I'd be doing this, until I was ruined. But after your marriage I never thought you'd be here with me."

She wiped her brow and continued pulling. "I'm actually glad. Remember when we were children and how all the others thought that it would be horribly shameful to be a sacrifice? Especially the way everyone gossips and speculates about it."

Boci colored. "I never liked gossipers. That's why I always stayed in the rectory."

"Yes," Seria grinned. "But I played with you anyway." She held out a pinky finger. It was their old code, acknowledging the equality of a Beatitude Sacrifice child to a noble bastard. He grinned at this solidarity, hooking his own pinky onto hers. They snapped fingers at each other and laughed. Boci settled back in the grass, reassured.

Seria continued weeding. "Truth to tell, I never thought to be here either. I was so relieved on my wedding day, proud that I'd been given to an honorable, righteous man... that is, until night fell. I was such a fool. Now my baby will bear the Solstice mark and she'll be welcome in any church. Like you, Boci. She'll never be a burden of shame for her father."

"I suppose." Boci plucked a chive stem and chewed on it. Babies were the last thing on his mind. "Do you think it'll hurt?" His buttocks tightened at the thought. He almost envied her femininity: she did not have to contend with such tightness of fit, and the priests could choose which way to enter her. After his rape he had bled for hours...

"We both know the answer to that." Seria paused in her labor. "I think the real question is, do you think it's possible for it to feel good?"

"I... don't know." Boci turned away and resumed his wood chopping.

Chapter 2
Renewal

The Solstice sun dipped in the sky. It was time to wash, to once again be anointed with holy water and oils. "If I'm never purified ever again, I can live with that," Boci whispered in Isaiah's ear. Again, the fresh white robes. Then all that remained was to wait, sequestered in the tower room. The sun was still inches away from the horizon. They languished, occasionally rising to pace. Isaiah sat in an introspective stance without expression, chaperoning as the minutes trickled by. Finally (finally!) bells below heralded that the church ceremony was winding down.

They both jumped as footsteps pounded up the stairs. Breathless priests began filing into the tower room. Aldrich came in last of all, still bedecked in his high-priesthood finery. He nodded to the western window and they all followed his gesture: the sun was perhaps half an inch away from the horizon. "Brother Yaan, light the incense. Brother Tabel, the chimes. Brother Farragon, you may proceed to disrobe. You pulled the shortest straw, so take your pick first."

Seria watched, transfixed in the bed, as priests assembled themselves. She felt as if she were viewing two different images spread before her. On the one hand, the brethren purified, chanted, chimed and anointed one another with graceful, practiced moves. Yet she also saw them as stallions: stamping hooves and rolling eyes, blowing out their breath as if they were about to bolt. Seria blinked. Though the brethren clearly attempted to stay focused on the ritual, their eyes flickered upon Boci and Seria with muted excitement.

As each priest disrobed, Boci eyed their roots, his lips spread in fascination. So many variations in one room: some were abbreviated, some small, or hooked, or thick. He watched others elongate even as they hardened. High Priest Aldrich, he discovered, was both very thick and lengthy, even at half mast. Boci tried to catch Seria's eye to see what she thought, but a naked priest had wandered between them, cutting off contact. The sun was now almost over the horizon, more than halfway down.

"Farragon, make your pick and take your stance," Aldrich intoned. Farragon's root turned out to be stocky and set at an odd angle, so Boci wasn't at all unhappy when he swung himself onto Seria's bed.

His own first turned out to be Kirr, the youngest of the brethren, skinny and freckled. Boci blinked as he observed the youth's awkward uncertainty. Perhaps Kirr was a virgin? If so, he was the only one in the room. Brother Cohose chuckled at Kirr's hesitation. "Ask the sacrifice to place his feet upon your shoulders, or you can have him roll over."

"Um, roll over. Please?" Kirr squeaked.

Boci did so and gasped as the man's oiled, blessed penis knocked against his buttocks. The young priest froze there, both hand on Boci's waist, waiting to thrust inside. They both glanced at the window, where the sun sank ever so slowly behind the mountain.

Seria couldn't breathe with Farragon atop her. He didn't settle his weight on her, that wasn't the problem. He was between her legs, his erect organ pressed upon her, waiting to enter. He was breathing hard. While she knew he had an affable nature—a kind soul who took pleasure in composting and cooking the parish breakfast—he was also a man who had complete power over her.

It was intolerable, yet she must endure this sundering. All her muscles were knotted with tension. She squeezed her eyes shut. Soon the sun would set and he would thrust inside her. Then she would be no one. She would sink her soul into the walls for escape, yet she would be hit and slapped even as she tried to leave her body.

Fourteen priests, two sacrifices and a eunuch watched the western window. An occasional cough, a cleared throat. Not even High Priest Aldrich chose to fill the time with scripture, his penis hard as mountain granite, his hands held tight behind his back. He would go last after his charges had expended themselves, breaking their fast. He could wait the longest.

Brother Tabel gripped the chimes hard as he stared into the last sliver of sun. To chime to early would mar the ceremony. One legendary Beatitude Solstice — in a different village, not Schoondack Brood — the ritual had been cancelled for a whole five years after the priests set upon the sacrifices early, when the sun still watched them. To be disciplined for such a lapse would be unbearable. The sliver slipped down, down.... It was down. Tabel chimed.

Boci gasped as Kirr entered him, filling him so hard with such force that he cried out. The young priest had awaited this night for so long; blood was rushing in his ears, sheer pleasure as he pumped. Boci bore the brunt of it, clawing at the carmine cushions in anguish. Kirr gasped with laughter above him and Boci felt a twinge of dislike for the man who caused him such pain... save that his laughter was of innocent joy, not cruel mockery. Kirr did not mean to cause him harm, he was just a young man with the penis of a bull. Boci gasped like a fish, thrust into the bed as if speared. The young priest cried out and collapsed atop him. Sweetness filled Boci, his limbs loosened from exercise. He'd done it.

Kirr rolled off him, clearly overcome with his triumph. "I did it!" he cried out. The other priests shot him quelling glances, their roots quivering with dammed seed. "I did it," the young priest whispered again as he hugged himself. But Boci was immediately rolled over and his feet were placed upon the shoulders of Brother Tabel, his anus wet and open as Tabel positioned himself. For Boci, the night had just begun.

Across the room, Seria found herself pleasantly surprised. Faraggon was compassionate, though not at all timid. His small girth fit inside of her, and the penetration lacked the sharp pain she associated with being soused cold and raw. Intrigued, she reached around and grabbed his back, pressing him down upon her, inside her. He grinned in response, his languid pace almost an outright compliment. But finally he arched his back and gasped, then leaned his whole weight upon her to kiss her on the mouth. She accepted the kiss and licked her lips with regret as he pulled out.

Then another man set upon her, and she gasped, feeling the differences immediately. This priest, Yaan, was like clockwork, pulling in and out at a set pace, his narrow face contorted with concentration.

Not sweet... but not frightening, either. Seria discovered, to her shock, that she was having an exceptional time.

Boci moaned as Brother Tabel thrust inside him. This time consummation didn't hurt nearly as much. He remembered that Tabel had spoken on his behalf during the inquest. The man had fought for him, if only with words. Boci touched his face curiously and Tabel gasped in reaction.

Boci found himself moving in time with the priest. It felt so intimate. Intimate and a little frightening, to match rhythm and breath, as if their souls were aligned with their bodies. Boci decided he liked the feeling. It was like diving into a sulfur spring: deep and warm, effervescent and welcoming. Tabel reached down and grazed Boci's root with his knuckles, sending him into the aether. His seed spilled between their undulating bodies even as Tabel burst within him, ripe as a black plum. Oh, but now Boci wanted more. More, more, more...

The stars appeared before all thirteen priests had taken their first dip — six in Boci, seven in Seria. High Priest Aldrich had watched them all with fatherly grace. His penis was so prodigious — solid as a grindstone and set at an ascendant angle — that Boci quelled at the sight of it, shivering with excitement. Which sacrifice would Aldrich chose? Seria lay boneless upon her bed, the same question rising within her mind like a bubble rising from a lake bottom. She was too relaxed to mind his size, but wondered what his manner would be like. The other priests, who had formed an irregular circle around the beds to await their leader's release, fell silent.

Aldrich glanced from one bed to the other, then seemed to reach a conclusion. He gestured to the priests at either end. "Push the beds together."

Boci and Seria eyed one another with bewilderment as their beds were jostled together foot-to-foot. Would he ask them to fornicate with one another? That would be blasphemous. Aldrich gestured to them. "Each of you stand and lean over your own bed, with your backs facing me. Stand side by side, close enough to touch."

The brethren murmured at this but none sought to intervene. Boci and Seria each followed his directions shakily, uncertain of what was to come. High Priest Aldrich poured oil over his hands and contemplated the two buttocks spread below him, male and female genitals distinctly marking one sacrifice from the other. Seria and Boci, side by side, touched hands and waited.

Then Seria cried out as Aldrich entered her civet, pumping her with the speed and rigidity of a waterwheel pump. Only one oiled hand gripped her belly to secure her. Beside her Boci gasped and moaned, writhing. What was Aldrich doing with his left hand?

Boci had never had so many fingers up his rectum; the previous purification ritual had been three at most. Now Aldrich seemed to be pushing into him with force, his thumb tucked against his palm. Boci cried out as the man pushed his whole hand inside. Oh, but that was tight. It was tight. Boci spilled across the bedsheets, but the pressure did not cease.

Then he gasped as the hand pulled out, and Seria simultaneously groaned, let loose. Boci had no time to breathe before he was entered by that tremendous, breathtaking penis. He groaned under the weight of it. Aldrich's hand held him in place, slippery with cast-off from his rectum. Now Seria screeched as the man's right hand found her opening, already wet and oiled, and pushed inside her with the same pressure he'd used on Boci. She hadn't known this was even possible. She hadn't known. It hurt but in the best way possible. Seria was weightless, free from the pull of the Castora. Her body was barely moving, still leaning over the bed in the same position. But her soul was flying as his hand rooted within her like an oak tree. It was nothing like being a ghostly shadow... more like how a chickadee must feel in the woods. Seria grinned, savoring her ability to fly.

An eternity later, the darkness now complete save for the bright candles lighting the tower, Aldrich stood back and held up his hands — each replete with bodily fluids: one male, one female. "The first rite is complete."

"The first rite is complete," the brethren intoned. The beds were pushed apart and cheerful murmuring commenced as fragrant dishes and chalices were passed about. Special food and drink was part of this night: seeds ground to oily paste and stuffed inside merchant-supplied dates, miniature breads shaped like genitalia, apple slices topped with honeycomb, and fried balls of meat from the testicles of a bull. Ample mead had been brewed by Brother Anik. Fourteen priests and one eunuch partook without reservation, determined to enjoy their one night of true hedonism to the utmost.

They made sure Boci and Seria had their shares as well. Seria drank mead with secret pleasure, as the forbidden drink was designated for men. Boci's anus hurt and he ate absently, worrying that he was bleeding all over the sheets. He asked Tabel if it were so. Tabel examined him with goodwill, declaring him whole if widely stretched. "You'll be feeling this night for days to come," he noted with a laugh. "But Seria will feel it for nine months, so count yourself lucky."

The second rite was far more relaxed than the first. The priests were not so intent upon release now that they'd broken their fast. Even Isaiah partook, his fingers cunning though his crippled genitals remained flaccid. They had all night to indulge in every variation afforded them by their sacrifices.

Seria felt as if she were glowing like a candle in the dark. Her late husband had treated her like chattel and she had believed him, understanding herself as lacking in value. Now the priests planted value within her. Each part of her was made sacred by their attention. Her benighted breasts were pushed together by Brother Anik: he mounted atop her and vigorously fountered the cleft they formed. She squealed as seed struck her chin, delighted that her body could squeeze juice from reddened fruit.

Still reeling with ecstasy, she gasped when Brother Farragon placed his penis upon her lips. Seria watched him for clues, uncertain. His expression was mild and gentle as always, his hands caressing her hair lovingly. She was safe with him. Emboldened, she opened her mouth to accept him. "There you go," he murmured as he pushed within her. "Lips over your teeth, like that."

Seria discovered that she loved the taste of him; more than that, she loved the trust he placed in her. She grew attuned with each thrust until she was moving in time with him, taking him inside her. In her enthusiasm Seria forgot about her teeth. Brother Farragon chuckled through his gasps. Then he threw his head back, moaning as Seria drank of him. She looked up and discovered he had tears in his eyes. "So beautiful," he murmured. She believed him. Her body was a church, beautiful and holy, and they worshiped within her.

Across the room Boci had passed through all emotions. Pain and pleasure were one. He was a chasm, his mouth and anus open without reprieve, his penis licked and slapped as he was milked of seed. It wouldn't end. He wasn't sure he wanted it to. He didn't know who he was anymore, his soul floating above his head. Boci couldn't figure out if this was good or bad, and indeed his ability to think had been shorn from him. But he took penises freely, feeling them as if they were extensions of the priest's souls penetrating his own.

As the church bells chimed the third hour, Boci saw... oh. Oh, lord. He saw the infinite. God stood before him. Without decorum, God placed an enormous hand upon his brow (ignoring the priest in his mouth) and pushed his fingers inside. Boci accepted him readily, receptive to his will. Abruptly, Boci felt his own intellect reenter his body. It seemed larger, as if it had unfurled above his prone form and was now twice the size.

God smiled upon him. "You will be my priest and I will accept your services unto me."

"Yesh, lor'," Boci gasped through the priest's penis.

God paused, as if waiting. The priest impaling Boci from behind loosened his seed and pulled free. The priest in his mouth pulled out as well, growling as Boci's teeth grazed him. God climbed atop the bed, his heavenly form solidifying. Boci glanced about the tower room, wondering if the others saw what he did. No... the priests were chattering and laughing with one another. Brother Kirr was even on his knees, playing his tongue over Brother Yaan's root. Seria was surrounded by men on all sides. None seemed aware of their visitor.

Boci glanced over his shoulder, nervous once again, but God smiled upon him benignly. "Do you trust me?" he whispered in his ear. "I will cause pain, you know. All your life I will cause you pain. That is my nature."

"Take me, lord. I'm yours."

God's penis was regal, far larger than Boci's own body. The ethereal root filled not just his anus but all of him, up to the top of his skull. Yet despite the warning, Boci felt only love. God was inside him, as he had once filled his first prophet, as it was written in scripture. Then God began thrusting and all other thoughts fled Boci's mind. He was filled with God. The tower grew silent as priests stared. He was being bucked and rocked on the bed, and Boci knew all of a sudden that while they did not see the Lord, they understood the beatitude of what was happening. God grabbed his hair and Boci threw his head back, groaning as God came within him. Boci screamed as the seed of God filled his skull. It trickled through his body, blinding as the sun.

Boci lolled on the bed, emptied. Reverently, High Priest Aldrich clasped his hands around his own testicles, symbolizing the single testicle that God had cut from his being to create the Castora. The other priests did the same. Seria, watching from the other bed, didn't know what was happening. Why had Boci cried out? He had acted like a man from the village, who occasionally fell upon the ground shaking, mindless with angry ghosts. Yet the priests acted like something enormous had just occurred.

Licking his lips with apprehension, Brother Tabel lay beside Boci and began petting his hair. "Are you whole?"

Boci grinned up at him, tears streaking down his face. "I am now." He leaned over and kissed Tabel, his tongue slipping inside his mouth. Tabel responded, his body tightening once again. When Tabel mounted him, Boci discovered that penetration had become nothing but pleasure. He'd been accepted. His place in the Castora was secure: he need not worry about fitting in, not ever again. Boci shook his head like a cantering colt, laughing as Tabel fulfilled him.

As the night wound down, Seria discovered not God but herself. Her own preferences surprised her. To her excitement she crested many times over the course of the night. Fingers were wonderful and so were tongues. Every part of her was open to pleasure, even her anus, and she gasped under the pressure of a man within her rectum. It seemed filthy. It was filthy! She cried out as if she were in heat, writhing under the absolute intensity. Seria's muscles were shaking and exhausted, yet she was willing to take another man, and another, and another. Then Brother Anik mounted her rear while she sat straddled atop the enormous penis of High Priest Aldrich... and her pleasure knew no bounds, filling her. She screamed, her voice hoarse as she reached her zenith, then reached it again in rapid succession.

Less than an hour before dawn, High Priest Aldrich ceased planting his seed to ready the final rite. He clapped his hands when the church bells rang five, the light growing brighter by the minute. Priests reluctantly clambered off sacrificial beds, though those locked in consummation dared a few last humps. Only Cohose, atop Boci, managed a final climax. Then the sacrifices were abandoned as the priests began final rounds of absolution with oil and holy water.

After a time, Seria rolled over to contemplate Boci. It seemed to her that he was changed; he was smiling widely though tears still rolled down his cheeks and into his ears. "Boci? What happened?"

"God says I'm to be a priest!" he whispered back, grinning with awe.

"Oh. Well, I'm to be a mother," Seria couldn't help but point out. God praised mothers at least, though he seemed disinclined to interact with them much. Perhaps it was for the best. She rather thought she knew her own mind at this point. She wondered, absently, if she would bear a girl or boy. Or... twins tended to run in her family. Seria almost groaned at the thought. Her civet ached enough as it was!

Then it was their turn to be blessed. First Boci was called to stand, his body washed down with holy water, his brow anointed. He shivered at the holy touch. God had chosen him. He'd been resurrected and there was no going back. The priests smothered him in crimson robes and wrapped him tight with a belt of blackberry briars. Boci bowed his head in gentle acceptance as the thorns drew blood.

Though Seria was washed and similarly robed, she did not receive a thorny binding. Instead she was belted with a fence-like bodice made from cut willow branches. It reached past her waist and above her breasts. She bore the awkward bodice without concern, her body aching pleasantly. She touched the willow branches and grinned outright. Oh, but she would love her baby. She already did.

The sun rose over the rim of the Castora. It was the face of God lighting upon Schoondack Brood. Villagers stirred from their beds, their lives blessed by the sacrifices of purity. Within the tower, all turned their faces to the sun. They were bathing in auroral light.

"And now we are absolved," High Priest Aldrich intoned, his voice ringing in the silence.

"And now we are absolved," they echoed as one.

If you enjoyed this story, you can discuss it with other readers
and the author at the *Sacrifices to Ecstasy* **story page**
at http://forbiddenfiction.com/library/story/JLW-1.000109.

The Thief's Dungeon

Madeleine Swann

Madeleine Swann has had short stories published in The *Big Book of Bizarro*, Analogpress.net and ForbiddenFiction.com and writes in various forms from her home in deepest, darkest Essex, England. She has also had articles published in various magazines including *Bizarre*, ranging in topic from church restorations to the toe wrestling championships, and performs as part of comedy group Braintree Ways.

The Thief's Dungeon

"Are you certain nobody has died in here?" Marella wrinkled her nose.

"My Lady's quite safe, the stop-over rooms have been carefully chosen and prepared," soothed her lady-in-waiting, a note of apology in her rasping voice. The cobwebs stretching over the empty spaces of the sparse, darkening walls and the heavy dust on the wooden floorboards smelled like the attic in Marella's country estate; she checked herself, former country estate. The light from a candle lantern on the only desk flickered over thick ceiling beams and deepened the shadows in the corners. Her excitement at a new married life had faded with this inn room. She was to be married in a week to a rich man in a beautiful part of the country and all she wanted was her parents. She scowled at the thought of more travelling the next day.

"Oh, please don't fret, Elly," Marella sighed, her shoulders sagging, "I shan't complain further, though the smell is most odd. I simply thought a Lord and his son could have organized a better place to stay, no matter how temporary."

The worry in her servant's lined face softened as she guided her charge to the bed. "Have a seat, my love, and I'll give that hair of yours a good comb."

The creaking and clacking of hooves and carriages drifted through the open window as ostlers groomed horses and guests arrived and left for the night, and below them the screech of a cockatrice was followed by angry rebukes. "That made you jump," chuckled Elly, and Marella tried to smile despite a small sourness at being laughed at. She scolded herself; Elly had always been good to her.

Marella studied the bedcover's gold and moth-eaten grey trim as the wooden teeth were pulled through her hair. She idly wished the rest of her was as beautiful as her brown locks. Her features were pleasing but she knew they lacked something, the thing that made men excited. She had always felt indistinct; attractive but not the first to be noticed. She had imagined her future husband to have wanted her immediately, to stroke her skin and lift her skirts in secret, to sneak the top of her dress down and tug gently at her nipples, but Mervil had done little more than smile awkwardly on his visit. When she tried to imagine the moment she would reach beneath his starched uniform to find his erection she was met with a worrying vagueness.

Once dressed in her long white nightgown, she assured Elly she would sleep better alone. "If my Lady is certain, I will take my leave. But should you need me I will be in the small room at the end of the hall," she added quickly.

"Elly, I promise I'll be well," assured Marella, and Elly left with a relief so subtle most people wouldn't have noticed. Marella knew the servant would spend the night shut in her room, inhaling deeply from a long pipe billowing acrid smoke and lying for hours in a daze.

Alone, Marella went to the open window. Night had fallen and the laughter and conversation from the inn downstairs and town square sounded so vital. Dragons flapped their leathery wings high overhead, their masters guiding them towards places of action, while harpies circled the rooftops looking for scraps. After staring blankly at the glow of the market fire lamps in the distance, Marella sat in the wooden chair and sighed as deeply as a hound. Every moment of her days had been carefully supervised by school governesses, or Elly, or her parents. Marella studied her hands. A thought erupted in her head; every moment until *now*. Marella's next years would be spent carefully following her marital duty, but right now she was alone.

She rose again to observe what she could of outside. Her hands shaking, she grabbed her hooded cloak and scurried from the room, picturing herself safe in bed as Elly trundled in with breakfast in the morning. Adrenaline pounded through her blood with each step she took. She kept the hood pulled down low and the material wrapped tightly around her so people wouldn't see she was a woman travelling alone.

The inn courtyard was empty; light and the sounds of revelry streamed from the bar window. A dragon emitted a low snort from its stable, a plume of smoke drifting from its nostrils, and Marella flinched like a child caught in the act of destruction. She hurried onto the cobbled streets and kept her head down. Her travelling sandals were no protection against the night air but after a moment's trek she felt the heat from the town's heart. Figures bustled past her unseeingly and wood-smoke curled in her nostrils from fires in short metal stands. Some traders were beginning to pack up their stalls but plenty more were still hollering for passers-by to purchase fragrant spices, magic ingredients, and multi-coloured dragon treats.

Marella swallowed her uncertainty as she joined a small crowd watching a busker, a slender young magician in smart breeches tracing fire from his hands through the night sky and transforming a mouse into a butterfly. The watchers were wide-eyed, cheering him on, but Marella noticed the way the mothers held on to their children a little too tightly. Further up the road, a caged manticore swiped his lion claws and jabbed his black scorpion tail through iron bars, his wrinkled human head gnashing its yellowed teeth.

Marella's shoulder was roughly knocked. The surrounding crowds eyed her with suspicion when she cried out in a feminine voice and Marella realised how exposed she was. Her excitement draining, she turned sharply back for the inn. Following a curve in the road, she found herself before an unfamiliar ale-house filled with toothless women and barrel-shaped men. Panic flamed in her chest and fingers but she walked with striding steps to appear as though she knew her destination. Again she was met by a wrong turning and couldn't refrain from sobbing.

The eyes glancing her way became more frequent and she broke into a run past stray dogs and bored horses. A tethered cockatrice snapped its rooster's beak at her, its dragon claws scraping at the cobbles. A harpy swooped down to snatch a piece of hog meat and clipped her back with its claws. Marella cried out, her lungs struggling to fill with air. Her breath came shorter and sharper until her vision blurred and she felt as though she drifted from her body. On she ran, blindly, people openly staring at her terror, then everything went grey.

"It's waking up," growled a deep voice.

"No it's not, keep quiet or it'll start screaming."

Marella tried to stand and found herself stuck. "You were right.

Oi," rasped a voice, and Marella's eyes opened wide to see a dank stone cell lit by a weak candle lantern, with a tiny barred window at the top of a high ceiling. The shadows crept up the walls and prowled in the corners while clumps of straw lay filthily around her. Two grotesque figures with stooped backs and missing teeth leered at her prone body. "Gruel at sundown and His Lordship's girly son will see you later."

"You can't say that," said the other, his red eyes opening wide.

"Why not? It's true. His Lordship's not around to hear it. Not 'til next month anyway."

"His girly son is Lordship 'til his father returns and don't you forget it. We'll be on the menu if you ain't careful. What if she says something?" He pointed at Marella, who shook her head desperately.

The original speaker sighed in defeat. "Come on Davran, I'm gasping. Don't know why he doesn't just let it sit in darkness at least. His Lordship would have served her up by now," he muttered as they shuffled out, closing the heavy wooden door and pulling fast the metal locks.

Marella tugged at the metal cuffs clasping her wrists, pulling with her body weight at the long chains on the wall. She struggled to maintain her breathing as her chest tightened. Lowering her head, she tried to recall Elly's soothing voice until her muscles relaxed. Calmer, she surveyed her surroundings and immediately felt her skin flame again. Several more cuffs and chains hung from the stone bricks, the grizzled bones of skeletons pulling at them in vain. One cuff, she noticed sickly, held a meaty arm. It had been cut messily with a serrated knife near the shoulder.

"Somebody! There's been a mistake! Please, somebody!" wailed Marella, scrabbling for the door and falling short. Wildly she pulled again and again until realisation sank in; she wasn't getting out. She curled into a sobbing ball on the stone floor. When she was still, she lifted her cheek from the burning cold stone and shakily gathered what she could of the straw, forming it into a nest. As she drifted into sleep, bolts were noisily pulled back and the door thrust wide. Framed by the glowing light from the torches in the passageway was a bulky beast with wild fur, but as he stepped nearer she saw he was a young man with dark knotted hair to his chin. Though he wore common breeches his top half was wrapped in animal pelt. The two guards beside him bowed in deference, casting each other an irreverent glance as they shuffled away.

The young man knelt down beside her, Marella noticing he was more slender than the furs had made him appear. An insecurity and delicacy in the way his brown eyes flicked over her undermined the set of his jaw.

"You're making a lot of noise," he stated simply. Marella's voice sank to the bottom of her throat. "Not very bright for a person caught spying."

"Spying?" Marella spluttered, her voice found.

"Yes," he replied, his expression one of triumphant outrage. "Tyro thinks I wouldn't suspect a tart dressed as a high born lady and doesn't think to send accompaniment with her? His senses are dulled!"

"No, no," Marella shook her head desperately. He caught her hair in his hand and she flinched. He released her, seeming to regret his harshness. He pursed his lips, seeming uncertain of what to do next.

"What did he offer you?" he asked in a low voice. Marella didn't reply. He studied her curiously, the way an artist studies a painting. His breath was warm against her skin. Marella felt her nipples harden and a dampness grow between her legs. "I'll return tomorrow," he warned, "I expect information then." He slammed the door and pulled fast the bolts, and all the heat was sucked from the room.

Red welts appeared on Marella's wrists. When the sun rose through the tiny barred window she hungrily devoured her bowl of gruel and thought of last night's visitor. She envisioned beating him, gaining the key and removing the fur around his shoulders to feel the flesh underneath. Confused, she forced herself to think of beating him once more but her thoughts were beyond control. Eventually she sank to the ground and tried to think of nothing, concentrating on the cold stone floor, but the visions worsened. She longed for warmth and his skin with its musky hint of sweat and animal pelt.

When darkness again drew the shadows close one of the guards relit her candle lantern. The second grabbed her wrists with calloused hands and pulled her to her feet. The smell of him made her think of swamps and bogs and she turned her face as much as she could while he fixed her arms and ankles with iron grips against the wall. She stood helplessly, feet splayed and arms at her side, fixing her hatred on the two figures as they chuckled their way out of the cell.

She heard her own intake of breath when the fur-covered man again entered the room. He held himself forcibly upright, a tiny light of doubt in the back of his eyes. "Surely you've had enough of this place by now?" He asked her, almost pleading. He attempted to harden his eyes, "I could have you killed."

"I don't know what it is you want me to say," she said, her voice cracking strangely.

His shoulders sagged.

"So you wish to remain here with no food, no light?" She shook her head, forcing herself to hold back a sob. "The thieves in this city run on a delicate balance. They are looking to me to keep things running smoothly," he explained, "if the balance is disturbed, if someone gets greedy and sends in spies, there would be anarchy. I can't let that happen, my life would not be worth living," he bellowed, oozing raw fear and frustration. He caught himself and swallowed, his voice softening "So you see I can't let anyone off. We have to be seen to uphold the law at all times. With my father away I'm the one in charge. It's expected," he added, barely above a whisper.

Tears now coursed freely down Marella's cheeks. "But I don't know what you're talking about," she insisted, "I ran away from my minder. Oh God, why did I do that?" Through her watery eyes she saw him falter, a furrow in his brow. When he spoke again his voice had softened.

"We must get to the truth of things," he mumbled, deflated. He reached out a hand like someone reaching for comfort. His finger-tips brushed her robe and she could smell the scent she had waited for, skin and fur and sweat. Marella's muscles twitched and he glanced up to read her expression. When he saw no fear, he reached inside to stroke the bare skin of her stomach. Marella sighed softly, the iron cuffs holding her immobile as a lover's restraint.

His touch traced a line down to her pelvis. He reached behind her and slowly untied the lace of her robe, her heartbeat increasing with each tug until the material fell to the ground, exposing her to the cool air. Marella breathed in deeply; her fear churned and mixed with other senses becoming something new, something that warmed her lips and toes and blood and made her lower parts tingle. He paused a moment before completing his journey, then brushed his fingers against her private lips.

Marella sighed softly; male hands had never reached for her there. Her cheeks flushed with shame, she knew he would never believe her to be a high born lady with the wetness slick on her. With a pleased look he knelt down and ran an experimental finger along her private lips. His eyes were black when he raised them to hers and Marella's mouth opened slightly as his middle finger investigated her inside. Her breath slid out in a long moan and her pelvis bucked as he curled his digit forward, brushing against a spot that ignited her whole body.

He leaned forwards until his lips touched her private ones. A jolt ran through her; she had heard the coarse whispers of servants and experienced late night rubbings with experimental girls, but had never seen a person's mouth join to someone in such an odd way. She jerked her limbs against the metal clamps but her body was held fast. She watched him as his tongue flicked over the spot she knew brought pleasure, but his closeness embarrassed her so greatly she doubted the shuddering would come. His finger slid back and forth inside as his tongue sent ripples of heat running through her and, to her surprise, she felt the fire begin to build. Her breathing came quick and she rolled her hips with him. "Were you sent here?" he asked in a low voice.

"No," she breathed, still moving with him. He pulled his mouth away.

"I won't harm you, but I must know." His expression was determined and Marella's flame began to recede. "I'll carry on if you admit it."

"Yes," she whispered, desperate for his lips to ease her discomfort. "Yes, I was sent." He placed his mouth back over her and the flame resurged. "Oh, God," she called, and the fire shot from her private lips through her entire body, shaking and engulfing her.

He rose to full height above her and discarded his breeches. Curiously she gazed downwards and was immediately flooded with nerves when she saw him stroking his shaft. The tip was so red and engorged it made her think of angry faces, but she forced her shock down and lowered her eyes to watch and to learn. Her own body tingled when she saw the pleasure it brought him, his sighing and half-closed eyes. Her lower muscles pulsed as though she could already feel him inside. He frowned with concentration as he reached behind her to tilt her pelvis, and she pursed her lips anxiously.

His eyes held hers with concern but his breathing became quick and his cheeks flushed with eagerness. Marella's body tightened when she felt his erection press against her opening. She closed her eyes and thought of a calm place deep inside her, yelping as the tip pushed in. Despite her readiness it had felt as forceful as a jousting stick. He paused, and she opened her eyes cautiously as the pain subsided. He pushed further, gently, until his entire expression softened, the redness covering his face and his lips parting as Marella instinctively tensed herself.

He made several slow, smooth strokes deep inside and the sensation changed for Marella. Tingling replaced the fire and a burst of pleasure prickled her skin. "Oh," she moaned in surprise. He felt the new ease and moved with more confidence, the tip of him stroking her furthermost point. She encouraged him by groaning and nestling her lips through his hair to kiss the lobe of his ear, breathing in his feral scent of fur and forests. He placed his mouth over her neck and nipped gently, sending a spark down to where they joined. She responded by squeezing his shaft tightly and smiled when she felt him grow harder.

He leaned back to survey her face. He became more vigorous, gripping onto her tightly until he moaned his longest and loudest, his eyes pressed closed. She felt a hot rush inside her and knew it must be his seed. His shaft pulsed and withered and they were a single statue for a time, until she tried to embrace him. He felt her pull at her restraints and took a key from his discarded breeches, freeing her from the locks. She pulled at her arms to encourage her blood circulation, wiggling her fingers and toes. He lay back on her straw bed, motioning for her to join him.

"It's Markus," he said. "My name," he added when Marella grunted in confusion.

"Oh," she squealed as she curled into him, embarrassed. "Mine's Marella." She lay her head down against his chest hair and felt him sigh. "What will you do now?" she asked, her mind drifting to his soft warm bed and a place she could sleep next to him forever. Markus sat up, his eyes hard with suspicion. She was too shocked to respond as he pulled himself away from her, the wetness of their encounter leaking onto her open robe. She watched, unable to call after him or move to reach for him as he angrily slammed the door. She placed a hand over her mouth as a sob escaped it. She curled into a ball and fell into an uncomfortable, feverish sleep.

The night passed in discomfort until the rising sun from the top window prised open her eyes. She thought of everyone she had left behind and an eerie calmness pacified her. Her thoughts of freedom mixed with the sensation of Markus on her skin. She was certain he didn't want her to be trapped. As her body relaxed, her daydreams of being freed mixed with the memory of his fingertips and tongue. Torrents of heat travelled down her skin to her inner thighs and on to her still wet private lips. The sensation made her feel as though he was somehow still with her.

Rolling onto her back on the straw she cast her thoughts to a night at a neighboring castle. The Lord was a friend of her parents and she had shared the daughter's room for the night. While the parents sipped goblets of wine in the Great Hall and laughed raucously at their wilder days, Sillian had recounted fevered rumors and whisperings from older girls to Marella, rumors of secret pleasurable parts on the body that adults were unaware of. With eyes like burning coals she had convinced Marella they ought to discover it for themselves.

Marella had obediently lain back on the shared bed. Sillian's skin was luminescent in the candlelight, though Marella knew her memory had varnished her with extra sparkle. Her dark hair was pushed behind her ears and her fingers had nervously lifted Marella's white night-dress. When Marella's already dampened private lips had been exposed, the girl's eyes had met as they exchanged giggles. Sillian had breathed in deeply and gestured for them to be serious. "It is somewhere about here," she muttered as her forefinger had circled the air above the other girl's skin.

Marella had opened her mouth in surprise when Sillian's digit landed on the spot at the top of her private lips, where a circle of flesh twitched and swelled. "Here, I found it," Sillian had whispered.

Their parents in The Great Hall had no longer seemed so far away to Marella, but she tried to banish all thoughts of them.

The candle had sputtered for a moment and plunged them into darkness for the briefest of seconds. It had been enough for Marella to consider pulling away but Sillian was more determined, one finger circling over the twitching nub and the other hand holding Marella's thigh. The concentration on the other girl's face had quietened Marella and she waited to feel the thing she was meant to, laying back and counting the patterns on the ceiling. Somewhere around the fourth pattern the intensity of the rubbing had increased and Marella looked up at Sillian, whose mouth had formed a triumphant smile.

"It's so odd," Marella had breathed as dizziness swam in her head. Her hips had bucked gently against Sillian's fingertip, the point where their flesh met growing hotter.

"You'll feel it soon," Sillian had promised with a low voice.

Marella had felt something building like logs being heaped on a fire. It had grown and sparked from the nub to her fingertips and toes until it was exploding in a rush throughout her body, flooding her head. "Oh, oh, oh," she moaned as her brow furrowed and her gaze held fast onto Sillian's.

Lying on the straw, Marella could almost feel Sillian's breath on her thighs as her own fingertip circled the hardening nodule. The tingling spread outwards to her fingertips until it poured through her body and pulsed inside her head. Arching her back, she moaned deeply until the waves calmed. She melted into the ground and closed her eyes, expecting to fall asleep at last.

The bang of the door opening jolted her upright. All of her senses screamed at once, but shame shouted the loudest. The two guards snickered as one strode forwards to grab her by the wrist and pull her up. Marella didn't dare speak, her cheeks burning. Holding her breath against the bog stench she desperately matched their long strides through the dank dungeon corridors lined with smoking torch flames. Upwards they went on an incline until they emerged into a small, plain room, the strong rays of natural light making her eyes water. The sounds of market traders setting up their wares penetrated the walls. Markus stood in the middle of the room. He smiled when he saw her, but his eyes were forlorn. The guards left them alone, muttering between themselves.

"We received a letter this morning. My father is returning sooner than expected. He will have you killed," he whispered when the footsteps had dwindled. A shard of panic cut through Marella. "No, I—I'm letting you go. In secret of course," he explained hurriedly. The fear thawed from Marella's heart and the tension poured from her muscles, and she ached. She clasped her hands to her mouth and laughed with relief before noticing Markus' sadness.

He furnished her with a heavy new travelling cloak hanging from the wall. "Nobody will be able to tell if you're human in this let alone if you're male or female, and I've drawn you a map," he muttered, handing her a torn piece of scroll. His kindness refreshed the water obscuring her vision. "You must promise you'll leave here immediately, or you might be in danger," he said.

"Yes, of course," she agreed, refraining from mentioning her travelling party. A silence stretched before them until they stood on two sides of a great chasm. Eyes down, Markus embraced her tightly. She breathed in his feral scent for the last time and stepped through the door.

The morning was bright and the cobbled streets were empty of townsfolk. Though it was winter the skies were as blue as spring and the banter of merchants had already begun. The pull of Markus lessened slightly as she hurried past assembling market stalls and shopkeepers opening their doors. A young shepherd was unsuccessfully guiding a flock of sheep—some green, some pink, some purple and some blue—with a crook and exasperated shouts. Marella opened Markus' map and stopped still where she was, "I'll always remember," he promised underneath the directions. She bit her lip and drifted vaguely forwards. When the inn was in sight, she allowed herself a small smile.

If you enjoyed this story, you can discuss it with other readers and the author at *The Thief's Dungeon* story page at http://forbiddenfiction.com/library/story/MS1-1.000062.

Chaining Flame

James L. Wolf

James L. Wolf hails from the busy corner of sex and gender. In other words, he is a Radical Faerie with a degree in Women Studies. He has written hormone and surgery letters to help people transition from one gender to another, and has letters of his own. James lives in the SF Bay Area.

Chapter 1
Lack of Autonomy

Ilamaych shivered and kept his head down. He had no choice. The chain around his neck would bite if he moved too much. No iron collars this side of the Junipec Ocean, just a loose chain as if he were an animal. He could scratch his nose but not his ass. It was annoying. It was horrible. Ilamaych followed the slave wagon without reprieve, his bladder aching relentlessly. If only the slave traders would stop to water their ceros beasts. Ilamaych truly did not want to wet himself. His dignity may have been shattered thousands of miles away, but wet, stinking leathers would mean more chafing. More pain.

There were five other men chained behind the wagon, their gamboge complexions a dirty orange in the unforgiving sunlight. They were all strangers. Ilamaych had nothing in common with them save skin color. He had been separated from his own coterie in Wetshul. He wasn't inclined to make friends; they had discouraged making friends in the breaking camps. Ilamaych had been whipped with vinegar-soaked knots just for talking.

He glanced around at the sound of approaching jingling and — singing? Singing, as if this were a fine summer morning and not the brink of the Abyss? A man was overtaking them on the road. His wagon overflowed with a stack of wild fescue hay. Ilamaych eyed him covertly. He was bisque colored like the rest of the people in this benighted (though beautiful) land, his long, sea-tinged locks tied back from his face, his beard scruffy. He wore bright colors. His gelded ceros hitched to the wagon seemed well cared for, its horns adorned with multi-color ribbons.

The man paused as he regarded the slave wagon, song dying on his lips. He frowned as he caught Ilamaych's eye.

Ilamaych jerked his head down to gaze at his feet. He'd been taught by slavers not to make eye contact, to be passive and accept what was meted out to him. Nothing mattered. Not even the mesmerizing, sea-green eyes of a stranger. Out of the corner of his eye he saw the man scowl; he jerked the reins and the ceros broke into a brief trot. Ilamaych shivered, moaning low in his raw throat. The man was leaving him.... He bit his lip, repressing roiling, erratic emotions. Oh, but his bladder ached. Why can't they stop for just a minute?

There was some sort of discussion in the front. Ilamaych couldn't make out words between the clink of chains and squeak of wheels. Was the man talking to the slave traders? Ilamaych caught his breath. The man was negotiating with them.

Scant moments later both wagons rolled to a stop. A trader appeared, key in hand. Ilamaych didn't have time to think. The trader unbuckled his chain and led him forward, not unkindly. The scruffy man eyed Ilamaych as he rubbed his beard. He growled, "Take the chains off." His accent was understandable, anyway.

"You sure?" the trader said absently. The man made an impatient gesture and the trader shrugged, removing the chains. Ilamaych almost moaned as the burden was lifted from him, though he contained himself. He had no wish to seem more vulnerable than he already was.

Ilamaych stood uneasily beside the hay wagon while the traders started back up the lane. The chained slaves looked at him over their shoulders until they disappeared over the rise. Ilamaych tried not to stare at his—new master? The man didn't seem to be in a hurry. He nibbled on his grimy thumbnail, as if in contemplation.

"Well, that's done," the man murmured, clearly talking to himself. "You look whole, anyway."

"Your pardon, Sir," Ilamaych whispered in his tongue. "Might I have a minute? I need to make water."

The man stared. "You—speak—my—tongue?" he said in an elevated tone, enunciating each syllable with exaggerated care.

Ilamaych frowned. He wasn't deaf. "I do."

"Um, I see. Well, use a bush. I'd appreciate it if you didn't run away. My ceros is tired; we've been hauling hay all week."

As Ilamaych relieved himself questions flew through his head. Was the man married? Did he have a house? A farm? Did he have children? Maybe he was a member of a matron-led household, as was the custom in this land. Ilamaych eyed the man for clues as to his station in life. His blue and yellow clothing was less dandified upon close examination: the colors were darkened by sweat, musk and hard use. Though the man's skin and hair appeared clean, he seemed rather gaunt. It might be natural but more likely indicated that he cooked and cared for himself. He didn't have spots or unsightly lumps, in any case; far older than Ilamaych, yet healthy.

The man turned out to be the quiet type, not even offering his name. They pulled up to a tiny farm as the sun sank in the eastern sky. The barn had been maintained with loving care and featured a loft, the roof shingles tight. Off to one side — almost an afterthought — was a house of baked clay half buried in the hillside.

Ilamaych helped pitch hay with his master. Then under the man's direction he milked two palaeoth. The man spoke intermittently: giving directions, telling him where items were located, showing him how he preferred tasks completed. The man never once hit Ilamaych. He didn't even curse at Ilamaych, not even when an ornery palaeoth barked low in its throat and kicked the bucket over, spilling milk. Instead, the man scratched its head and sighed. "Going into estrus soon. You can tell by the smell."

Yes, the beast had a typical musky odor. Ilamaych rubbed his hands — covered in oily musk — on his leathers as the man lit a lantern. He led Ilamaych into the house where they concocted a simple meal of millet gruel. The man meted out equal shares and offered butter and milk without reservation. The taste reminded Ilamaych of home. He felt stunned. He had expected... something very different. More like his experience in the breaking camps or even the slave-trade ships. It was unnerving.

What did the man want with him? The man acted as if he'd been alone for years. And yet... Ilamaych thought he could guess. The man had yet to show Ilamaych where he was to sleep. There was only a single bed in this one-room house, covered by a ragged patchwork quilt.

After supper the man lifted a pot of steaming water from a hook above the hearth. He gestured to Ilamaych. "Strip and wash. Be thorough. Don't know what kind of bugs you have on you."

Ilamaych accepted a ball of soap (crackled with too much tallow, but at least it wasn't rancid) and a rag. He hesitated as he removed clothing, the same leathers he'd been captured in—over a hundred days ago? Yes, it had been well over a seasonal cycle. It had seemed like forever. His leathers were filthy beyond anything Ilamaych would have ever tolerated given a choice. He was embarrassed by the smell and nudged them into an abject pile with his feet. The man sat in a rough-hewn chair and watched, stroking his scruffy beard. He did not comment. Ilamaych bore his gaze uneasily.

When he finished he stood aside, uncertain what to do next. The man gestured to the bed. Ilamaych hesitated, then reluctantly slipped upon it, brushing dirt from his bare feet. Would the man take him now? Ilamaych didn't even know his name! His shoulders ached with tension.

The man stood before the fire a time, then banked the coals. He stripped and washed with the same water, his movements swift and certain. It was Ilamaych's turn to stare. Even in the dim light the man's body bore evidence of hard life. He had scars everywhere. His wiry muscles were well defined, as if he'd been laboring since he was young. There were a series of bizarre scars on his back; they looked like brands. Ilamaych licked his lips. Were they serf marks? Ilamaych had made a study of Ventris two years ago. He remembered the smell of rain and Goldenrod's low-pitched voice, instructing him in languages and etiquette, the cultures and customs of Mother Earth.

The man blew out the oil lamp and climbed into bed, still damp. Ilamaych wedged himself against the wall. Waiting. Waiting upon his master's pleasure. Would the man find him out? How would he react to Ilamaych's abnormality? Ilamaych's breath betrayed him, rapid and uneven. The man aired the quilt then draped it over both of them, pulling Ilamaych down beside him. Ilamaych did not resist. Maybe it would be easier this time if he were passive, yielding everything.

The man's hands—calloused and rough—began traveling over Ilamaych's body. They never lingered in one place. It was as if he wanted to know him through touch, trusting his hands more than his eyes. Ilamaych waited to be crushed and impaled, but the man continued exploring him, his pace steady. Ilamaych couldn't breathe, wondering when the man would make his discovery. The man hadn't touched his genitals yet.

After a time Ilamaych dared look over his shoulder into the darkness. "Why did you buy me?" he whispered.

Silence. Ilamaych could hear the man breathing. Then, "Not sure myself. Recognized something in your eyes, maybe. Lucky I'd sold the lystros shoats this morning. Don't usually carry coin."

"You have brands on your back," Ilamaych ventured. Would the man grow angry at the observation? But there was only silence and Ilamaych tried again. "Are you a freed serf? A houseman?"

The man barked an acerbic laugh. "Am a serf still. You're very knowledgeable for a coterie slave, young man. You know my language and can read household marks. Did they truly fish you out from Palister?"

"I... I... had a good teacher," Ilamaych stumbled over the past tense. He didn't want to remember what had happened to Goldenrod. His Flame teacher had been the most important person in his life. Now Ilamaych would never initiate in fire, never be Flame himself. His loss was unbearable.

The man rumbled low in his throat. "I belong to the Ywen Coed household over the hill. Always have, probably always will." His tone sounded resigned and worried, though Ilamaych couldn't see his expression in the dark. "Mmph. Haven't talked so much in a week. Been making hay over in the slough. Enough."

Ilamaych gasped as the man seized his penis. He stroked it energetically and Ilamaych's muscles contracted, his breath quickening with excitement and fear. The man couldn't miss his secret. His fingers were too cunning. Even now he cradled Ilamaych's ill-formed scrotum, his fingers tracing the unevenness Ilamaych had been born with. "Huh," the man whispered, his fingers slowing down. "You have... oh. Oh!"

He'd found it. The man slipped a finger inside his opening and Ilamaych mewled at the odd sensation. The man's hands were rough though his touch wasn't painful. Despite mind-numbing fear, Ilamaych was wet and ready; wetter than he'd ever been in his life.

The man emanated confusion in the dark. He drew back and

grasped Ilamaych's legs, forcing them wide apart. "It's not your anus," he wondered aloud, fingers still exploring. "It seems... deep."

"I was born this way," Ilamaych whispered.

"Does it — work?"

"I'm not sure," he said, his volume increasing with frustration. The man drew back uncertainly, though one hand remained wrapped around his ankle. Ilamaych bit his lip, repressing tears. "I was... a virgin until Wetshul. They didn't discover it then. I thought they would have, when they... but they didn't. I almost wished they had. It might have hurt less."

The man paused thoughtfully as Ilamaych sniffled, then let go of his ankle and settled again beside him, stroking his hair gently. Then the man stopped as if struck by thought. "Were you a Flame apprentice? Is that who taught you Ventris' language and customs? A Flame?"

"Yes." Ilamaych blinked with surprise. "You know my... the Flame?" He'd been about to say, my people. But he would never be one of them now. He'd never have the ability to shapeshift or to bathe in fire, gifts of the goddess Pelin. The ability to change his body had been tempting: to be female or male at will, not in between. Ilamaych had been studying to become Flame for ten years, almost half his life. The Flame were a gentle people, intelligent and educated. Not like the slavers who had so recently conquered them.

Now everything was gone.

The man snorted. "'Course I do. This is Ventris, boy. There's a Flame at Ywen Coed named Ficus, second only to the matron." Again, he seemed distracted and worried at mention of Ywen Coed. Ilamaych wondered who worried him more: the matron or the Flame in question.

Ilamaych licked his lips, realizing that he could talk. The man might even care. "I was supposed to initiate mid-summer, before everything... happened. Now I'm stuck as neither man nor woman. I dreamed of being both, to have the power of choice." And yet, despite his frustration and anger, he'd witnessed what had happened to Goldenrod. The slavers had bound her with leather masks and a cunning canvas coat with lengthy sleeves that could be tied together. They'd shut her up in a box on wheels. Though it had been shocking to witness Goldenrod trussed up like a lystros, to witness such disrespect afforded her, Ilamaych could see their rationale at work. A cold logic seemed to be behind the slavers' actions, for how else would you bind a shapeshifter? Ilamaych shuddered. He'd cried for days afterward just thinking about it. Had he escaped that far worse fate by remaining human?

Unaware of his thoughts, the man began fingering him again. "You said you were a virgin before... so you've never had anything in here besides fingers, right?"

"No," he whispered, shy again.

"I wonder if you'll bleed like a girl. Or get pregnant."

"I don't know."

The man inserted two fingers and Ilamaych gasped. By unspoken mutual agreement, Ilamaych rolled onto his back as the man half crouched above him. The man placed his hands on either thigh, bracing him as if he were a woman. Ilamaych's penis was hard as marble. The man knocked it out of the way — Ilamaych cried out — and worked his own penis into the opening. Oh, but it was tight. The man settled atop him, pushing inside until he could push no further.

All words, all thought ceased. The man penetrated him vigorously as Ilamaych squealed and writhed. How could an act be so magnificent and painful simultaneously? It was too much.

Ilamaych's eyes filled with tears and he arched his back, rigid. His mind spattered: he couldn't think or breathe as wetness gushed from his penis. But it wasn't over. The man's rhythm increased, one hand grasping Ilamaych's hair. He threw his whole weight onto Ilamaych, taking him without reprieve. Then the man quivered and grew still. Ilamaych could feel the spreading wetness in him. They lay gasping, the man draped atop him.

The man rose after a minute, graceful in the dark. Ilamaych stayed put on the bed, boneless and spent as the man returned with a rough clay pot. "Drink carefully or we'll be sleeping on a wet tick," he instructed. The pot was filled with clean water and Ilamaych drank greedily. The man pulled it away after a minute, laughing. "Don't want to go out in the dark. Probably fall down my own well."

As the man drank, Ilamaych found himself growing bolder. His fingers wandered up the man's hairy, wiry chest, stroking his nipples with wonder. The man gasped a laugh and choked on water. Ilamaych was sprayed with a fine mist.

"Good thing I'm not Flame or that would have hurt," Ilamaych murmured, brushing himself off. At least now that he couldn't initiate as Flame, he'd never burn in water. He'd always thought of a severe vulnerability to water as the least desirable part of bargaining with the goddess Pelin.

"Warned you." The man settled next to him again. His body was comfortable as if they'd been sleeping together for years. "Wish you had tits. Then you'd be perfect."

"You never even told me your name." Ilamaych complained as the man threw an arm around his shoulders, embracing him gently.

"Oh, you worried about that? I'm Earen. Now quit your questions and let me sleep."

The next morning Ilamaych woke to discover he was alone. He reluctantly slipped on his benighted leathers and went searching for Earen, but the man was nowhere to be found. Earen's ceros was missing and the other animals seemed cared for. The day was sunny so Ilamaych decided to make the most of his time. He found a burlap sack in the barn and fashioned it into a temporary loincloth, his chest bare in the chilly morning. Ilamaych boiled his leathers in a metal bucket that he'd also found in the barn. The roughness of burlap was preferable to the filth that darkened the wash water. He dumped the bucket and boiled his clothing three times more before the water stayed clear.

As he worked he thought about Earen. Ilamaych felt like he was only seeing a tiny piece of a larger picture. After all, how else did you judge a person than by their family and friends, their coterie? Ilamaych was alone now, though not by choice. Earen... Earen was a different story, he rather thought. How had the man come into his serfdom? After all, Ventris serfs were not born into their station. They were made: captured men from coups, the sons of traitorous women. It wasn't necessarily a station for life as some did earn an elevated status to houseman. The serious scholar in Ilamaych knew the households were based on a matriarchal hierarchy, almost exactly like the coteries back home. Except... his home was gone now. Ilamaych closed his eyes against tears.

An hour later Ilamaych was laying his leathers out on the rough-hewn fence to dry when he spotted Earen coming over the rise. Earen rode his ceros bareback and whistled a cheerful ditty. "Ah, what a pretty picture you make, my fine slave," he called out.

Ilamaych smiled uncertainly, tense and vigilant. Earen dismount-ed and strode up to him with an almost reckless confidence. Ilamaych shied away. He tripped over a stump and landed on his backside. Would Earen laugh at him? Roll Ilamaych and take him right here? But Earen threw himself onto the turf beside Ilamaych and tucked his hands behind his head, grinning. "She wasn't home," he said, relief evident in his voice.

"Who wasn't home?" Ilamaych squeaked.

"The matron, of course. She took her Knights across the Ventricle Channel. Bothering the neighbors again. I can keep you a while lon-ger, eh." He reached over and rubbed Ilamaych's naked chest. "Mmm. You're warm."

Ilamaych tucked his head, accepting the touch with heightened awareness. Earen found a nipple and Ilamaych gasped. He wasn't sure how he felt about Earen. Earen seemed to know it, too. He raised his head and eyed Ilamaych, then stood. Earen towered over him: Ila-maych gazed up him as if he were a mountain top.

"Take off that sack," Earen commanded, his face expressionless. Ilamaych slowly obeyed his master, tossing the burlap aside. He felt exposed under the open sky. Earen's eyes narrowed, surveying his body. "Now undo my laces."

Ilamaych's breath sped as he reached for his master's waistline. His fingers shook. Earen's penis, freed from confinement, spilled out. It was already hard. Ilamaych swallowed, his entire being focused upon that penis. Earen's expression remained stern but his eyes glis-tened with enthusiasm. "Take me in your mouth," he said.

Licking his lips, Ilamaych moved in and delicately accepted the end upon his tongue. The texture was unbelievably soft and it tasted salty, musky. Masculine. Ilamaych's penis grew hard and his body quivered as he accepted more. He felt as if hot sulfurous water were coursing through his veins. Earen grabbed the back of his head and used it as leverage, pushing fully inside his mouth. Ilamaych moaned. Tears filled his eyes. He licked and suckled, his hands reaching to grasp Earen's buttocks to pull him closer still. Earen threw his head back and Ilamaych heard him laugh.

Ilamaych grinned in response and Earen gasped. "No teeth, no teeth!"

Earen pulled out of Ilamaych's mouth and pushed him back onto the turf, climbing atop him. This time Ilamaych was ready when Earen penetrated him. The pressure and movement were invigorating and Ilamaych rocked with Earen's rhythm. Earen grew wild at this. Ilamaych threw his head back, enfolded as he was ground down into the turf. He felt every stone beneath him, every stem, yet he didn't care. He came messily, his semen shooting between their undulating bodies. Earen cried out and came within him.

After a time Earen rolled off. "Let's try that again. No teeth this time."

Ilamaych had known his leathers would take all day to dry, but it was nine days before he put them on again. Earen wanted him naked and naked he was. Naked doing the chores. Naked while cooking or scrubbing the floor. At first the wind felt odd: his body hair stood on end at times. After a while he grew used to it, then began to enjoy the particular freedom it afforded him. He just wished he could choose to put on clothing or not.

Sometimes Earen simply watched him in motion, eyes dancing with excitement. Sometimes Earen knelt and took him right there on the floor, or wedged Ilamaych against the barn posts. Once, after milking the palaeoth, Earen smeared their musky oil inside his rectum and took him from behind. Ilamaych screamed at that, but afterwards he felt so light that he could have flown without wings.

All the while Ilamaych wondered at Earen's manner. He could have sworn the man was playing a game: his cheerful mood and mirthful expression were indicative of a boy playing a prank. He often grinned friskily at Ilamaych, as if Ilamaych were in on the joke. Ilamaych wasn't sure what to make of this. What would Earen do if

Ilamaych defied him? Ilamaych fingered his own scars and frowned. He'd learned obedience in Wetshul. And to be honest, he was enjoying the attention Earen gave him. Earen's touch was vigorous but pleasurable, and his terse words were kind. Surprisingly so, in fact. Was the man his lover or master?

On the ninth day Ilamaych was carrying rope between the house and barn when a stranger appeared from over the hill. She rode a saddled ceros with an air of absolute self-assurance. Ilamaych stared as if sun struck. The style of her clothing was bold, nearly militant: puffy pants of a bright red and orange pattern folded into high muddy boots with steel caps; a vest of orange stripes over a leather bodice that showed off her ample breasts much as it laced them tight. She dismounted at the gate, frowning at him. Ilamaych nearly choked when he remembered that he was naked.

"Niixpachway," she called out. Good afternoon. Ilamaych could not have moved if the earth shook out from under him. She spoke his tongue! What was this? How could she know the language of the coteries?

The stranger seemed to take in his bewilderment, sighed and removed her hat. She was completely bald. Ilamaych breathed out, his whole body filling with relief. She was Flame. No wonder she understood his language. He let go of the rope he'd been carrying and dropped to one knee. "My good Flame," he said, head bowed.

"Apprentice?" she asked, her tone curious but also somewhat suspicious, as if he claimed status she knew was false.

She was right. "I'm sorry," Ilamaych whispered, awkwardly regaining his feet, embarrassment rushing to his cheeks. "You... can't help but submit when you're chained. I'm, um, no longer able to initiate." Especially since Earen had been vigorously enjoying his every orifice at will. Pelin only initiated virgins, after all.

She sighed. "My condolences on your loss. My name is Ficus; Earen may have spoken of me. By the by, where is Earen? And... your clothing? He didn't burn them, did he?" Her eyes narrowed and Ilamaych's hands crept to his crotch.

"No, good Flame. One moment, I'll—um. I'll fetch him."

"Do that."

Clothes came first, he decided. Inside he discovered that his dried leathers were now stiff as wood. By the time he'd managed to crack them and wrestle them on, voices outside assured him that Earen had found Ficus on his own. Ilamaych emerged from the house to find an argument in progress.

"...lack of autonomy. That money was not yours to spend!" Ficus growled, her arms crossed. "These are not your animals. This is not your land. You forget your station in your solitude."

Earen looked sulky and stubborn. "I need help to maintain the plot properly. It seemed a reasonable solution to me."

"Ah? Is that why he's walking around without a stitch on him? You haven't appealed to the matron for another serf to maintain the property, in any case." Earen mumbled something under his breath and Ficus raised a smooth brow, one hand cupped around her ear. "What was that?"

"I said, I wouldn't have liked her choice of companions."

"You are not here for your personal comfort. You are here to work this property at her will. You realize what's going to happen next, don't you?" Ficus shook her head. "Just like a man. Always thinking with your member."

Ilamaych wanted to creep back inside the house or turn invisible. But when Ficus turned to him, it was with a smile. "Earen said your name is Ilamaych, correct?" He nodded shyly. Her smile grew wider. "I formally invite you to come with us to Ywen Coed. I suggest that it may be of benefit to you to meet the matron. These are her lands. She might find a place for you in the household. We do not recognize this foreign notion of slavery, in any case. We have our own system here and like it just fine."

He licked his lips. "Will you... I mean, does Earen get a place, too?"

She shot Earen a frown. "He has a place, a place he has forgotten in his avarice. He will be duly reminded. And punished. Oh yes, he will be punished. However, you can relax. You haven't done anything wrong, Ilamaych."

So it was that Ilamaych found himself riding tandem with Earen, Ficus leading them forward on her own ceros. Earen remained silent, his expression stoic, but Ilamaych could feel that he was shaking. Ilamaych looked over his shoulder back at the little farm as they crested the hillside. Had he been happy there? Yes, he decided. He'd been happy with Earen. Yet he had an unsettling feeling he would never see the farm again.

Chapter 2
Branded Bottom

Earen had forgotten how raucous the great hall of Ywen Coed could be, especially when the matron was holding court. It had been quiet on his farm. His farm... well, there was the problem, wasn't it? Ficus was right, though Earen would never admit it. He'd started thinking that just because he planted and harvested, cared for the livestock, cut the hay and maintained the buildings, that it was his farm. That he was a houseman rather than a serf.

Now... the noise was tremendous. Earen bore it silently, willing his eyes not to water in the smoke. Beside him, Ilamaych stared with obvious bewilderment and curiosity, gazing up at the soapstone columns and walnut beams high above them. Earen wished he could touch Ilamaych's hand or shoulder; some form of physical contact. After being alone for so long it had been astonishingly easy to draw someone into his little world. So easy to hold and talk to. Yet it wasn't like he minded the solitude. Again, Ficus had put her finger on it: he could have asked for another serf to help maintain the property anytime, yet he hadn't. Earen had chosen Ilamaych personally, handpicking a companion for himself. He'd been in charge for once. Now he'd lost Ilamaych, too. Best keep his hands to himself.

Iron pounded iron, setting off sparks between hammer and the matron's traditional anvil. The room quieted. Matron Gund need not rise or yell to draw eyes to her. Sitting in the traditional iron chair, her pregnant belly bursting through armor plating, she commanded attention. Earen was struck by how little she'd changed since last he'd seen her. Perhaps her hair had more grey, that was all. Yet Earen couldn't help but think that soon she would bear no more children. Though he didn't care, he couldn't help but be drawn back into household thoughts, household customs. It was annoying. It chafed his sense of himself. Any independence he might have felt on the farm was gone here, shattered to the common hearth that claimed him.

"First order of business," Matron Gund said in her booming voice. "My Knights came home with a bonus. Bring forth Regori's heir, girls!"

Massive cheering filled the hall. A youth was pushed to the forefront of the hall. His fallow-colored skin and curly black hair marked him as different, his clothing well made in the Tache style with lots of puffs and flourishes. Of course, now his clothing was ripped and bloodied. Earen thought him good looking in a spoilt kind of way. The foreign heir gazed around him with pride and fear as Knights beat their breastplates and tankards. A victory chant filled the hall. It was too loud. Earen put his fingers in his ears, and felt vaguely pleased when he noticed Ilamaych had done the same.

The matron banged her anvil. "We've showed up those snotty Tache miscreants but good. Regori and his ilk think women are for naught but spilling out children and cooking their suppers. So now Regori's heir is going to serve us! Ura, you and your ceros colleens castrate him tonight. Then he'll fill his place by serving in the hall and the scullery."

This statement was met by more victory chanting. Earen's stomach dropped as he surreptitiously glanced around for Ura. He'd rather fancied her when they'd both been young, and now she was the beast mistress of Ywen Coed. A position so far above him she might as well reside among the stars. Before his mother had betrayed the household — thus condemning her underage male children to serfdom — he'd thought to offer Ura his sword and shield someday, as was the custom. That had been long ago. Earen had since learned to swallow bitterness of his burnt dreams.

Not seeing Ura, Earen stole a glance at Regori's heir, whose face had drained of blood. The foreigner was staring at the matron with a glazed expression, as if wondering if she were bluffing. Earen knew full well she wasn't. Over the years he'd witnessed castrations of his fellow serfs, though he'd never merited such displeasure himself. His hands crept to his crotch all the same. Ficus had promised he'd be punished. He doubted castration was in his future, yet... who knew? The matron had been known to be unreasonable, deep in her cups.

I just wanted to make my own choices, he thought. Be master of my fate... well, master of more than my own fate. Was that so bad? Serfs had occasionally been known to achieve elevation to houseman status. It didn't happen often, usually due to great deeds or selfless acts. Earen had hoped... well, that wasn't going to happen now, was it?

"Next order of business," Matron Gund belched. The heir was made to step aside while Ficus approached the chair with the intense self-confidence Earen had always admired. She spoke in the matron's ear. The matron's eyes locked with Earen's as she took another drink of malt from her ceros horn. Ficus stood back as the matron crooked her finger at Earen.

Earen stepped forward until he reached the spot where the unfortunate heir had stood. Matron Gund smiled toothily at him. "Ah, Earen-bachgen. You've been very naughty. Very naughty indeed. Trading household coin for one of these newfangled slaves. For years you've been pretending to be made of wood. What changed?"

Earen considered telling the truth: that he'd looked into Ilamaych's eyes and seen himself reflected.... No, that would never do. He shrugged. "Got lonely."

The matron snorted. "Very well, let me relieve you of your loneliness. Ura, take the serf. You and the colleens can enjoy him after you rid Regori's heir of his scrotum."

Earen blanched. He glanced to where the matron gestured and saw Ura at last. She looked good. Weathered and tanned as any member of the household ruling circle. Her expression was acerbic, though. The matron appeared not to notice. "Make sure to brand Earen, a strike for every lystros shoat he wasted. Tomorrow and thereafter he can shovel out pens. I'll find another serf to farm that slice of land."

Earen's stomach plunged as his whole life burned away, leaving only ashes. Well, he'd survived complete decimation before, here in this very hall. Such a familiar feeling. Yet he wasn't the only one at stake this time. "Your pardon, Matron Gund. What of Ilamaych? My — friend."

Ficus stepped forward. "A willing lad and a good worker, I imagine. I'll take personal responsibility for Ilamaych. He was in training to become Flame in his homeland. He'll do well under me as an assistant, I believe."

Matron Gund waved her hand in dispassionate assent. "Very well. Next order of business."

Earen found himself surrounded by three comely young women. He didn't know them: it had been eight years since he'd lived in the household proper. They must have grown up in his absence. The women were wearing the accouterments of ceros colleens: leather bodices, canvas split-skirts and iron-toed boots. They giggled as they hustled him away. In the hallway one took a leather collar and wrapped it securely around Earen's neck. Her fingers were cool. He gulped, his penis stiffening as the leather was cinched tight. The other two bound his hands behind his back. He shifted, uncomfortable at the loss of control.

"Now he fights back," one laughed. "Let's tether him with the foreigner until they're done."

The day had grown overcast, Earen noted glumly. Who knew what shape he'd be in next time he saw the open sky? At least Ilamaych would be all right. Earen hadn't wanted anything untoward to happen to him. Earen was led to a building he recognized as the tack shed, a common gathering spot for livestock caretakers. The shed was dark but a figure jumped up at their entry, chains rattling with his movement.

"Cool off, boy. We'll get to you soon enough," one of the colleens said, slapping the foreign heir on the ass.

Earen was tied next to the heir. The women drifted outside but the door was left open; Earen could hear them talking in the yard. He glanced at the foreigner, eyes adjusting to the dim light. The heir seemed to feel Earen's gaze, for he snapped around. His expression was intense, enraged. "My father will move God-Plane and Abyss to avenge me. He'll come. You'll see."

Earen kept his peace. The man continued muttering vengeance under his breath as night fell. Punishment was a long time in coming. Earen slumped, deep in thought. What would it be like to be tortured by a woman he'd once held affection for? After being branded a serf, everything had changed in the household: women who'd been kind to him became cold, housemen silent. Only Ficus, secure in her position, remained charitable. Ura had been several years older than Earen and therefore had never acknowledged his presence, even before his mother's treachery. What would Ura do to him now? Earen felt himself growing involuntarily erect at the thought. His punishment, it seemed, would be self-punishment as much as anything else.

Earen woke abruptly from brooding when other voices joined the colleens outside. The band of women entered the shed, bearing lanterns which they hung from rafter hooks. At their heart was Ura. Earen watched her with rapt, nervous attention. She glanced at him with the same exasperated expression she gave Regori's heir. His heart fell.

"Unstring the foreign lad first. Zulenne, you're on clamps. You three, hold him steady. Don't want him bucking like that ceros colt yesterday, do we?"

The colleens were practiced in their movements: castration was apparently a chore they knew well. Earen winced but couldn't look away, though bodies and shadows barred his view. The heir swore, threatened, struggled, pled for his future children, and finally began screaming. Earen vowed not to scream whatever they did to him. He wasn't some milk-fed whelp who'd thought to be lord someday. Serfdom had few opportunities for self-respect, but pain tolerance was one of them.

"Well done everyone. Boy, cease that caterwauling. You weren't skinned alive, you know," Ura said with a trace of exasperation. "Honestly, Gund keeps saddling us with the dirty work. It's not as if we don't have a full complement of livestock to care for day and night. You'd think that Flame could take on responsibility beyond coppersmithing around here, but no."

Ura sounded tired. Maybe she'll be too tired to bother with me, Earen thought as the foreigner was led out of the shed, limping and silent at last. His fragile hope was shattered as Ura turned her wry gaze upon him. "Ah, there's the lad I remember. What are you now? Forty, forty-five? And you still forget your place. I recall that when you were younger, you earned every mark on your body. Seems to me you need a better memory."

Earen couldn't help but look away at that. He'd never known what she'd thought of him. Now he knew. She only saw the serf in him, no more.

One of the colleens giggled. "He broke matron's law for the other foreigner. The comely one."

"In love, were you? In lust, more like." Ura smirked. "I never understand how serfs conveniently forget that they cannot choose a partner like housemen do. Well, guess it's time to remind another one. Girls, strip him, then let's have him dangle from the rafters."

This was it, then. Earen considered struggling, then rejected it. Struggling would not change his fate. His hands freed, he helped the young women take off his clothing. One even blushed when his pants came off. He chose to consider this a good sign. Nevertheless his hands were restrained with rope, the other end tossed over the rafters. He was pulled upward, his body stretched. At least his feet still touched the dirt floor. For now.

Ura sighed. "A few stripes first, I think. Pass me that crop."

Earen gasped as the first blow connected, then bit his lip. Another blow, then another. He closed his eyes tightly. She grabbed the leather collar around his neck and pulled him backward. He screeched, fearing for his life and breath.

"Ah, you're paying attention after all," she breathed in his ear. The lack of air had another effect on him: his penis hardened as his buttocks clenched together. The colleens around him whispered and giggled.

Ura noticed. "Go get a string of bells, Zulenne."

To Earen's horror, the string of bells was for his penis. Zulenne tied them on firmly: her ministrations served to harden him until his penis tilted upwards like a ship's bow. Their laughter made his face hot as he writhed from the rafters, struggling against his own shame. A blow came from behind and he yelped, caught off balance.

"That's better." Ura let loose a string of blows, each stronger than the last, until Earen was dancing in place. The bells tinkled wildly. They were freezing cold and oddly heavy as they struck his penis, out of sync with his movement; the sensation was both disturbing and erotic. Earen was moaning, now. Even the blows from behind had grown pleasurable in their fury. Ura knew how to punish with a whip as much as words.

Then Ura grabbed his buttocks with her hand. She squeezed his reddened flesh. Her touch was too personal, too much. Earen was used to pain but not the twisted pleasure Ura evoked in him. He screamed, overcome by ecstasy and shame. Semen spurted in the air as he came.

"You have juice in you after all, wood man." Ura let go and sat down with a grunt. Young women around her were chattering excitedly, their eyes shining as they regarded him. Earen gasped limply. He imagined he looked the part of a dead fish hanging from the rafters. What would they do to elicit a response from him next?

Ura seemed lost in thought. Then she turned to a colleen. "You know the wooden insert we use to inspire semen from the ceros stallions? Fetch it, please. And bring the grease bucket, too."

Earen gazed at her with horror, guessing her intent. This was worse than he'd imagined. The other colleens seemed to catch wind of this statement and bounced in place, clearly excited. They were about to see a show. When the colleen returned, Earen know his guess was correct. The wooden insert was a penis-shaped object with a handle. It was enormous.

Ura grinned wryly. "We use this to harden ceros stallions before setting them on our mares. It helps what can be an arduous process. You enjoyed that poor boy, didn't you? I wonder if you asked his favor, like a civilized houseman, or if you took him like a criminal. We're going to return the favor." She dipped the wooden penis in the bucket and came up with a staunch ball of waxy, yellow grease.

Earen couldn't help but lean back on the tips of his toes as she approached him. Then he scrambled forward when she disappeared behind him. She slapped his ass and he jerked in place. The audience loved it, their mouths open in apparent fascination. She rubbed the greasy tip of the wooden dildo into his crack. Earen moaned. The grease was soft and easily warmed by his body, oily against his skin. His muscles were tense and shaking, yet he was growing hard again. The bells were tinkling with the movement. She inserted the tip and he braced, teeth clenched.

"Hmm." Ura said, pausing. "Not yet, I think. Let's make sure he remembers this lesson for a long time. Girls, everyone dip a finger into the bucket and smear grease on his body. Every part of him should be covered."

Now Earen struggled in earnest. It was one thing to be at the mercy of Ura; it was quite another thing to be the object of a lesson. Young women approached him with fascination, each with a warm dab of grease on her index finger. One chose an armpit, another his lips. His beard was a popular target, and other rubbed grease in his hair. Many took to his chest and nipples. A few got his thighs, and he gained dollops on his back and shoulders. Two women had the audacity to attack his penis, the bells ringing wildly as they played with him. His scrotum, too. His yelps and gasps made them giggle further. When they stepped back he found himself utterly oiled with grease.

It was humiliating. He was harder than he'd ever been in his life.

Behind him, the tip of the wooden penis was inserted. Then Ura dug into him, one hand clasping his scrotum for control of his greasy body as she forced the full length inside. Earen screamed. The pain was stupendous. He struggled in earnest, writhing. The bells tied to his penis hit him with astonishing force and speed; the sensation added to his panic. At one point he lifted himself off the floor, legs kicking as he hung by his wrists. But the pain did not cease. Ura began pumping him with the wooden penis. Its unyielding nature, its girth and breadth, were too much. Too much.

Earen came in a wild clanging of bells. Ura didn't stop even then. Earen gasped, dangling and oily. She grabbed his penis directly and pumped him, the bells clamoring around her greasy hand. At her ministrations he grew hard again. The twisted pleasure was agony. He came with a low moan, not by choice. Not by choice at all.

Movement ceased and Earen hung, feet forgotten beneath him.

Ura sighed and rubbed her greasy hands on her trousers. "We are long past our bedtime, I think."

A colleen stirred and objected, "But Ura, you haven't branded him yet."

Ura swore. "Forgot that. Very well, someone fetch a hot poker from the kitchen. Take a lantern and be careful, please. I don't want you hurting yourselves in the dark."

Earen couldn't think. He couldn't believe it. After all this he had to endure more torture? More humiliation? He licked his greasy lips, tasting rendered lard with nausea. He had no choice.

Chapter 3

Choice of Companions

Earen blinked, willing himself not to cry from exhaustion and fear. Ura had collapsed onto a straw bale and tossed aside the wooden phallus as the colleens chattered around her.

"How many strikes?" someone asked, her tone curious.

"Matron said one for every lystros shoat," someone else noted, her voice as precise as a lawyer's.

"How many's that?"

"Six is the typical litter."

Earen licked his lips. "Four," he rasped out.

"What?" Everyone looked at him.

"It... was... a litter... of four."

Ura snorted, her expression worn. "Six is typical, yet you say four. Fine. We'll split the difference at five."

Earlier Earen would have argued. But here he was a serf strung up for their pleasure, not a man. Not a man at all.

A woman returned with a poker, its tip red hot. Earen found he still had enough energy to be afraid.

"Where should he be marked?" someone asked as Ura rose and took up the poker.

"We want him available to work, so no hands or feet. Nor somewhere fragile where he'd be too damaged. No, we'll be traditional about this. Girls, wipe him off then surround him, please. He's not boxed in enough to suit my taste. Buttering him up was one of my less intelligent decisions," she grumbled, and the colleens agreed with undertone complaints.

The colleens rose to obey as she disappeared behind him once again. Earen struggled reflexively as Ura and the colleens wiped off grease with rough cloths. Their ministrations did little to clean him. Earen vividly recalled his last branding; he mewled under his breath like an animal. What little self-containment he had left fizzled as women grabbed every part of his body to restrain him.

Then Earen felt a horrifying, agonizing strike to the small of his back. The women around him renewed their slippery grip as he bellowed, his hands — the only part of him free enough to move — writhing in anguish above his head. He felt another strike. It was worse than the first, for now he was mired in the raw extreme of pain. He forgot to scream or struggle. He forgot everything, even consciousness. Earen woke while they were letting him down, his back throbbing, his nose bristling with the smell of burnt flesh.

For a few days afterward, Earen managed stilted, painful movement. Mucking out stalls took much longer than it should have. His back protested every movement, and of course his back was connected to the rest of him. Even his toes ached. Ura and her colleens didn't bother him, in any case. They seemed to feel sorry, almost ashamed, as if they'd gone too far that night and knew it.

Soon enough his body set about recovering. His mind, however, was a different matter. As he shoveled manure Earen simmered with anger and despair. He'd lost... everything. Sometimes he spotted Ilamaych from a distance, ducking in or out of the coppersmithy. He seemed well enough. He was not limping or stumbling throughout his days. Though it was unfair, Earen couldn't help but feel resentment as summer drew to a close.

On Luck Day, the traditional day between seasons, Ura poked her head into the lystros pen Earen was mucking. "The matron said you can have today off like everyone else. Get cleaned up. You're even welcome to the festivities this afternoon."

Earen tossed the shovel away without a word. Even the prospect of Luck Day fireworks didn't cheer him up. After washing, he lay on the straw that was his bunk, hands folded on his stomach, bereft of direction. At least mucking out had been something to do. He should go spend time with what friends he had here. He should enjoy the day, but the idea left him cold. What did he really want?

Ilamaych. He wanted Ilamaych.

Reluctantly, he set off for the coppersmithy. It hadn't just been Ilamaych that Earen had been avoiding; he'd also been avoiding Ficus. She'd been so upset with him, earlier. She'd been such a benevolent presence in his life that her anger had caught him off guard. Earen wondered if the source of her outrage was that he'd pretended to be Ilamaych's master. He'd meant no harm by the charade. Perhaps it was natural that Ficus take slavery so personally, when Flame were apparently being enslaved in Palister.

It seemed a likely explanation. And if it were true, then he was an idiot. Earen sighed. He owed them both an apology. If... if either of them would even accept an apology from him.

The fires were banked low in the coppersmithy. No work today. Despite this, he could hear noises from within the building. His face grew hot as he realized what the noises were. Envy rippled through him. Of course Ficus would take it upon herself — or himself, if he'd changed gender for the occasion — to enjoy Ilamaych, just as he had. She had the perfect right and freedom to choose any partner she wished. Earen had lost that right the moment he'd been branded a serf. He stood bereft. It was hopeless. He should walk away. Instead, he crept toward the noise. He wanted to see for himself. It might not be them. Anyone could be back there.

They were lying on a pile of straw in the corner. Ficus was on top, straddling Ilamaych. Ficus moved with scintillating gratification. Ficus was still female, though she'd changed her face and figure since he'd seen her last. She now matched Ilamaych: her skin color and features were of the gamboge race, as if she came from Palister herself. It figured she'd do that. It also figured that she'd make herself beautiful. Her large eyes were offset by a hatchet nose and high cheekbones. Generous hips. Insult to injury, she seemed to be enjoying herself tremendously.

Earen swallowed. He wanted them. He wanted them both, yet his aching, scabbed-over back told a different story. He was not free. He could only accept, not initiate. Never dominate. Earen turned away. Blinded by stinging eyes, he accidentally kicked a pair of copper-shaping tongs lying on the floor.

Ficus twisted around, her elegant features startled. "Earen!"

Ilamaych gasped from under her, his voice muffled but clear. "What? It's Earen? At last! Earen, wait. Don't go."

Earen paused though he didn't turn around. He heard the sounds of frantic scrambling from the straw pile, footsteps scampering toward him. Then reassuring warmth as Ilamaych embraced him from behind. "Missed you," he whispered. "Missed you, missed you."

"Really?" Earen's breath stopped in his throat with... was that hope? He ignored the pain radiating from his scabs.

"Really. Why didn't you come before? I wanted to look for you, but...." The young man seemed embarrassed. "I wasn't sure what they'd done to you. Or if you were allowed to talk to me. Didn't want to get you into more trouble."

Earen gulped. "I got myself into trouble. I'm sorry, Ilamaych. I didn't mean to force you into anything you didn't want to do."

Ficus snorted and Earen glanced her way. She'd stood and thrown on a colorful cloth, draping her delectable figure. Her arms were crossed, her expression darkly sardonic. "Now you apologize?"

He flushed. "People do so many things to me that I don't want. I thought... for once... he didn't even understand my station."

She dropped her gaze. "Yes. I can see that. Doesn't make it right, but I can see that," she sighed. "I'd just like to note that I've never done anything to you that you didn't want."

"That's true." He shot her an appraising glance which she returned. He realized that he'd missed her out on the farm.

Ilamaych glanced from one to the other. "Does this mean that we're all right?"

Earen didn't reply. Instead, he approached Ficus with the confidence he'd always admired in her. It was the first time he'd had the courage to try this—criminal dominance—with anyone from the household. To his delight she responded to his energy, her whole body opening like the sun, her eyes soft. Earen realized that Ficus was slightly shorter now than she usually was: she must have used the extra body mass to shape those hips, those breasts. He touched her under her chin and tilted her head up.

She smiled up at him. "How do you prefer me?" It was a traditional question.

"Male," he said decisively. He was tired — oh so tired — of women.

Ficus's mouth twitched upward, eyes twinkling merrily. She dropped the colorful wrap and began changing. He watched as she shifted fat and muscle, her skin rippling and stretching. Her breasts receded, her chin thickened. No longer female, Ficus formed scrotum and penis even as Earen watched. The Flame raised a smooth brow. "Bigger? Smaller?" he asked. Even his voice was lower.

"A little thicker. Bigger at the end. Yes, right there." Earen grinned. He savored the feeling of being able to request what he wanted. He looked up and down the Flame, appreciating his musculature and strong chin with a notch in it. Only Ficus's acerbic, knowledgeable eyes remained the same.

Over his shoulder, Ilamaych stretched luxuriantly, yawning. Earen glanced at him, then realized why the young man wasn't alarmed or surprised at these changes. Ilamaych had been studying to be Flame, so of course he knew what they could do. He knew better than Earen. Ilamaych embraced him from behind and Earen relaxed into his arms, readily ignoring pain from the branding. Earen laid his head back on Ilamaych's shoulder, fully accepted. Then Ficus embraced him from the front, rubbing against him playfully.

It was perfect.

They moved like a single, pleasurable being. After a time Ilamaych began undressing Earen, taking his time. Then Ilamaych gasped and paused, hands hovering in place. Earen glanced over his shoulder: the man was staring at his lower back. At the new brand marks. Ilamaych touched the scabs hesitantly.

Earen sighed. "It doesn't hurt."

"Like the Abyss it doesn't. Don't lie to me. I know what torture feels like," Ilamaych growled at him.

Earen sank down onto the hay, then deliberately lay on his back so Ilamaych couldn't see the marks. "Well, I don't want to think about it right now. I want to think about you. Want to go for a ride?"

Ilamaych glared at him, and seemed about to protest when Ficus grabbed his buttocks from behind. "Go on," the Flame breathed. "I'm going to take you from behind while you're on top of him."

Earen's penis stiffened at the thought and he breathed deep, stretching in the straw. Ilamaych was hard as well. He mounted Earen like a puppy, all wiggling energy. Earen gasped as he was enveloped. He relaxed, enjoying the feeling of being inside Ilamaych's cunt. Ilamaych in turn moaned as Ficus fingered him from behind, then mounted him.

It was like being immersed in hot water; all ripples and tides. They moved in time with one another. Ilamaych moaned and rocked, sandwiched between them. Earen reached out and squeezed Ficus's hand, and was squeezed in return. He was embraced and accepted. Earen couldn't hold himself back. He arched his back, coming. Then he lay still, his penis spent though still immersed in Ilamaych. Ficus continued on, his rhythm self assured and steady. After a time the rhythm affected Earen and he grew hard again. Ilamaych gasped as Earen began thrusting up diligently from his reclined position. Earen grabbed his nipples and Ilamaych screamed, semen bursting between them. Earen came again, grinning as Ficus, too, arched his back.

They lay in each other's arms, motionless. Moving seemed improbable and Earen didn't want to try. He was soaked with sweat and covered in semen, his whole pubic area bathed with Ilamaych's juices. Ficus seemed to be thinking along the same lines, for he murmured, "I'm so glad bodily fluids don't hurt."

"Mmm. Pelin would have had to be crazy to make bodily fluids burn like water," Ilamaych put in. Earen hadn't given the goddess Pelin much thought, but both Ficus and Ilamaych snorted simultaneously at the notion.

Loud bangs resounded without warning nearby. Earen startled, then he relaxed. "Just fireworks for Luck Day," he sighed, scratching his scrotum with a free hand.

Ficus shook his head and climbed to his feet. "That's not fireworks." The Flame ran across the coppersmithy and stared out a narrow window, absolutely still as he gazed outside. "Sounds like rifles. How on Mother Earth did Regori get so many?"

"What? Why do you think Regori is out there?" Earen paused as he heard screams. He struggled upright. The banging was right outside the smithy and the screams were more rapid. Though the household had been taken by surprise, some were apparently fighting back. There were sounds of yelling and metal clashing on metal.

Ficus turned from the window and grabbed a sword and shield from the walls. "Hide under the straw, you two," he growled.

Something inside Earen snapped. "No. I make my own choice for once," he said. He rose and grabbed a sword from the wall. Ilamaych also scrambled to his feet; he, too, reached for a weapon.

"You haven't trained for this," Ficus began, then snapped his head around as strangers appeared in the doorway. Men in Tache-style clothing were poured into the coppersmithy, holding short-nosed rifles.

"Drop the swords." The foreign-accented men cried out.

There were too many. Earen's stomach dropped as he made one final decision: he let go of the sword. Ficus and Ilamaych followed suit, though Ficus scowled fiercely, unrepentant in his nudity. Earen shut his mouth as his arms were grabbed and pulled taut behind his back. The feeling of hempen rope on his wrists was vehemently familiar. His brief respite from pain was over.

Chapter 4
Trussed Up

Ficus ducked one fist and rolled away from another, only to feel a sharp slap upon his back. He fell with a cry. The dock boards were rough beneath his cheek, his whole body stinging from the blow. Ficus realized he'd been slapped by the flat of someone's sword. His eyes teared up, though he would not cry. He wouldn't let them see him cry.

"That's the third time he's tried to escape," one of Regori's men growled at their leader. "We should break his legs."

"No," the leader said. "Broken legs mean we won't be able to sell him. He's got enough bruises and cuts as is. No, go borrow a bucket from those fishermen."

Ficus glanced up as footsteps faded, alert to the possibilities. He discovered that the leader had one of those sophisticated rifles prepared and pointed directly at his face. "Don't you even think about it," the leader growled at him. "If I'm not going to make a profit off you then I don't care what happens. Understand?"

Ficus decided not to give him the courtesy of an answer, instead letting his head sink back to the warped, sun-warmed boards of the dock. He gazed out the Ventricle Channel, forced into passivity. The beauty of the river was profound: green and wide, the mountainous, wooded banks of Tache hazy in the distance. The warmth of the day should have calmed Ficus, save river water would burn him should it touch his skin. Save that he was captive, his choices narrow and severe.

These men are such idiots, Ficus thought resentfully. They'd tried tying him up to no avail. Ficus smirked: they should have known better than to attempt to confine a Flame. Then his smile faded. Though he (and other members of the ruling circle) had expected retaliation from Regori, the mid-day raid had been an unusual gesture. And on Luck Day of all times. Disrespectful, to say the least. Ficus rubbed his swollen knuckles and crusted eye ruefully. Revenge for Regori's bruised pride and the treatment of his heir; such were the eternal relations between Ventris households and Tache lords. With only the five-mile wide Ventricle Channel between them and warring gods urging them on, Ventris and Tache had been feuding for over three thousand years. Now Ficus himself was caught in the middle.

Why me? he thought. The serfs were fair game for coup captures, certainly. But why him? What could they want with him? Unless... it was this slavery concept that Ilamaych had described in alarming detail. He glanced at the other captives, not far away. Ilamaych, Earen and four other serfs returned his gaze, their expressions ranging from sympathy to acerbic. They seemed to say without words, You're one of us now. We're equals. Ficus looked away, ashamed.

The man returned, bucket in hand, his boots making the boards vibrate underfoot. The leader filled it with muddy river water. Ficus's shoulders grew tense. If they want to sell me then they cannot burn me badly, he thought, seeking reassurance. Yet he shuddered as the leader knelt down. The bucket's wooden sides were dripping wet.

"Don't try that again or you'll get more than this." The leader dipped his hand and shook droplets in Ficus's direction.

Ficus squealed and rolled in a ball, his dignity shredded worse than the squalid rags covering his body. Oh, that burned. He wiped off what wetness he could, then sat blinking—not crying—over his stinging palms. His breath came too fast; he breathed in and out with conscious effort, focusing his mind. Ficus caught the leader's eye and growled, "Why mark me further if you wish to sell me?"

The leader grinned at him. "I know how this works. I run a fiery torch over any of your burns or bruises and the wounds go away. You get healed."

A tooted horn caught his attention; Ficus, too, glanced down the river channel. A riverboat was approaching the dock. "At last," said one of Regori's men. "Warguf's late."

Ficus frowned at the riverboat. It seemed not so much designed for elegance as for bald function. The boat was flat and broad, boxy cabins built atop the deck. It was powered by one of those newfangled paddlewheel mechanisms churning water at the rear—the aft, Ficus supposed. Steam puffed from a smokestack. Though he'd traded household goods for decades, Ficus had rarely ventured near the Ventricle Channel itself. Even the sight of that spraying, churning wheel made his heart fall.

When the riverboat docked and men began unloading freight goods (barrels, plate glass packed in straw and milled boards,) the captain wandered over to speak with Regori's men. Ficus knew him for the captain straight off, even from a distance, because of his stance and gait. Only a leader of men could move like that. Up close the captain seemed to have swirling blue skin. Then Ficus realized what he was seeing: the man was marked by detailed tattoos over every inch of his fallow-colored skin. The two colors clashed so violently that his whole face seemed to be crawling.

Ficus blinked. He rather thought he recognized this man. Ficus had been trading household goods long enough to know Tache merchants, if not their ships. "Captain Warguf?" he called out.

Warguf paused, wide eyed. "Isn't that the Flame from Ywen Coed? What's he doing here?"

Regori's leader stepped forward. "We're selling him. We've got a few serfs left, too old for other traders. All in good health. Also got an orangie if you're interested."

"Certainly I'll take the serfs and boy. I'm on my way to Allistair." Despite his offhand words, Warguf's eyes were for Ficus alone.

"I can make you a very good offer on the Flame. If you're going to Allistair, he's sure to have some kind of value up there."

"A little roughed up, isn't he?"

"No broken bones or permanent damage, I assure you."

Ficus cleared his throat. "Whatever you pay, I assure you we can double it for my safe return back to Ywen Coed. Triple it, for the serfs and boy as well. My word is vouchsafed with the matron herself." Matron Gund wouldn't be happy to pay for her own serfs, but Ficus could hardly abandon them.

In response the leader reached for the bucket; Ficus flinched away involuntarily. The two men began the dickering. Ficus kept his mouth shut, though it grated upon him to do so. The price they finally arrived at was paltry and beneath contempt. Ficus handled more money every day in the raw metals of his smithy. Was that all he was worth? He knew what serfs went for these days, and the price they'd come to was fair, but he'd thought himself more valuable than that.

"Return us to Ywen Coed and I'll throw in a bronze wristlet for every one of your men," Ficus said as he and the other captives were hauled to their feet. Everyone ignored him.

Captain Warguf's men were certainly brawny types: Ficus counted six and wondered if there were more. As two of them laid hands on him, he considered that their penises must be tiny in comparison to their musculature. Then Ficus shivered, realizing with a start that he might discover if his supposition were true. Ficus gulped nausea as they were hauled into a cabin like so much cargo, and blinked in the sudden darkness. The boat rocked gently. He realized with a sinking heart that he was surrounded — absolutely surrounded — by his anathema. He quelled the feeling of vulnerability with difficulty.

Captain Warguf entered with a lit lantern, which he hung from an overhead hook. In the light Ficus noted that the space was half filled with crates and odd-shaped packages wrapped in oilcloth and twine. The captain gestured toward the others. "Chain them in a row. Chain the Flame separately with those extra heavy manacles."

Hah. There was no chance in the Abyss that would hinder him. Ficus fought not to grin as the riverboat men leapt to obey. The manacles were quite heavy, and the men carefully screwed in the pins so they fit upon his wrists. They would be childishly easy to shape out of. Ficus sat still, seemingly placid and defeated. He made sure to note that the captain pocketed the manacle keys in his vest pocket. If Ficus laid hand on those keys, they could all escape.

His smugness lasted until Captain Warguf stepped forward and began undoing his trouser laces. His meaning was obvious. Ficus's lip curled in repugnance: no one touched him without his consent. No one. The captain turned to his men. "Leave us alone. Don't enter even if you hear shots fired."

"Awww." The muscular deckhands left reluctantly with many a backward glance. Ficus noted that they didn't argue further. Apparently Captain Warguf was a man who did not tolerate debate by underlings in his command. Ficus had a feeling he was about to find out how Warguf enforced his rule.

Warguf strode forward and grabbed Ficus's bald head with his open hand, tilting it upward. Ficus gazed up at him, teeth clenched tight. "You're so proud, you little household sluts," Warguf purred in his low baritone. He pulled out his half-erect penis through loosened laces. Warguf laid his hand flat upon Ficus's head to control him. Then Warguf slapped Ficus's face with his penis. Ficus felt the weight of it against his skin, the intensity of Warguf's unwashed smell hitting his nose. The slap was an absolute insult, grating against his pride. Warguf did it again, clearly enjoying himself. "Take it. Take me in your proud little mouth."

"You'll lose it if you try," Ficus growled through his teeth.

The captain chuckled. "Above everyone, weren't you? Now you're brought low. Wanted to be Flame myself when I was a child, but Pelin wouldn't have me. Now I have one of you at last. You take it or you won't like what happens."

"Abyss to that." It wasn't an auspicious moment but Ficus didn't care. He wouldn't be insulted this way. He shaped his wrists and ankles at the same time, slipping out of the heavy manacles. They jingled as they hit the deck. Ficus grabbed the man's testicles and twisted — hard.

Captain Warguf fell over backwards and cried out as Ficus scrambled upon him, pressing his advantage. Ficus had his testicles in a death grip. Still outraged, Ficus slapped Warguf's penis — hard — with his other hand, taking out his outrage on the flaccid organ. Then he grabbed the root of Warguf's scrotum in both hands, digging his nails into soft flesh.

"You'll take us back to shore or I'll castrate you with my bare hands," Ficus snarled. It was a good bluff, anyway. Ficus hated the idea of getting blood on himself, though he wore only rags. Bodily fluids may not burn like water, but they were messy.

The captain squeaked and scrambled to reach... into his back pocket? He pulled out a short rifle, or rather, one of those fantastic new pistols. Ficus couldn't react quick enough. Instead of aiming at Ficus, Warguf aimed at the nearest serf, a man named Aghy. He fired.

The shot reverberated through the cabin. All breath left Ficus's body as he realized what had happened. He raced to the serf's side, sinking down to his knees. Aghy's eyes were open, his chest a bloody mess. Warguf had excellent aim. Ficus couldn't do anything for Aghy. Nor could Earen, who was chained beside the dead man. Earen caught his eye, his expression horrified as they heard a death rattle. They'd both known Aghy since he'd been a youth, captured during a coup many years ago. On the other side of Earen, Ilamaych began crying softly.

"Now you know I'm not joking," Warguf said. He'd regained his feet, tucked his penis away and began rummaging through the cargo. "Each time you spurn me I will shoot another serf. They mean little to my bottom line."

"Why don't you just shoot me?" Ficus asked. His voice was oddly devoid of emotion, as if all feeling had been wiped from the world.

"First off, you are mine. What I inflict on you will be personal." Warguf lifted a small crate out of the corner and dusted it off. "Second, you will fetch a fine price in Allistair. Flame presently have mighty value on the exchange. I'd prefer to sell you undamaged."

Ficus rubbed his face, then drew away when he realized his hand was smeared with Aghy's blood. How had that happened? No chance he could run his hand over fire here, on a boat in the middle of the abysmal Ventricle. Was this what slavery consisted of? If so, Ficus didn't care for it. Not one bit.

Meantime, Captain Warguf had set the crate down before the line of serfs and thoughtfully reloaded his pistol. It was an involved process: first he measured black powder, which he dumped into the barrel. Then he pushed in a bullet, followed by a flannel rag. He un-clipped a cunning ramrod from the pistol's length and tamped it all down. Ficus realized through his shock that he should have acted — done something! — before the man was ready to fire again. Yet it was too late, the pistol already loaded. Anyway, there was no guarantee that Warguf didn't have another weapon in his boot or vest.

Ficus sighed. He had his own bottom line: he didn't want more serfs to die. Not for his sake. Warguf had too many hostages lined up.

Warguf opened the crate and drew out a canvas garment with lots of buckles and cords. Ficus frowned, uncertain what it was. Ilamaych, however, cried out, as if involuntarily. The young man gazed with dismay at the garment, his face pale. "No," Ilamaych whispered.

"It's not for you, boy," the man said, his tone bemused. He drew a cigar out of his vest pocket — where the manacle keys were, Ficus realized with a start — and lit it from the lantern. The puffs of fine smoke made Ficus feel nostalgic for fire. Then he blinked as Warguf shook out the canvas; he suddenly understood what those straps, buckles and cords were for.

"You're mad if you think I'd donning that... thing," Ficus said. During their days (and nights) together, Ilamaych had reluctantly told Ficus what had happened to his former teacher, Goldenrod. Ficus had barely believed the boy. It seemed so outlandish, more a nightmare than reality. Yet now the evidence was before his eyes. This was the same sort of canvas coat that had bound and subdued Goldenrod. Ilamaych must have reacted with terror because of that memory. Ilamaych must think that a second Flame was about to be bound and subdued in front of him, while he was helpless to change anything. Ilamaych... might not be wrong, little as Ficus liked admitting it.

"As you wish," Warguf said quietly. To Ficus's horror, Warguf drew the pistol and pointed it at Ilamaych, perhaps drawn by his quiet sobbing.

"Wait!" Ficus jumped in front of Ilamaych, hands out. "Don't. Please don't."

Warguf smiled at him. Ficus met the captain's eyes... and slumped. Not defeated — never defeated — but outmaneuvered. For now.

Warguf tucked the pistol into the back of his trousers. He reached for Ficus, grabbed the tattered rags he wore and ripped them violently from his body. Ficus stood still, withstanding the humiliating treatment. Only his breathing was fast. Warguf held out the canvas: it was built like a backwards coat with oversized sleeves. Reluctantly, Ficus allowed himself to be wrapped in it, his arms enveloped. The canvas felt rough and untreated. Ficus hated it instantly. Warguf secured the sleeves by buckling them to the opposite sides of the coat. Ficus tested the strength of the garment covertly, then less covertly. It was effective, he had to give it that. Not badly designed by any means.

Could he shape out of it? No. Ficus blinked, heart falling. Pelin granted much flexibility, but Flame could not flex their skeletal structure to the extent that this coat would require. His arms were trapped, helpless.

"That's better," Warguf murmured. Ficus realized the man was standing back, smoking his cigar and watching the — show — with evident enjoyment. Warguf opened the crate again and drew out a tiny, leather piece with dangling strings. "Since the slave trade began I've been collecting supplies in case I ever laid hands on one of you. Isn't this pretty? I had it cut special."

Ficus couldn't figure out what the leather was for until the man knelt before him. Warguf caressed Ficus's penis. Ficus gasped, startled by his gentle touch. Warguf grinned and took Ficus's penis in his mouth. Ficus let loose a groan, aroused by the treatment. Warguf's tongue was skilled, his fingers doubly so.

One of Warguf's hands slipped behind him and caressed his anus. Ficus moaned as Warguf penetrated him with a finger, then another. Like all Flame, Ficus could withstand such penetration without need for oils or ointments; one of the advantages of being a shapeshifter. Pelin was a thoughtful goddess who enjoyed anal sex and didn't understand why humans had been assembled so poorly in that respect. Her Flame could be wet and ready at either end. Ficus threw back his head, feeling his penis growing erect. It was wrong to be so aroused by such an evil man. So wrong.

Warguf drew back and hit Ficus's penis, hard. Ficus yelped and fell over backwards. He landed on his ass without hands to cushion the blow, forcibly wrapped as they were around his waist. Ficus glared at Warguf, wishing he could rub his bruised behind or stinging member. "What was that for?"

"Make your ramrod bigger. I know you can," Warguf ordered.

"Absolutely not." Ficus didn't want to give the man more of a target to abuse and arouse.

Warguf punched Ficus's penis so hard he almost lost consciousness. "Do it. Remember what I said about spurning me."

Ficus remembered. He ground his teeth and shaped the largest penis he'd had in... well, the largest he'd ever had. It was more than a foot long and quite thick. He had to shrink his overall height to accomplish the feat, becoming so skinny that his bones showed. There was only so far his body mass could extend, after all. The captain smirked, his own groin noticeably pointed through his trousers. He wasn't the only one. Many of the serfs' eyes were like saucers. Ficus noticed that they, too, were aroused at the sight. Even those who were not attracted to men couldn't help but react to his alluring smell, designed by his goddess for sexual interest. Ilamaych still had his eyes shut tight but Earen, like the others, was obviously aroused, though his expression radiated shame and embarrassment.

The captain grabbed hold of the leather piece and folded it around Ficus's enormous penis. Ficus groaned. Oh, that felt astonishing. He could feel too much through such a large organ. Now the leather was being laced up around his penis like a corset. Ficus was being squeezed out either end. Warguf tied off the stays around his testicles. So tight. Ficus shivered, literally wrapped in pain and pleasure.

Warguf reached into his small crate and drew out a... packet of embroidery needles? And several mismatched brass earrings. Ficus stared, taken back by the ordinary objects. "Always wanted to try this," Warguf murmured, grinning like a boy with something squirming in his pocket.

Try what? Ficus thought as he struggled within the canvas coat. Though he knew perfectly well that he couldn't shape out of it, he tried anyway. If he elongated his fingers, could he undo the buckles holding the sleeves in place? No, not from the inside. What if he...

Warguf took down the lantern. He removed the glass chimney and ran an embroidery needle over the open flame. Ficus frowned up at Warguf; his actions made no sense. If he wanted to burn Ficus, then hot metal should be the last thing he would use. Warguf knelt over Ficus with an expression of intense concentration, focusing on his penis. He grabbed hold and pierced Ficus's penile head.

Chapter 5
Bone Crunching

Ficus screamed and swore, writhing with pain and outrage. The needle pierced his penis all the way through. While the heat felt wonderful (indeed, he could withstand far higher temperatures) the penetrating needle was agonizing. Yet Pelin's gifts flowed through his veins. Fire still healed him. So he wasn't surprised when the needle ceased moving, his flesh closed — cauterized — around the red-hot metal.

"Huh. Wasn't expecting that." Warguf bit his lip and withdrew the needle with force, then pushed it in and out of the hole.

Ficus yelped, his mouth dry. Warguf inserted a brass earring into the newly forged opening. It felt... rather alarming, to be controlled in such a manner. Warguf gave the earring a tug and Ficus moaned, writhing as soreness coupled with unexpected pleasure. Warguf regarded Ficus much as a man would smile upon a freshly gelded ceros. A job well done upon a witless animal. Then Warguf began heating the embroidery needle once again.

There were four piercings in all. Three in a row along his penile head: top, tip and bottom. Ficus lay helpless on his back, wiggling like a beetle as he withstood sharp agony and astonishing pleasure the earrings evoked in him. Such a fascinating exercise. Someday Ficus might try this again, though in a slower, more consensual manner. Now he bore the sheer exhilaration bonelessly, though he couldn't help but scream when Warguf pierced his testicles. It was the most painful piercing, his flesh extra sensitive. Perhaps Warguf had hit a particularly soft spot.

Warguf stood above him, lantern in hand, surveying his handiwork. He was obviously aroused by the sight. Ficus watched, muscles contracting with anticipation as the other man shed his clothing. There was a clatter as Warguf's trousers hit the deck. Ficus realized that the pistol — loaded and ready — was somewhere in that heap. It lay near Ficus's right foot. But Warguf was atop him now. He grabbed Ficus's legs and spread them, placing Ficus's feet upon his shoulders. Ficus gasped, trussed and spread, waiting to be speared.

Warguf bore into him with force, taking him without reprieve. Ficus cried out and squirmed. Warguf grabbed Ficus's penis hard, squeezing him through the leather corset. The stays dragged upon his ball sack, pulling it upward. Ficus's tortured flesh screamed as Warguf tugged the brass earrings. The sensations were shocking. Warguf's tempo increased; he was plundering Ficus, spilling into him. Ficus screamed as he came, his orgasm a teeth-clenching mixture of pain and ecstasy.

Warguf lay bonelessly atop Ficus, face sweating in the shadowed light. "That was something. We have all the way to Allistair to practice that."

We indeed. Ficus bristled at the implication. That had not been sex. It had been no more than masturbation with an unwilling accomplice. He realized his feet had released from Warguf's shoulders. His right foot was once again resting upon the muddle of soft fabric and a hard rod. The pistol. His foot was lying upon the pistol.

Ficus's eyes went wide as Warguf rolled off of him. Will he notice? Ficus wondered wildly. Will he get dressed? Warguf reached for his clothing and Ficus held his breath, but the captain riffled through his vest and came up with another cigar. Warguf must have noticed where Ficus's foot lay... though perhaps he thought nothing of it. Ficus blinked, mind grinding like a mill wheel. He'd never tried shaping his feet to hold something. Could he? Even if Ficus could, he'd never handled a pistol before. He could hardly aim with his feet! Puffs of expensive cigar smoke filled the room as Warguf puttered somewhere in the hold, humming to himself. Ficus sighed. He had to try it. He had to.

Ficus poked his right foot under the cloth and began reshaping it. His big toe needed to pivot around like... like that, in a way it had never been meant to go. Like a thumb. Ficus breathed through his teeth, eyes tearing from the pain. Inhuman shaping hurt, as inflexible bones protested the changes. Ficus stretched his other toes to be longer, more versatile. This part was easier: he liked long toes and had often sported them. But now they grew long as fingers. He flexed, wincing. Now, how to pick up the pistol? His ankle needed adjustment to grow flexible as his wrist.

Warguf had settled down again beside Ficus's torso. Warguf began playing with Ficus's penis, flipping it this way and that as if it were a game piece, even as Ficus fine-tuned his ankle. Ficus gazed upon him with disgust. He wished Warguf would just leave him be. Ficus was wet with semen, chafing and uncomfortable, and the leather corset cut into his flaccid penis. His anus was soaking, muscles clenched in anticipation of more penetration. Yet Warguf seemed less rushed than before. Not a bad tactical situation, Ficus decided after a moment. After all, Warguf was close. Better here than at a distance. At this angle Ficus probably wouldn't hit a serf, though he might accidentally hit himself.

Maybe he could position Warguf? "Straddle me, would you? Rub me with your piece." Ficus said breathily, as if he enjoyed the man's company.

Warguf grinned. "I had to tie you up to make you obedient. Now you like it, eh? Good. Very good." To Ficus's satisfaction Warguf climbed atop him, both of his hands occupied with penises, pulling on the brass earrings as he rubbed them together.

Ficus gasped and rolled his head for show, ignoring the sensations as best he could as he concentrated on the pistol. He couldn't quite get a grip... and where was the trigger? There. It shook uncontrolled in his foot; he needed to steady the weapon. Grimacing, even as Warguf batted his penis playfully, Ficus shaped his left foot in the same manner. Oh, that really hurt. But at least he could firmly grip the pistol. He aimed haphazardly. Warguf was grinning, his expression open and relaxed. If Ficus missed... he gulped and gritted his teeth.

Now.

The explosion was shocking. Ficus was splattered with warm liquid. A heavy weight dropped upon his bound torso. Ficus couldn't breathe under such weight. His right foot hurt. Hurt, hurt, hurt. Was it broken? Ficus opened his eyes and gazed into the dripping, staring, dead face of the captain.

"You got him! You got him in the head!" someone was crowing. Serfs were cheering and simultaneously shushing one another. Chains rattled as they tried to move about.

No one could pull the body off of Ficus. He'd have to do it himself. Ficus coughed, compressed within the canvas coat. The dead body was dripping blood and bits of brain upon him. Shuddering with disgust, Ficus managed to roll the deadweight off. He sat up, abdominal muscles protesting. Yes, his right foot was sincerely broken. He reshaped it best he could, wincing as he did.

"The keys! Get the keys!" Earen hissed at him.

Right, the keys. Why did he have to do everything? Ficus used his left foot to poke into the vest pocket for the keyring; he tossed it toward the serfs with a kick. Then he lay back motionless as they unlocked themselves. Two knelt beside him. Ficus blinked up at Ilamaych and Earen. He realized he was crying. He hated blood. He hated it. And his foot was broken, and the penis corset pinched, and they were still captives in the middle of the abysmal river.

Ilamaych's eyes were shining, his expression relieved as he helped unbuckle the canvas coat. Ficus bet he wasn't even thinking of the struggle to come. Earen was, though. "The others are looking for weapons," he said as they helped Ficus upright.

"Get me the lantern," Ficus groaned, rubbing his face with his filthy hands. He found something wet dangling from his ear. Ficus cried out and threw it across the hold, his skin crawling.

The lantern helped, fire burning off the blood. So did getting the penis corset off. Ficus decided not to touch the earrings now. Later, he'd deal with them later. Ilamaych shook out the captain's clothing and handed them over. Ficus reshaped his body to fit. Nothing on Mother Earth could make his right foot fit into a boot: it was swelling, the big toe still jutting at an awkward angle. Running it over fire did little — as always, bones were beyond Pelin's aid.

Ficus looked up from his self-ministrations to find serfs excitedly planning to ambush the riverboat men. "No, we must wait until they're asleep," Ficus said, overriding their excited argument.

They glared at him. Earen frowned, the captain's pistol dangling from his hand (he'd been attempting to reload it with much swearing). "That's cowardly, killing people when they can't fight back."

"We're outnumbered, out-armed and at a disadvantage. It's their boat. We—wait—until—dark," Ficus snarled.

They began arguing... then cut off abruptly as footsteps trod near the cabin door. "Everything all right in there, captain?" a voice called out.

They stared at one another, wide eyed. Ficus swiftly reshaped his throat and tried to approximate the captain's baritone. And accent. "Fine. Fine, thank you."

"Captain, we're approaching the locks but it'll be dark in an hour. Should we drop anchor here?"

Ficus could feel his blood pumping. What would Warguf do? It seemed a reasonable request. The river locks would be filled with other riverboats and dockworkers, he imagined. "Do that. I'll be here all night. Don't disturb me," Ficus growled.

"Yes, captain."

Silence as the footsteps trod away. Then Earen whispered, "Do you think he suspects?"

Ficus could only shrug. Then he turned to the serfs and stared them down. "We wait. Keep looking for weaponry." They glanced at one another and complied. Ficus wondered how long it would take them to realize they were no longer obliged to obey him... if they hadn't realized already.

A crate of fine cooking knives satisfied Ficus well enough: sharp, close-range weapons were more to his taste than loud gunfire and complicated reloads. Meanwhile, Ficus had Ilamaych bind his bad foot with strips of canvas dipped in a pot of glue. They spent the next few hours whetting knives on leather strops and planning in whispers. When they emerged from the hold into the darkened boat, they did so in silent, intent order.

Finding the sleeping hold took time. Breathlessly, Ficus limped behind the others. He sighed with relief when they found men sleeping soundly in their hammocks. Snores cut off abruptly off as serfs cut throats. Their efficiency was everything Ficus had hoped for. Ficus counted six dead men in the cabin. Were there more? Ficus limped onward, knife in hand, as they slipped through the dark riverboat.

He was on deck by the great paddleboat wheel when Earen cried out, pointing the captain's pistol in his outstretched hands. "Ficus—

duck!"

Ficus dropped to the deck as an explosive shot rang out. A man dropped bonelessly from the balcony above, his pistol discharging as it hit the deck. So loud. Ficus froze, breathing shakily. The body didn't move. "Are you hit?" he finally asked Earen, who seemed to be shaking worse than he was.

"No. You?"

Ficus shook his head. "That makes seven men. He must have been on watch."

"Good thing I reloaded this right!" Earen laughed.

Good thing he's a lucky shot, Ficus thought acerbically, though he declined to say so aloud. Next time might not be so lucky. Another serf shushed them, wide eyed with anticipation of other lurking enemies. Despite their caution, another sweep of the boat turned up no more surprises. Their luck, it seemed, had turned.

Later they found a small rowboat strapped to the side deck. They loaded up and rowed toward the Ventris shoreline by dawn's light. Ficus could only be grateful that the wind was low and the water smooth as plate glass. He huddled under a tarpaulin anyway, rightly fearing droplets from the oars. The serfs scattered once they drew to shore, each carrying a bundle of valuables and food from the riverboat. Ficus could only wish them luck. He turned to Ilamaych and Earen, eyeing them, curious what they would choose.

"I'd love if you both came home with me," he said. From a practical standpoint he could sure use the help. His right foot throbbed terribly.

"I'd love to come," Ilamaych said. His whole body was relaxed, his expression lively with covert joy. Ficus could guess why. The pain he'd known seeing Goldenrod captured was lessened, now that Ficus had escaped his bounds. Ilamaych hadn't had his world torn from him again.

Then Ilamaych's face grew still as he looked to Earen. Ficus, too, gazed at Earen. Earen's mouth was set at a stubborn angle. "I would not return as a serf."

"You saved my life last night. I will formally ask the matron to rescind your serfdom." Ficus would exaggerate Earen's deeds to the point where the matron could not ignore his worth. One lucky shot could become auspicious for both of them. "I'll talk her around. You'll see."

Ilamaych smiled shyly at him. "Please, Earen? I know they hurt you but you can be a houseman in Ywen Coed. A real man, not a serf. Just think about it."

Ficus reached out and took his hand. "I know you'll make a fine houseman."

Earen met his eyes... and a smile broke through his face, like the sun coming out from behind clouds. "So I shall."

If you enjoyed this story, you can discuss it with other readers and the author at the *Chaining Flame* story page at http://forbiddenfiction.com/library/story/JLW-1.000120.

Fools Rush In

Elizabeth Schechter

Elizabeth Schechter is a stay-at-home mom who lives in Central Florida with her husband and son. Her first novel, *Princes of Air*, was published in 2011 by Circlet Press, and her second, a steampunk novel entitled *House of the Sable Locks*, was released in June, 2013. Her most recent work, the *Tales from the Arena* duology, was published in November, 2013.

Chapter 1

Rash Promises

"And I'm saying it can't be done!" The current object of my attentions snapped. Not at me, thankfully. I was sitting at a table in a tavern with a pair of bickering women. The one sitting in my lap was the only one who really held my interest. I'd lost her name somewhere at the bottom of the first bottle of plum brandy, but that didn't bother me. What was important to me right at that moment was that she had the most amazing tits. I was a simple man, then. Nice tits, nice ass, pretty smile, red gold in my pocket and good wine. That was all it took to make me happy. And let me tell you, that night, I was really happy. I had plenty of the last two, thanks to a very profitable heist back in Tarsis. But things had gotten a little too warm for me back in my home town, so I decided to come to Arraki for a spell. For my health, you understand. Which was how I found myself in a tavern in the Thieves Quarter that night. With her.

Now that I look back on it, I honestly don't remember just where she came from. It was like she was just... there, cooing over the tales of my recent exploits and paying me just the right kind of attention. She was a short, buxom blonde with gorgeous blue eyes, and she'd giggled when I'd first pulled her into my lap and told her that she was conveniently pocket-sized. After the first night with her, I wondered if all the whores in Arraki were that pretty and that pliable. After the second night, I stopped wondering about anyone else—female or male—entirely.

"What can't be done, Darlin'?" I asked, tightening my arm around her waist and glancing over at the woman across from us at the table. That one was dark, and she had a hard, rangy look that told me that she was in my line of work. She was young, though. No older than seventeen, I guessed. Old enough to know how to survive on the streets, but too young to have made her name.

"Lace is going to try to break into Kai's Temple," my lovely companion told me. "And it cannot be done!"

Now, telling me that someplace can't be broken into was like telling a devotee of the God of Lust that a woman was virtuous. All that does is give us something that needs to be proven wrong. I picked up my glass and took another sip of plum brandy. "And Kai is...?"

"Kai the Formless," the lady in my lap answered. "The Arraki patron God of Thieves. The Temple is sealed to everyone. I've heard that there is supposed to be a cloistered priestess, but no one knows for sure, because no one ever goes in there."

"I've also heard that the mosaics on the interior walls are made with gemstones, and everything in there is dripping with gold," Lace added. "I need to make my name, and that's how I'm going to do it."

Dripping with gold, hm? I've always wanted to be dripping with gold. I leaned back in my chair. "You really want to throw your life away?" I asked nonchalantly. "Don't fuck with the gods, sweet. You'll live longer."

Lace sniffed at me. "And who are you to be handing out platitudes?" she demanded. "Some kind of priest?"

I laughed, "No, sweet. I doubt there's a god out there that would want me as his priest. I'm just someone who has been doing the old snatch-and-grab a lot longer than you. My name is Davi."

Lace's jaw dropped, "Davi? Davi of Tarsis? Davi the harem thief?" Her voice spiraled up on the last few words, and the tavern fell completely silent.

I smirked, reached up to twirl my mustache, realized at the last second that I'd shaved it off before I ran for my life... excuse me. Before I decided to take an extended vacation in Arraki. I settled for stroking my chin. "You've heard of me?"

I could see Lace now had a serious case of hero-worship building, and my lovely lady was smiling at me in a way that sent heat rushing to all the fun parts of my anatomy. Once again I thanked the Trickster that I'd paid extra for a private room. We'd certainly made good use of it.

"Of course we've heard of you!" Lace gushed. "Who hasn't heard of the Master Thief who stole the thousand emeralds from the Sultan of Tarsis' harem?"

I clucked, fishing under my shirt for an emerald the size of my thumb that I wore around my neck. "Thousand and one," I corrected her as I flashed the stone. Of course, this particular emerald hadn't been stolen. It was a gift from the Sultan's intended bride, a truly stunning eighteen-year-old virgin named Naras. Call it... payment for services rendered. I got entry into the harem and access to the emeralds, she got a way out of a marriage contract she had no desire to go through with. Everybody won. Well, except for the Sultan.

The rest of the night in the tavern was a blur. It seemed as if every thief, grifter, pickpocket, cutpurse, pimp and whore in the place just had to buy me a drink. In return, they all wanted me to breathe on their hands. For luck, they all said. So I went from being a little bit drunk to being very drunk, and I swear by the Trickster that I remember nothing about the rest of that night.

I woke up the next morning hung-over, wondering if it would be worth it to turn myself in to the Palace guards so they could chop my head off. No, I decided. If they did chop my head off, it would still hurt. It would just hurt way over there.

"Drink this."

I didn't recognize the voice, but I drank anyway. Maybe I'd be lucky and it would kill me. The room took a sharp turn to the left, wheeled around three times, settled gently on the ground and spit me out like a peach pit. "What is this?" I gasped.

"Trust me, you don't want to know." The bed creaked and settled, and I turned to see my lovely lady with the pretty tits sitting next to me. She was completely, gloriously naked, except for a pair of wide gold bracelets that she seemed to wear all the time. A brief check under the coverlet showed that I was as naked as she, and I wondered what I'd missed. How to find out...

"I am very disappointed in you, Davi," she said, folding her arms over her chest.

Well, I suppose that's one way.

"I'm sorry, Darlin'," I said, sitting up and letting the coverlet slip down. "I shouldn't have drunk those last two dozen whatever-they-were. What was I drinking, anyway?"

"You don't want to know that, either," she answered. She looked down at me and sniffed. "You really don't remember anything, do you?"

For a minute, I wondered if I'd started something with her that I hadn't been able to finish, then shook off that thought. "Not a thing. What did I do? Or not do?"

"You swore by the Trickster that you and you alone would be the one to dare Kai's Temple," was her answer.

"Oh, I didn't!" I gasped.

"You did. Your exact words were that you would be the one to relieve the god of gold that He was never going to use," she told me. I groaned and rubbed my hand over my face. That did sound like me when I let the bottle do my thinking for me.

"And... how many people heard me say that?" I asked.

She sniffed at me, and didn't answer, which told me more than words could have. If I didn't at least make an attempt on the Temple, I might as well leave town. I sighed dramatically and reached out to take her hand. "So, let me get this straight. I got drunk and stupid, swore to do the impossible, and then you brought me back up here so that I could snore at you. Is that right?" She nodded without looking at me. "Sorry, Darlin'. Is there any way I can make it up to you?" She sniffed again, then squeaked in surprise as I pulled her closer.

"What are you doing?"

"Attempting to make it up to you," I answered with a smile. I ran one finger down her cheek. "Sapphires, I think. To set off your eyes."

"Sapphires?" she repeated, those amazing eyes as wide as saucers.

"Once I've done this job, I'll see you draped in sapphires," I whispered, running my finger down her throat and over her collarbone. "Sapphires and silver and nothing else."

She smiled in return and leaned closer, "You're really going to try it? And you would do that for me?"

I drew her into my arms and lowered myself back onto the bed, holding her to my chest as I did. "Oh, yes, I'm going to try it. And, Darlin', you just wait to see what I'll do for you after this job."

She giggled, running her fingernails over my chest, "How about what you'll do for me now?"

That was just what I wanted to hear. I ran my hand up her throat and into the curls at the back of her head, pulling her face down and kissing her, making it hard and possessive, the way I'd learned she liked it. She moaned against my lips and squirmed against me, her hands trapped between our bodies. I loosened my hold on her long enough for her to get all the way onto the bed, then caught her in my arms again and rolled, pinning her underneath me. She giggled, her cheeks flushed, her lips red as rubies. Once she was settled, I pushed up, bracing myself on my arms so I could look down at her.

"What are you waiting for, oh Harem Thief?" she asked. "You're wasting time."

"Since when is it a waste to admire the woman I love?" I asked. She caught her breath and sat up, so fast that she almost caught me in the chin with her forehead.

"What?" she demanded. "What did you say?"

I smiled at her, reaching out and tracing the bow of her upper lip with my thumb. "I said I love you."

"Oh..." she breathed, looking stunned. "Oh, Davi..."

"Now, are you going to let me show you how much?" I asked, pushing her back down onto the bed. She giggled and raised her arms, embracing me as I lowered myself down over her.

"I love you, too, Davi," she whispered in my ear as she held me. I kissed the side of her neck, then started moving down her body, admiring her every curve, worshiping her beauty with lips and tongue until she was breathless and whimpering under me. When I found her jewel with my tongue, she moaned, arching her back and wrapping her legs around my head. Gently, I pushed her legs up and back, rolling her into a ball and leaving her open and spread so that I could drink deep. It amazed me how good she tasted — like honey mead warmed in the sun, mingled with the finest spices in the world. I could pleasure her like this for hours, and it was incredibly tantalizing to watch her as she writhed underneath me, moaning and screaming with the force of her climax and then going completely, bonelessly limp. I stretched out next to her, studying her as she slowly rose from the depths of pleasure and returned to awareness. When she smiled at me, I leaned down and kissed her.

"You taste fantastic," I told her. She blushed and giggled, then ran one finger down my chest.

"Your turn," she said in a husky voice.

Just what I was waiting for. I kissed her again and moved back between her legs; she hummed softly and raised her knees, hooking her legs over my hips and pulling me towards her. She was primed and ready for me, and I let her set the pace as I teased the entrance of her cunt with my cock. She moaned softly, her legs flexing as she tried to pull me deeper.

"Davi, don't tease," she whispered, her voice catching as I thrust into her before she finished speaking. She was still wet, tight from her orgasm, and for a moment, I wished that this would never end. Then she found my nipples with her fingers, and I gasped and started to pump, hard and fast. I could feel her cresting again, growing wetter, growing tighter. She locked her ankles behind my back, digging her nails into my arm as she pleaded with me in a broken voice to not stop, never stop, more, please, please. I could feel my orgasm, feel it in each thrust, in the way she tightened around me, her cunt throbbing and squeezing me. When she started to shriek, I lost it, pounding into her until I burst, riding wave after wave of ecstasy until I collapsed over her, spent.

I stayed there for a moment, keeping my weight on my arms so I wouldn't squash her, then rolled to the side and pulled her into my arms. She cuddled against me, her head resting on my shoulder. When her breathing finally returned to normal, she murmured, "When?"

"When what?"

"When are you going to try the Temple?" she asked.

"Oh," I answered, and considered the question. Then I shook my head, "Soon, I think. Before the gossip hits the wrong ears. Where is this Temple, anyway?"

She raised her head and smiled, "I'll take you."

Chapter 2

Into the Temple

It was just after midday when we stopped outside what she called the Temple Wall. Which was pretty accurate. It was, indeed, a wall. I left her standing there and made my way around it, a longer walk than I'd expected, finally coming back to ask the obvious question, "Where did they hide the gate?"

She laughed, "That's the usual first question. There is no gate. Hasn't been for as long as anyone can remember. We told you last night — the Temple is sealed. No one goes in there."

I remembered someone saying that, but I'd thought it hyperbole. Instead, I was faced with a real challenge. I found myself oddly excited. This might be fun! "No supplies? No food or anything? No deliveries?"

She shook her head, "There's a rotating portal to let supplies in."

"I saw that. Not very big."

"Exactly. It isn't big enough for a man. And I don't even know why it exists, because the Temple is the same. No gate, no door, no anything. The only opening is... well, come with me." She led me down the street to a small park, then pointed back at the Temple. "Look just under the dome."

Now, there's a reason I don't do second-story work, and it has nothing to do the fact that, for some reason, most people usually hide their valuables in either the root-cellar or that crock right up on the top shelf of the kitchen. You know, the one with the crack in it that you can't put mead into anymore? Yeah, that one. No, the reason I don't do second-story work is that it involves climbing, which makes me dizzy and ill. So I do not, under any circumstance, climb anything other than stairs. The idea of scaling the side of a building made me nauseous, and here I was, about to do just that. I'd backed myself into a corner, and if I didn't go through with this, word would spread. I didn't think that my sweetheart would actually tell anyone, but if we weren't stinking rich by dawn tomorrow, then everyone would know I failed. So I really didn't have a choice.

I squinted and nodded, seeing the regular dark spaces in the gray marble, "Windows?"

"For ventilation. That's the only access."

I frowned and looked at her, "How do you know that? If there isn't any way to get inside the gate, how do you know that there isn't a door to the Temple?"

She dimpled, "Because I scaled the wall and took a look around the Temple grounds last year."

I coughed, "You?"

Her smile vanished. "Yes, me. I thought I'd try my luck at that treasure, and I decided that it was too much trouble to take the risk."

She folded her arms over her chest and turned away from me. I gave myself a good mental kick and went to rub my hands up and down her bare arms. She didn't shrug me off, which I took as a good sign.

"Darlin', I didn't realize you and I were in the same line of work," I said. "I apologize."

"Some of us like to keep our doings a bit more discrete than the Harem Thief does," she snapped back, looking over her shoulder at me. "Now, are you going to listen to me?"

I stepped back and bowed, "I yield to the expert. How do we do this?"

She relaxed when she realized I wasn't being sarcastic, taking my hand and leading me to a bench underneath a tree. A nice place to sit and talk, and if any of the people passing by were paying attention to us, we would look like a pair of young lovers making up after a spat. I pulled her close and whispered in her ear, "Didn't take you for a thief. You're very good."

She smiled and rubbed her cheek against mine. "Yes, yes, I am," she whispered as she kissed me. She rested her head on my shoulder and murmured, "Now, there's a place where the outer wall is rough.

There are wonderful handholds, and it takes less than a minute to get up and over. It's an easy drop on the other side."

I buried my face in her golden hair, "What's the watch schedule?"

"Every twenty minutes. Plenty of time." She tipped her head back and gave me a lazy smile, her blue eyes sparkling. "And I'm going with you."

I couldn't react to that statement without calling attention to us, so I forced a smile and said, "No, you're not," through clenched teeth.

She laughed and tapped me on the nose, which would have been adorable if I didn't want to strangle her right then. "You need me. You'll never get into the Temple without me and my equipment," she said in a soft voice, then pulled free from my arms and stood up.

"I'll meet you here an hour past sunset. I'll have everything we need," she purred, then turned and walked away, vanishing into the greenery.

When I returned to the park that night, she wasn't there. I sat down on the bench and waited as full dark fell, wondering if I'd been made a fool of, and I nearly jumped out of my skin when she appeared out of the darkness as if she'd been conjured there. As I tried to slow my heart down, I noticed what she was wearing. Gone were the low-cut bodice and hiked-up skirts; now she was in breeches and boots, with a long-sleeved jacket that came down to her knuckles and a heavy-looking bag slung over her shoulder. Everything she wore was mottled black and gray, and her face was smudged with dirt or soot, the better to hide in the shadows.

"Come on," she said softly. "We don't have a lot of time." She pulled me from the bench and into the shadows, shoving a bundle into my hands. "Put this on. The guards have just passed the Temple. Once they pass the park, we'll have just under twenty minutes to get over the Temple wall and up the side."

I didn't answer, shaking the bundle out to reveal clothing in mottled gray and black, similar to what she was wearing. I stepped back into the bushes and stripped, pulling on the shadowy clothes and wondering just how she had been able to get something that fit me as if it had been made for me. I rolled my own clothes up and left them under the bush. I could retrieve them later, if all went well. And if it didn't go well, I wouldn't need them anymore, and whoever found them was welcome to them. I kept my emerald, though, tucked under the jacket. For luck.

When I rejoined my partner, she was standing in the shadows of the trees and was almost impossible to see. She nodded when she saw me, and fussed over me for a moment, pulling the jacket's hood up over my hair, then rubbing her hands all over my face. Whatever it was that she smeared on my skin itched. I grimaced.

"You can wash it off later," she whispered. "Stay in the shadows. The guard just passed. Let's go." She flowed out of the shelter of the trees, moving like a ghost. I followed her, not quite as gracefully. This morning, the walk from the Temple to the park had taken two, maybe three minutes. Now, it seemed to take half the night, and I was sweating by the time we got to the wall. She gestured to the left, and I followed her lead until we reached a place that didn't look any different than the rest of the wall, until I rested my hand on it and felt the uneven stone. She grinned, her white teeth flashing in the darkness, then swarmed up the wall and over. I heard a distant thump as she landed on the other side.

Well, if she could do it, so could I. I fumbled my way up the wall, certain that at any moment someone was going to grab onto my ankle, pull me down and haul my ass to prison. I almost fell over the top of the wall in my haste to get out of that imaginary guard's reach, and I dropped down on the other side and kept going, sitting down hard and panting.

"There, that wasn't so bad, was it?" she cooed. I glared up at her, but the effect was lost in the darkness.

"How did you say we get in there?" I asked, knowing the answer and not wanting to believe it. What had I gotten myself into? And was there any way to get out of it? She pointed up, and I grimaced. "How about we agree to say we did it, and never speak of this again?" I offered.

"Really? The Harem Thief is giving up?" she said with a snicker. "Afraid of heights?"

"It isn't the height that bothers me. It's the stop at the bottom when I fall," I muttered, staring up at the distant dome of the Temple. "So, are we going to fly?"

"Not so simple," she answered. She started rummaging through her bag and pulled out a hand crossbow and a quarrel with a thin cable attached to it. The rest of the cable dropped to the ground in a coil.

"That is never going to reach the top," I said as she took aim.

"It isn't meant to. I did some scouting after I left you today, and there's a ledge halfway up. We'll go in stages." She fired the crossbow and I watched as the cable unfurled until just a few inches were left on the ground. She tucked the crossbow back into her pack, picked up the end of the cable and tugged on it, then pulled harder. "It's ready. Let's go." She handed the cable to me.

"You go first. I'll keep you steady." Trapped. Nowhere to go but up. I tried to cover the fact that I was completely, absolutely, terrified, giving her a quick grin. I took the cable from her... and the next thing I knew, I was standing on the ledge with her arms around me.

"Idiot!" she scolded. "Why didn't you tell me you have no head for heights?"

I looked at her, a much more pleasing view than the ground all the way down there. "How did we get up here?"

"We climbed. You did fine. When we got to the ledge, you turned around to help me up and froze. You don't remember?" I shook my head slowly, and she sighed and kissed my cheek. "It's fine. That happens, sometimes. So I hear. Now, do you want to go the rest of the way up, or back down?"

"I came this far. Maybe I won't remember the rest," I joked, forcing out a laugh. She grinned and coiled the cable up, repeating the process of setting the line. And again, the minute I took hold of the cable, I blanked out, coming to myself this time standing in one of the windows at the top of the temple. Looking down into heaven.

The entire inside of the temple glittered in the light of torches that ringed the interior of the space. In the flickering light, I could see bright flashes of red and blue and green, like brilliant stars below my feet. And for once, I didn't mind looking down.

"Oh, me," she breathed next to me. "It does look amazing from up here..."

"Incredible," I agreed. "If we come out of here with even a fraction of what is down there, we'll be set for life." I looked down at the vast wealth below me, and then at her. "Darlin', when we get out of here... what would you say to staying with me?"

She looked at me oddly, "I am staying with you."

"I mean..." I hesitated, then decided that if she said no, I could always fling myself down into the gold below. "I mean marry me. Raise up our own little thieves guild. You'd have to teach them the second-story work..."

She stopped me, "You... you're serious?"

I nodded. "Dead serious. Sapphires and silver and a wedding ring."

"Oh..." she looked down, then back up at me, a gamine grin on her face. "Shall we get down there?"

Thankfully, I didn't remember a minute of the trip down, either. I found myself on the ground, the cable still in my hand, wondering just how I'd managed to get all the way down without remembering the stop in the middle. I heard a soft thump, and turned to see her straightening and coming towards me.

"Darlin', I have never seen anything so beautiful," I said as she walked into my arms. She smiled up at me and put her arms around my neck, drawing me down to kiss me.

"Davi, I want you," she murmured against my lips.

I had sudden visions of rolling around with her, naked on a pile of gold the size of a feather bed. I laughed and pulled her tightly to me. "Oh, I like the way you think, Darlin'."

She ran her hands over my chest and pushed me back. "Over there, in the corner. There's a pile of silk."

I turned away to see what she was talking about, and gasped in pleasure and surprise as she came up behind me and wrapped her arms around me, caressing my chest through my jacket, running surprisingly strong hands down my belly and over my hip, her body pressed against my back. For a moment, I thought there was something strange. Her body felt... different. But then one of her hands started working its way down into my breeches, and I gave up on thinking and reached back, running my hand down over her flank.

"Darlin', you'd better give me a chance to get laying down," I said over my shoulder. Her answer was a low chuckle. I turned in the circle of her arms, and found myself looking into blue eyes that were full of amusement... and on the same level as my own. That stopped me long enough that I noticed the beard. I yelped and jumped backwards, pulling out of her—his!—arms and staring. He was my size, wearing mottled gray clothing similar to mine, with shoulder length blond hair, brilliant blue eyes and a rakish grin that looked familiar. A glint of metal caught my eye; I saw the wide gold bracelets on his wrists and my jaw dropped.

"I..." I started, then coughed and cleared my throat. "That's... a nice trick, Darlin'. Someday, you have to show me how you did that."

Chapter 3
Tricks and Tricksters

He laughed again, "Oh, I do like you, Davi. I'm going to enjoy having you around. Welcome to my Temple."

"Your...?" I started to repeat, then shook my head. "Oh, no! No, no, no! You're... you're him, aren't you? What's-his-name...?"

"Kai the Formless. Yes," he answered, grinning at me. "Patron of thieves. You call me Trickster, and I like that. You're one of my most devoted sons, you know."

"Thanks. I... uh..." I had been about to apologize for breaking into his Temple, then remembered that it hadn't really been my idea in the first place. "You tricked me!"

He grinned, "That's what I do."

"I never told anyone I was going to try and rob the temple, did I?"

"No. I told you that, and made you believe it," he shrugged. "Truly, I couldn't think of any other way to get you here. If I'd asked you nicely to come here, would you have?"

"Ah..." I looked down and away. He had a point. "All right. So you tricked me into thinking you were a woman, manipulated me into thinking I had to rob your temple, and I've no doubt that you did some kind of magic to make sure we got past the guards so that I got in here in one piece. Not to be rude, but why?"

He sighed dramatically, just the way I do when I'm about to try and sell someone their own shoes. Before he could start, I held one hand up. He looked surprised, then nodded. "All right. I had to. I couldn't lose you, not when you were finally close enough for me to reach. The form you were so intrigued with was that of Arna, my priestess. She died recently."

I frowned. Arna. Not usually a woman's name, that. And for some reason, the name sounded familiar. I didn't know anyone named Arna, so I wasn't sure why. It would come to me, eventually. "Sorry to hear that," I said while I thought. "What does that have to do with me?"

"Do you remember what you told Lace? That you doubted that there was a god who would want you as a priest. You were wrong." He looked at me, starting down at my boots and working his way slowly up until his eyes met mine again. He smirked at me and said, "I need a new votary."

I was about to repeat myself and ask what that had to do with me, but that was the moment when I remembered where I'd heard the name Arna before. And the Arna I knew hadn't been a woman. He'd been a thief, a legendary one, one who'd made his name before the age of twenty and had never stopped making his mark on the upper echelon of Tarsii society. No one was safe from his reach, right up until he vanished. Which had happened over five hundred years ago.

"Wait... you're telling me that your priestess was Arna the Rogue, the most famous thief in five generations," I said slowly. "And he ended up... here. As a woman?"

"Sometimes. Sometimes he was a man," Kai answered and shrugged. "It depended on our moods, really. I think you can agree that he made a most fetching woman, didn't he? Of course," he looked down at himself, "He wasn't bad as a man, either."

I nodded slowly, wondering just how far up the cable I'd be able to get before Kai stopped me. Which raised another question. "You... you did something to me. To get me up the side of the Temple."

"I was running out of time, and you never said a word about being afraid of heights." He rested his hands on his hips. "Davi, let me finish. I need a votary. It doesn't have to be a priestess. It can be a priest. I just need to have someone here in the Temple, someone to serve me, see to my needs. I'm... well, I got into a bit of trouble, a few millennia back. And Mother... grounded me."

"Grounded?" I fought the urge to have a giggle fit—it wasn't often that I heard a god admit to having been sent to his room and told to play nice.

"Well, I couldn't help it! I am what I was made to be, and Fersis' shield was so shiny…"

"Fersis?" I did laugh this time. "You stole the Sun God's shield?"

Kai pouted at me. He actually pouted, and when he spoke again, he sounded like a small child who'd been caught with his hand in the date jar. "Yes. But I gave it back, and said I was sorry. Anyway, Mother got upset. She always did like Fersis better. So I'm confined to my Temple until she decides I've learned my lesson."

I shook my head, confused. "But you came out! You were with me!"

"Loophole. I can walk outside for one mortal week to find a new votary when the old one dies. But I have to find a new one within that week, or I'll be alone. Do you know what happens when a god is alone? We need to have someone to actively worship us, or we fade away into the darkness." He looked at me, and I saw a hint of desperation in his eyes. "You're my choice, out of all the thieves in Arraki. I want you. I like you. You're funny, and you're interesting, and…" He stopped, looked down, then looked back at me. "You can stay with me, be mine. You'll have every luxury, everything you desire, anything that is in my power to grant. I'll keep you alive far longer than you would otherwise live, keep you young and handsome. You'll serve me, be my priest. Or priestess, if you want to try that. I don't mind either way. Please say you'll stay?" Kai leered at me and took a step closer, "I can promise that you will never be bored."

My mouth went dry, and I think I whimpered. "I…"

"You just spent most of a week with me in your bed. You promised to drape me in sapphires and silver. You were ready to take me right here, right now," his voice dropped, became lower, sultry, seductive. "You asked me to marry you. You're already half in love with me."

"More than half…" I croaked.

"Do you object to men, Davi? I can be female for a few hundred years. Tell me what you want, Davi." He closed the gap between us, standing close enough that I could feel the heat radiating from his body. And a small part of my brain was dying to know what he looked like under those clothes. "You aren't the only one who fell in love, Davi. Be mine. Please. And let me be yours."

"Or...?"

He sighed, "Or... I will cloud your memories of me and transport you out of my Temple. I will not force you. I will not try to coerce you. I had to bring you here, so that I could make the offer. But if you do not want to stay, I cannot keep you. There's no point—if I keep you here against your will, you're not a votary. You're a prisoner. You won't worship me, you'll hate me. And I don't want your hate. There are no tricks now, Davi. No magic, no manipulation. Just me, asking you to stay." He paused, then turned away, but not before I saw disappointment plain on his face. "If you want to go..."

"I didn't say that," I whispered.

He looked at me over his shoulder, wide-eyed as a startled deer. "You'll stay with me?" he asked, looking into my eyes.

I nodded slowly, wondering what I was getting myself in to. He smiled at me, and the joy in those eyes made me not care.

"Take this, my priest," he murmured, taking from his wrist one of the wide bracelets. "Take this and be marked as my own." He took my left hand in his and slipped the bracelet onto my arm, and I watched in wonder as the metal warmed and shifted, forming itself to the shape of my wrist. I admired it for a moment, then smiled and slipped the emerald off, dropping the cord over his head and settling the stone onto his breast.

"Now you're marked as mine," I said, smoothing the stone down and touching the skin underneath.

He covered my hand with his. "You promised sapphires," he reminded me.

I grinned up at him, "I'm a little short on sapphires right now." I had a thought, and the question fell from my mouth before I could stop myself, "Kai, you're using Arna's face now, right?"

He nodded, turning slightly, "Both of them. I thought... my powers are limited, outside these walls. But from what I could see in your mind, I thought she would appeal to you."

"Oh, she did." I smiled slowly. "So... what do you really look like?"

The minute the question was out of my mouth, he changed. Sharp-faced, high cheekbones and eyes like storm-clouds under unruly black curls, he was a little taller and a lot thinner, wearing a wrapped shirt and loose breeches instead of the shadowy clothes that he'd worn as Arna. He looked down at himself and shrugged. "This is the form Mother gave me when she made me." He said, his voice a wonderful baritone rumble. He peered shyly at me through ridiculously long lashes, and I felt my heart stutter as I recognized the look as one of hers. That made me look harder at him, and I studied him for a long time, long enough that he started to fidget. "Should I change back?" he asked quietly.

"No," I answered. "I like this face." I cocked my head to the side and smiled at him. "Emeralds suit this face better. And you're right."

"Right about what?" he asked.

"I really was more than half in love with her. With you, I mean. It was her face, but it was you behind the eyes." I crossed the space between us and reached up, cupping his cheek with my hand, feeling his skin grow warmer under my touch. I had no idea that gods blushed so beautifully. "I like this face," I repeated. "Because this is your face." I slid my hand to the back of his head, running my fingers through curls like warm silk, and pulled his head down to mine. His arms wrapped tightly around me, and the kiss was as warm and welcoming as any that he'd given me whilst wearing his female disguise. I slid my arm around his waist, laughing against his lips as he started tugging at my jacket.

"Impatient?" I whispered as I pulled away from his kiss and slid my hand out of his hair and down to his shoulder.

"You have no idea," he answered, then scowled slightly. For a moment, I was afraid he was annoyed at me, then I felt a cold draft against my skin, and warm skin against mine where our bodies touched. When I looked down, every stitch of clothing that we both had been wearing was gone. The only things that remained were our bracelets and the emerald, flashing green in the torchlight. I looked up at him to see amusement and desire in his eyes. "Clothing only gets in the way," he growled.

"It does," I agreed, shifting my hips against him and feeling his cock pressing hard against my stomach. I ran my fingers over his side and down over his hip. "You said something about a pile of silk in the corner?"

He laughed, taking my face between his hands and ducking his head to kiss me again. I'd never before been kissed by someone taller than I was — even when I'd been with men, I was usually the taller one. It was interesting, if a little hard on the neck. I ran my hands up his back, tightening my fingers over his shoulders as he ran one hand firmly over my ass. Then he grinned and took my hand, tugging me after him. I followed, surprised when Kai pushed aside a tapestry and revealed a large door. He looked at me over his shoulder, then led me into what I knew had to be the main sanctuary, a room decorated with more gold than I'd ever seen in my life. At the center of the space was the altar, glittering with inlaid gold. As I watched, Kai raised his hand — there was a flash of light, and the top of the altar was piled with fur and shimmering silks.

"Better than a pile of rags in the corner?" he asked, pulling me towards the altar without waiting for an answer. Laughing, we clambered up onto the makeshift bed and he pulled me into his arms again, his eyes meeting mine as he stroked my sides and back.

"I wasn't expecting to fall in love with you, you know," he said. "I wasn't expecting you to propose marriage. Or to take my bracelet so easily. I'm amazed." He pressed his lips to mine, then started moving down my jaw and over my neck. I preened under his attention, until curiosity got the better of me. I pushed him back gently and asked, "What was that about the bracelet?"

He smiled lazily and stretched like a cat, then held up his left arm. "This is what ties me to the Temple. So long as I wear it, I can't leave, except for that loophole I told you about. Now that you're wearing one, you're bound here, too." He must have seen something in my face, because he sobered and propped himself up over me. "I'm sorry. Should I have told you that before?"

"Yes..." I said slowly. He blushed again, looking chagrined.

"Does that... would that have made you change your mind?" he asked in a small voice.

I considered the question, then realized that it would have made no difference. I had always wanted to be rich. Now I was, beyond my wildest dreams. I'd always wanted to be a legend, like Arna. I'd made that name for myself by becoming the Harem Thief. I'd wanted her, the girl I'd somehow fallen madly in love with, the girl that turned out to be the god who was watching me, waiting for my answer.

"No. It wouldn't have made me change my mind," I told him, and watched the worry fade from his eyes like mist in the morning sun. I leaned forward and kissed him, then pushed him onto his back.

"What are you doing, Davi?" he asked.

I leered down at him as I straddled his legs. "I want to see if you taste the same," I answered, leaning down and kissing his throat. I worked my way down his chest, stopping to pay lavish attention to his nipples, making him moan and squirm so much that I had no choice but to pin him down, my hands on his upper arms as I nibbled and licked him into a frenzy.

"Davi!" he groaned, a delicious sound. "Davi, don't tease!"

I laughed with my lips pressed against his skin and continued my exploration of his body, pausing for a moment to ponder his navel — why would a god have a navel? — then traveling further, until I reached my goal. He gasped and thrust his hips up as my mouth closed over his cock, his hand tangling in my hair and pressing gently. His skin was salty-sweet, and surprisingly different from how he'd tasted before. I swallowed him entire, then rose up and started to play, swirling my tongue over the head of his cock, sucking the first droplets of nectar from him before moving on to lick the shaft from base to head and back. He had a magnificent cock, and I couldn't wait to feel him. But it had been a long time since I'd been with another man...

I raised my head and asked, "Where do you keep the oil?"

He groaned and looked at me, his eyes glazed, "You stopped!"

"Kai, where do you keep the oil?" I repeated. I had to ask the question once more before he understood enough to ask, "Why do you want oil?"

"For this," I answered by running my finger down his length. "You're a monster, and I can't take this without something to ease the way."

He grinned, "Oh, you want me to fuck you. We don't need oil, Davi." He shifted and sat up. "Lay down. On your back. I want to watch you."

"Kai..."

"You've never been with a god before," he said, cutting off my protests. "Trust me. We don't need oil."

He had a point. I never had been with a god before. How could I know what I needed? I nodded and lay down, rolling onto my back and looking up at him. "Now what?" I asked.

"Now?" he asked, smiling down at me. "Now you let me play. It's been a long time since I last had a man like this. Arna didn't care for it." He ran his hands up my legs, then slid his fingers under my knees and lifted them, pushing them towards my chest and positioning himself against me. I felt the head of his cock probing against me, and fought the urge to push him away. I couldn't get past the fear that this was going to hurt....

Then he entered me, and it was as smooth as if he had used oil. There was no pain, nothing but the pure pleasure of being filled. I gasped as he moved, looking up to see him smiling down at me. Then he started to pump, and I closed my eyes and moaned as he pressed down on my legs, pinning me in place and holding me there with his power. I struggled for a moment, straining against him, and heard myself whimper.

"Like that, do you?" he murmured, his voice husky, his hands sliding down my legs and over my chest in a soft caress. "I'll have to remember that. There are chains around here somewhere. Would you let me bind you, Davi?"

Just the idea was enough to make me moan with need. I nodded, unable to find words, then cried out as he thrust harder into me, his cock hitting just the right spot. Without warning, my right hand was freed.

"Touch yourself, Davi," he ordered, bending over me and bracing himself with his hands on my shoulders. "I want to see you come."

I did not need to be told twice. I reached down and wrapped my hand around my cock, fumbling for a moment until I got the rhythm and could pump in time with his thrusts. He moaned his approval and started moving faster. His movements were becoming more erratic, his moans more strident, and his fingers on my shoulders tightened. I yelped in surprise when it suddenly felt as if his cock was growing inside of me, expanding, filling me completely. It was that sensation that drove me over the edge, and I screamed my climax to the distant roof as my seed splattered all over my chest. A moment later, Kai followed me, cresting with a wild cry before slumping over me. He released me from his power, and I sighed happily and curled into his side. "I think I'm going to enjoy this," I mumbled.

He chuckled, running his hand down my spine. "It shouldn't be too much longer before Mother remembers me and releases us."

I nodded, then raised my head, "Kai, who is your mother?"

He blinked and looked surprised. "You don't know?"

"There aren't any goddesses worshiped in Tarsis, and I don't know the local gods. I didn't know about you until... well, you told me about yourself in the tavern."

"Ah," he said as he nodded. "I'm surprised you don't know, though. Mother was... everywhere. Sirina, the Mother-Goddess? I thought she was worshiped in Tarsis, too."

All at once I went cold. "You have been here a long time, haven't you?"

He frowned, "I don't know how many mortal years. I've had... four votaries. I think it's four. Why?"

I let out a long breath, "And Arna lived over five hundred years ago, according to the stories I've heard about him. Four votaries... two thousand years. That explains why I didn't know you, and why you didn't know...."

"Didn't know what?" Kai asked. I grimaced. There was no easy way to say this.

"All of the temples of the Mother-Goddess were destroyed almost two hundred years ago," I answered slowly. "The followers of Fersis rose up against her. Her priesthood was wiped out, all of her followers put to death. Her worship is still outlawed. My grandfather told me that there used to be a Mother-Goddess worshiped once, but I didn't know her name until you told me." I swallowed and rested my hand on his stomach. "Kai, how long before one of you... how long before a god fades, like you said?"

He shuddered, closing his eyes. "I'd wondered..." he murmured. "I'd wondered why she never came for me."

"I'm sorry," I said.

He nodded, then looked at me and smiled. "I have you, though. You'll be here with me now, and I will love you for the rest of your life."

And that's how I came to be Kai's High Priest. I've been here a long time now. Long enough that I'm not even sure anymore just how long it's been. They haven't been bad years. Far from it. The food is the best I've ever eaten, Kai's company is wonderful, and the sex is amazing. The first time he turned me into a woman was a little strange, I will admit, but I got used to it after a few years.

The only problem is that I'm getting older. I can't help it; there's only so much aging that he can stop. I just can't keep up with him like I used to, and I know my time is almost up. In a few years, I'll be gone and he'll be going hunting again. That's where you come in, whoever you are, and that's why I wrote this journal. To tell you about what you'll be facing, and to ask something of you.

Be gentle with Kai. I know that sounds strange, given that he's probably tricked you into his arms. He's easy to love, once you get to know him. So give him a chance, at least. He's lonely, and he's trapped here. He needs you.

Welcome to the priesthood. Take care of him for me.

If you enjoyed this story, you can discuss it with other readers and the author at the *Fools Rush In* story page
at http://forbiddenfiction.com/library/story/ES1-1.000174.

Milk

Claryssa Berg

Claryssa Berg is a Norwegian writer of smutty fairy tales of various kinds, who has been published in English since 2004. When she is not twisting myths and ravaging fairy tales, she lives a quiet life in a smallish city in the middle of Norway, together with her son and her cat.

Milk

They always held a fascination for me, the arts of pleasure and pain. Even as a young princess I cared little for hearts, broken or whole — but I cared for this: the craving of the flesh, the hunger in a kiss, the power and thrills of ecstasy...

I first met my mistress when I was a child, appearing to me as an old woman with withered skin and ragged hair who looked out on me from the swirling depths of a mirror, brought to me as a gift from afar. A land of sun and desert, they told me, where the princesses lived in tents of brightly colored silk.

I used to look at her in the glass, and her ice yellow eyes were measuring me in return. Then she started to come out when I was alone, slithering across the gilded, jewelled frame as a white serpent and curling up in my lap. She told me her name was Zela, and that she had been imprisoned by magicians — tall men in embroidered robes who had cursed her for her wicked deeds. The silvery looking-glass was her prison — her coffin.

I was never afraid of my scaled friend. And as I grew older, she told me secrets — like who was planning to poison whom at my father's court and — more importantly — the secrets of the body, and who was doing whom behind closed doors. Her serpent tongue taught me much. She was my mistress in all, and for all the secrets she taught me, I gave her my affection in return. And she changed: in the mirror the old woman was gone and in her place was a goddess: white diamond skin, her hair a waterfall of white silk. I thought her so beautiful, every glimmering inch of her, down to the tips of her fangs, gleaming like polished ivory. To keep her that way, my confidant told me I would have to feed her my blood or my pleasure. I chose pleasure. Hiking my skirts up every night before the mirror, bringing myself over the edge with lust, I fed her all my passion. When she slithered out from behind the frame I gave her my milk, coaxed from my core. She licked it from my fingers, and when back behind the glass — she smiled.

When I was quite grown up, at the height of my beauty, Zela gave me the most precious gift of all: power to defy age, eternal youth in exchange for my services. To show her my gratitude, I had a rod made of quartz crystal with a carved serpent's head at the top in her honor. It became my steady companion in my explorations of pleasure, pain and the realms in between. Dripping with carnal wine, pleasure for her to feast upon, it was my gift for her, a token of our alliance... I am no fool; I know what Zela is, and what she wants — ever since she first approached me, I have known... But she is as useful to me as I am to her — ours is a perfect match...

I brought my first lovers to her, enjoying them in front of the mirror. It looked at those times as just a silvery slate in an ornate frame, but I knew better. Zela was in there, watching me at play: big men chained on the floor, spears erect and eager; me, a waif maid with red-golden hair, bringing my whip down on them. I rode them till they burst, and fed my serpent its spoils from my fingers. Those were happy days for us. But for a little while I feared they would be over. It was a marriage; of course, I was to marry a king. I did not know him at all, had only met him once and did not remember much of it. But I was a princess of some value, politically and economically, and I would have to face my fate as all maidens of my standing must. The fact that the king in question was old and probably all dried up did nothing to inspire me. And I feared for my nights — they had always been mine to do with as I pleased. Perhaps with an old husband it would be different. Maybe my nights had to be spent with ointments and teas of bitter herbs just to make him work as he ought to? My fears were many, my future looked grave, but that was before I met *her*.

I had heard of her, of course, she was renowned for her beauty already then. Skin like snow, they said, lips like blood and hair the color of ebony. They called her Snow White, though her real name was something quite different. I liked it though, as snow is the purest slate, so easy to taint — and tainting it soon became my greatest desire.

I was to be her queen, her stepmother, but she was just a few years younger than me, a woman just come into her bloom; her petals slowly opening to reveal the temptation inside. To men, the temptation was toxic, leaving them with bleeding hearts; to me, it was a challenge. I could meet her with temptation of my own.

True, she was a beauty, a beauty with hungry eyes. There was always a restlessness about her, even when she stood still. She reeked of her desire, yet unfulfilled, a passionate young woman, ready to be picked. As she first saw me at the reception in her father's great hall, her gaze lingered at my cleavage, her nostrils flared when her shiny, black gaze caressed my neck, my hair, my waist... Her fingers shivered slightly when she greeted me.

"You may kiss my ring," I dared her. The girl only smiled, and did it.

As dull as the father was, exciting was the daughter.

I could not help but tease her: touch her whenever I could, a brief hug, a hand on her wrist, her shoulder ... she felt so soft, supple, pliant... And she blushed so prettily, little hands trembling, whenever she came in touch with my skin.

As I was the new queen she was expected to wait upon me with the rest of the ladies at court, and I picked her — always her, to help me undress, get dressed. I revelled in the heat I saw rising in her when she saw my naked body. Her gaze was always drawn, as by an invincible force, to the coppery hair at my crotch, the swell of my breasts — nipples puckered and hardened before her eyes.

I had Snow White watch while the maids oiled my skin, spoke to her about everyday things: dinners, hunting parties, weather, cakes, and smiled inwardly each time she lost the thread, licked her lips, shifted on the floor beside me. Then I let her lace my dress.

"How beautiful you are," she said in her sing-song voice. "You hair is so red, your eyes are so green ... like emeralds, almost." She smiled her lovely smile.

Snow White was so kind, they said. Good-hearted and compassionate. A pleasant and well-behaved queen-to-be. And, yes. She was. But no one but me seemed to notice how it pleased *her* to do those kind deeds. How it ignited her fire to serve and obey. Her eyes lit up, her body relaxed and a heat rose in her cheeks every time I asked her to redo the lacings, comb through my hair again, adjust the ribbons on my shoes... Her lips would part slightly then, when she knelt before me on the floor, and she would wet them with the tip of her tongue, her bosom heaving beneath the exclusive fabrics of her dresses, while she adjusted the silly ribbons, one by one, and then once over again.

I wondered what lived in her heart... How much darkness, how much light. How much pleasure and how much pain... Would she be willing to let me have my way?

Zela coiled up in my lap, her fangs affectionately nibbling the skin on my hands. "As beautiful as you are, my queen," she teased me, "the girl is prettier still. I think we would want her milk."

Snow White was quite ripe for picking when I decided the time was right. I had been teasing her for weeks and her old father had already grown tired of his new bride, preferring to spend his night drinking wine and playing chess with the lords instead of trying to please me in bed.

I asked her to help me get ready for sleep, told all my other maids to leave. And as my dress of heavy, green silk came off she said, quite out of the blue:

"My father has been married twice before. I will never regard you as my mother."

It could have been haughty, even insulting, but I got her meaning at once.

"And I," I told her, "have never seen you as a daughter."

Our gazes met in Zela's mirror. For a minute we just stood there, looking at each other. Then she broke off the stare and I said: "Why don't you take off your dress as well?"

She gave me a shy glance and then she did as she was told, as I expected her to do. Off came the blue gown, down to the floor. She was quite naked underneath. I closed my arms around her neck, skin like expensive velvet, and we kissed, soft at first, then passion began to rise in me and I pried her lips open with my tongue. Kissed her sweet, open mouth. Licked the moist cave with my tongue. I caressed her breast with my open palm, and felt her eager hand upon my own as I tugged at the nipple, weighing the breast in my hand. I pulled her closer and inhaled the scent of her: sweet like flowers with something else underneath; spices and fur, sweat and fresh juices.

I turned her to face the mirror, told her not to be shy... She knelt between my thighs and arched her head backwards. Lips like blood, tongue like a snake. Her hot, moist breath was on my skin. My fingers in her hair, ebony tendrils of silk around my wrists...

You may say that I was cruel ... but *she* was surely wicked. She licked me like a queen with her sugar mouth and honey tongue. Swirling, playing, eager, so eager ... and then, tasting, licking my milk. Drops of salt and pleasure. Her fingers slipped inside of me. She was good at it, knew exactly what to do, coaxing it out of me, a harsh cry and then — I clenched around her hand, pressed her face to my crotch and she lapped it up eagerly, every drop of milk I gave... She was a good girl, Snow White. Good girl, indeed.

How bruised her lips looked afterwards, her eyes were glazed with heat. I said, "Bend over!" And she did, balanced on all fours before me — legs spread. I picked up a supple twig of willow from my bed and smacked it across her bum, that delicious white apple of meat spread out before me, once, twice... I could smell her sex; sweet apple milk. Another smack and she sighed. Her breasts in the mirror swung with the impact. Strawberry nipples and supple flesh. Yes, I hit her hard. Red swells, ridges of passion. I put the twig down, picked up my crystal rod and pushed it inside of her, crouched down behind her and worked her hard from behind. She sighed, moaned. I reached for one of her breasts and squeezed it in my palm. Pinched the strawberry peak with two fingers until she cried. Worked her even harder with the rod, let her nipple go to smack her bottom with my hand. Hard. Unable to restrain myself, my head dipped down and I bit her

— where I'd hit her, drew blood from one of her delicious cheeks. She came then, with a cry.

Afterwards I cleaned her with my tongue, licked the sweetness from her crotch. She watched me in the mirror ... awed.

You may say that I was wicked, but she came to me almost every night after that. Wanted me to tie her up and slap her hot and wet. She was my precious princess, and took such pleasure in my games. Kneeling obediently at my feet, offering me her breasts, her behind, to do with as I pleased. All that creamy snow white skin was entirely at my disposal. I savoured every inch of it. The flowing juices of her sweetest meat, I dutifully offered to Zela. She was pleased. Grew even more brilliant, more beautiful in her prison.

I gifted my raven-haired princess a bead of polished onyx for each time she made me come. Her reward, her naughty gems. She had a rosary made of them and brought them to mass, praying her wicked wishes before the altar. Sometimes I caught her smiling, eyes closed, while she caressed the black pearls in her lap. I could see her blush: pale pink roses in her cheeks, and I knew she was aroused. Knew she would come and see me then, naked under her gown, and beg me to treat her like a naughty child: fingers inside of her, slaps on her bum, punishments performed by her tongue... Keep her on a leash of braided silk, silver clasps on her nipples — it was an art; to keep her satisfied took all of my cunning. To master her I had to be perfect in my demands. To rule a future queen, one must be mighty as a goddess. A constant challenge ... and how she loved me...

The rosary is in the coffin with her now, clutched between her fingers. My dark angel of wicked wishes is lying there on display. It was another marriage, of course, that put an end to our games. Snow White was to marry a prince who lived far, far away...

She cried in my arms on the night that her father told her; my plump, juicy apple wanted to remain my slave. And I — I told her it would never happen, promised her we would never be apart ... but after she had left me, I almost cried as well: Zela's plan had gone so well, I could not bear to have it ruined by an insignificant prince. Zela herself watched me from the mirror. She had a cunning expression on her beautiful face.

"Do not fret, my girl, it is time," she said. "I am strong now, have taken so much from her... I am sure it can be done." Then she came slithering out from the mirror.

The next night, when Snow White came and undressed by my bed, I sat up to my knees and offered her my breast, squeezed it between my fingers. A few drops of milky white appeared on my dark red nipple.

"Drink it," I urged her.

For the first time I saw hesitation in her gaze when she looked at me.

"Drink it!" I bid her again. "Think of my breast as a candied apple," I told her with a smile laced with promises of pleasure. "Suck at it as you would a piece of sugar; swallow it down like wine."

And she did it: drank and swallowed Zela's toxic milk, suckled me almost dry — before she fell to the floor, deathly pale. Gone.

Dead now, she is in the dungeons among her forefathers, in a coffin made entirely of glass. The spirits of seven departed knights are keeping watch at my command, making sure that no one but me touches her body. The fair skin, perfectly preserved, the ebony hair ... and the lips as red as blood...

And when the day comes that my sordid husband is dead, and the power in this realm belongs to me, I shall go down there. I shall bite my lip until it bleeds and kiss her cold, red mouth. She will open her dark eyes and smile at me then. A goddess freed from the glass at last. Never again shall we be apart, separated by cold frames and reflective windows. She shall be my goddess for real then, dressed in the prettiest flesh we could find. No more a snake in my lap, or a dream, caught in the swirling mists of a mirror. Zela shall be my princess. And I — I shall kneel before the only one worthy of my love, and ask her, pleadingly, to let the red and blue tokens of her affection rain down on me from above.

If you enjoyed this story, you can discuss it with other readers and the author at the *Milk* story page at http://forbiddenfiction.com/library/story/CB1-1000013.

To Market

Elizabeth Schechter

Elizabeth Schechter is a stay-at-home mom who lives in Central Florida with her husband and son. Her first novel, *Princes of Air*, was published in 2011 by Circlet Press, and her second, a steampunk novel entitled *House of the Sable Locks*, was released in June, 2013. Her most recent work, the *Tales from the Arena* duology, was published in November, 2013.

Chapter 1
The Goblin Market

"We must not look at goblin men,
We must not buy their fruits"

My name is Conn, and I am no man's son. My mother claimed to have gotten me from one of the Gentry. I don't know the truth of that, if my father was indeed one of the Sidhe, or if he was simply a silver-tongued peddler who never thought again of the girl he left behind him in Hunter's Dell. All I know is that for my whole life, it was just my Ma and me in our little hut by the edge of the forest. Ma... well, the folks in the village called her Wise Meg, or Uncanny Meg, or Meg the Witch, and they came to her for their charms and simples and all the things that made the parson look down his long nose at us when we came to market. Ma told their fortunes and read their palms, made their love charms and uncrossed their cows, and before she died, she taught me her art. Now the village comes to me. That was how it all began.

I had been in my garden that morning, trying to convince the small patch of stubborn dirt that I needed radishes more than I needed rocks. When I saw the rider coming up the road, I knew that he was coming to see me. I leaned on my hoe and waited, and was surprised to see that it was Patrick Grady who was riding up to my gate. The richest man in the village, Grady looked down at me from atop his tall horse like I was something he'd rather not have found under his boot. Then he swallowed his pride, nodded a curt greeting, and cleared his throat, "I've need of an uncrossing."

I nodded. "Is it a cow or a horse you're asking for?"

The expression on his face wouldn't have been out of place if he'd swallowed a live toad. "Neither. 'Tis my daughter."

I dropped my hoe. "Something's happened to Bess?"

He didn't answer, turning his horse back down the road. "Will you come?"

He must have known that I wouldn't have said no, that I would never turn my back on Bess. She was my childhood playmate, a bold, headstrong girl who'd been willing to defy her father because she wanted the village bastard for a friend. She'd wanted to have me as something more, too; the night of her sixteenth birthday, she'd brought me into the hayloft of her father's barn. Grady and his men found us there, both of us half-dressed; Grady dragged his daughter off to the house, leaving his loyal pack of rowdies with instructions to "deal with the bastard." They did, hanging me by my wrists from the hayloft and laying my back open with a horsewhip, then leaving me there until one of the stable-boys took pity on me, cut me down and took me home. A few days later, Grady had ridden up to our gate, and told my mother that if he ever caught me near his girl again, he'd kill me himself.

Since that day, I'd avoided the market, avoided going into the village. I couldn't bear the thought of seeing Bess and not being able to go up to her, talk to her, share everything with her the way we had since we were small. But I never stopped thinking of her, dreaming of her, recalling the few precious moments that we'd had in the hayloft before we'd been found.

What in heaven's name must have happened to her that could bring Grady to look for *my* help?

Grady's house was the finest in the village, and every time Bess had brought me here, she'd brought me in through the front hall to sit in the drawing room like an honored guest. This time, I went to the kitchen door, and found a familiar face there. Moira, Bess' old nurse, met me at the door, wringing her hands as she escorted me into the house and up the servants' stairs.

"Conn, you can help her?" she asked, her voice cracking with fear.

"I don't know, Moira. I will try," I answered, trying to keep my own voice steady. "Where are we going?"

"Miss Bess' bedchamber." Moira led me to the second floor, and down the hall. Grady himself was waiting outside a door, and as I reached it, he opened the door and gestured me inside. I walked in and stopped, stunned at what I saw. Bess lay in the center of the wide, curtained bed, writhing and moaning like a woman possessed. Her fair hair was dirty and matted, and her fine gown was filthy, tattered and torn. Worst of all, her arms were spread wide, her wrists lashed to the bedposts.

I turned to Grady, "What happened here?"

At the sound of my voice, Bess turned. She saw me standing in the doorway, smiled with delight, and called my name. I'd heard her say my name like that once before, and it had made my blood race. Now, the heat in her voice and the wildness in her eyes horrified me. I couldn't imagine what could have caused this. Grady gestured for me to join him in the corridor, closing the door firmly behind me.

"Tell me what happened," I said, trying to ignore the fact that I could still hear Bess through the door, whimpering and crying, calling my name.

Grady shook his head, not meeting my eyes. "We don't know. She went for a walk one evening, and didn't come home. The next morning, we found her wandering in the sheep pasture on the east side of the village, looking like she'd lost her wits. The doctor has been here, and the parson. She attacked the parson, tried to get out of the house. That's why she's bound." Grady stared at the door. "It's been three days, and she only gets worse."

I nodded. He was lying about something, but what, I had no idea. "Let me back in," I said. "I need to look at her, see if I can see anything."

Grady pushed me none-too-gently towards Bess' door. "Moira, go with him," he growled. Then he turned and stalked down the hall.

Moira held the door open for me, then followed me into the room. Once she had closed the door, I turned to face her. "What is he not telling me?" I demanded.

She looked at me and whispered, "He'll have me out on the streets if he finds out I've told you anything."

I met her eyes. "Moira, tell me what I need to save her."

She stared for a moment at the struggling girl on the bed, then nodded. "The Master has arranged a marriage for Miss Bess. To Lord Faraday."

I hissed at the name. Lord Faraday was our liege lord, but that didn't mean I had to like the man. He was a heavy-handed man, I'd heard, and he'd buried four wives that I knew about. Moira nodded again.

"When he told Miss Bess, she refused. She told him..." she paused and then looked at me. "Conn, she told her father that if he forced her, she'd go to the goblins. They didn't find her in the sheep meadow. They found her at Hunter's Oak."

I turned and stared at the bed in shock. She had gone to the goblin market?

If you were to wander in the gloaming towards the hollow where the tree that the old folks called the Hunter's Oak had once stood, you would hear the goblins, calling to the unwary: "Who will buy? Come and buy!" No one knew for certain when they had first come to Hunter's Dell. There were some, my mother told me, who were foolish enough to go into the hollow and take what the goblins offered. But when they returned to the hollow, seeking more of the same, they found it empty; the goblins never came twice to someone who had tasted their wares. All of those poor souls had died horribly within a few days, refusing food and drink, pining for whatever they had found in the hollow. Ma had told me once that she thought there might have been a way to save them, if there had been someone brave enough to try it. I wasn't brave, but I cared for Bess, and I was bound to try and save her.

I crossed to Bess' bedside and sat down next to her; she leaned towards me as much as her bonds would allow, whimpering softly.

"Conn," she moaned. "Touch me, please." Her eyes met mine, and I was stricken to not see the joy that usually shone from behind her eyes. There was only need there, and want, only what the goblins had thrust upon her. I cupped her cheek and leaned forward to kiss her forehead.

"I'll bring you what you need, Bess," I whispered. "I swear it." Then I pulled back, reaching into the satchel I wore over my shoulder and pulling out a small, brown bottle that I handed to Moira, "Give her this, a full dram mixed into some milk. It will make her sleep. I should be back before she wakes, or very shortly after."

Moira looked at me in horror. "Conn, what are you going to do?"

I looked back at Bess, who was crying and calling for me to come back. It near broke my heart to turn away and leave her.

"I'm going to the goblins."

I took a long breath, gathered my courage, and walked down the hill into the hollow. I could hear the goblins calling from somewhere down near the stream, but until I came up to the remains of the oak, I couldn't see them. And once I did, I had to stop and stare.

Ma had never told me that goblins were beautiful. I'd been expecting monsters. Instead, I was facing angels. They were tall and thin, taller than any man, and covered from head to heels in sleek, glistening fur that reminded me of the otters that played in the forest pool. They were dressed solely in long, beaded loincloths that swayed in the evening breeze, and they moved with a fluid grace that made them look like they were gliding on air. When one of them turned to look at me, I could see its eyes were golden, and slitted like a cat's. It came closer, the setting sun turning its mottled gray and black fur into flame, and when it reached me, it crouched slightly so that it was closer to my height.

"Welcome to the goblin market, young mortal. Will you come and see our wares?"

I nodded, too awestruck to say a word, letting the goblin take me by the hand and lead me into their market. There were carts and baskets full to overflowing with fruit, most of it impossible to find this early in the spring—there were apples piled up next to peaches, full bunches of grapes lying next to cherries and figs, strawberries in baskets with pears and quince. The goblin escorted me from one end of the market to the other, and when we reached the end, it waved one arm expansively. "What will you have, young mortal?"

I shook off the spell that the goblin's beauty cast over me. I was here for a reason. "There was a girl, a few nights past. What did she choose?" I asked.

The goblin laughed, "The golden girl! Yes, she came to me, and greatly enjoyed her choice. You wish to have what she had?"

I nodded slowly, not sure what I was agreeing to. The goblin took my arm and led me off; I could feel its sharp claws pricking me through my sleeve.

It led me away from the market, into a copse of young willows that grew along the banks of the stream. In the center of the copse there was a clearing, and it was there that the goblin stopped, turned towards me and smiled again.

"Take off your clothing, pretty mortal," it said, running long fingers through my hair.

I whispered Bess' name like a prayer as I unslung my satchel and took off my shirt and breeches; the goblin must have heard me, because it cocked its head to the side and studied me for a long moment.

"The golden girl, she is your lover?" The cat eyes narrowed. "No, not a lover. But beloved, none-the-less. Why have you come?"

"Because I love her," I answered.

It laughed, resting one long hand on my back between my shoulders, "Intriguing. Come here, mortal, and see what your golden girl bought at the goblin market."

The goblin led me to a mossy bank, guided me gently down onto my back and then stretched out next to me. It said not a word to me, arranging my arms and legs as if I were a doll, until I lay there with my arms flung over my head and my legs slightly apart. It nodded, seemingly satisfied, and then sat up and made a long, low trilling sound. Immediately, I felt something cold curling around my wrists and my ankles; I tried to jump up but was held fast to the turf as slender green vines rose from the moss, wrapping around my body and holding me fast. The goblin laughed, moving so that it was again lying next to me, soft fur rubbing against my side as I struggled against the vines.

"Pretty mortal," it crooned, and smiled, showing all of its sharp, white teeth. Then, to my shock, it kissed me.

When I was twelve, a minor lord who had sought my mother's aid rewarded her with a flagon of fine brandy. Ma had let me taste the wine, and I had always remembered the smooth warmth, oak mixed with wood smoke and peat and apples. The goblin's lips tasted like that, like brandy, heat and desire; I found myself drunk on that taste, forgetting my fear. When the goblin pulled back, I strained up, wanting more, and heard the creature laugh.

"Patience, little one. Patience." It stood, and loosened the belt around its hips, letting the loincloth fall to the ground, revealing to me finally that this goblin was male. His cock was erect, long and curved, and as thick around as my wrist. He looked down at himself, running one hand down his length. "So, you see now what goblin fruit your little golden girl enjoyed? Would you like a taste?" he asked, and laughed again as he lay back down, running his fingers over my skin in swirling patterns that left fire in their wake. I could feel myself responding to his touch, until I ached with desire. He laughed again, sliding down over my body until he lay over my legs, his breath warm on my cock.

"You are a virgin?" he asked. "You've never lain with a woman before, or a man?"

"I... yes. No." I was addled by his breath and his warmth, and wasn't sure what question I was answering. He trilled softly, sliding his hands under my ass.

"Untouched fruit is the sweetest. What payment do you offer, young mortal, for your taste of goblin fruit?"

Payment? I couldn't clear my head, couldn't think of anything but his kiss and his touch and his breath on my aching, throbbing cock. He ran one finger down my shaft, and I gasped at the sensation.

"Barter, perhaps? Will you give me seed for seed?" Without waiting for an answer, he lowered his mouth over my cock, swallowing me whole. It was like nothing I had ever felt before, and I howled as he caressed me with his rough tongue and slid one long, slender finger into my ass. I strained against the vines, trying to move, wanting *more*, even though I had no idea what more would be. I felt him laugh again, and he stopped and raised his head, sliding up to cover my body with his own and kiss me again.

"You taste magnificent," he murmured, licking my ear and then nibbling my neck with his sharp teeth. "Shall you have your taste now?" He got to his knees, shifted, turned around until his cock was suspended over my mouth. I heard him laugh again, "Do to me what I did to you. Do not bite." He took me into his mouth again, and lowered his hips so that his cock tapped against my lips. Uncertain, with only his direction to guide me, I lightly touched his cock with my tongue, feeling his hum of pleasure as a jolt through my own cock. Encouraged, I kept on, gently bathing him with my tongue until he groaned and shifted his hips lower, raising his head so that he could whisper, "Take me."

Obediently, I opened my mouth wide, and he slid his cock between my lips, filling my mouth and cutting off my voice. His cock tasted of honey, salt and something wonderful and exotic, and I eagerly swirled my tongue over the head, wanting more. The goblin moaned, increasing his own efforts until I was thrashing under him, moaning, sucking, licking, finally screaming as I spent. Laughing, he licked me clean and then trilled something; I felt the vines on my arms loosen and fall away.

"Touch me," the goblin said, and I could not tell if he was commanding or begging. I slid my hands up the fur of his thighs, luxuriating in the softness, hearing the goblin moan and trill as he started to slowly pump in and out of my mouth. Inspired by what he had done to me, I wrapped my arms around his hips and slid one hand over his ass, running my fingers down his cleft, seeking the hidden entrance there. The goblin yowled like a cat in heat when my fingers found their target; he went rigid, and I felt his cock pulsing, growing impossibly thicker. My mouth filled with warm liquid, thick, sweet-salt, honey and brandy; I swallowed, drinking deep, lost in pleasure. Then I lost myself in a soft, warm embrace as I fell asleep in the goblin's arms.

I woke feeling soft fur under my cheek and long fingers in my hair. For a moment, I was confused, then everything came back to me and I jumped up to see the goblin looking at me.

"You are truly magnificent," he murmured. "There is something to you, something different. You are not like the other mortals I have tasted. You are more like my own people."

I couldn't speak; I stared at him for a moment, then turned away.

I'd failed. Worse, I'd condemned myself to the same fate as Bess.

A soft arm encircled my shoulders, "Whatever is wrong? Did I not please you?"

His voice sounded truly concerned. I looked up into his golden eyes and decided to trust. "I came here because I needed to bring the goblin seed back to Bess. To save her life. I failed her." I didn't add that I'd condemned myself, too.

The goblin cocked his head to one side, "I don't understand. Your golden girl is ill?"

I blinked, "You don't know? You don't know what happens when mortals come to the goblin market?"

"No," the goblin answered. "Among my own people, I am considered very young. I have had very few of your kind. "

I tried to gather my wits. "When a mortal comes to the goblin market, when we taste the goblin fruit, we... pine for it. And we die, in a matter of days. My mother, she thought that if we could get another taste, it would cure the need, but no one who has ever been here has ever been able to find you again."

The goblin reared back, and I could see horror in his eyes, "Die? The golden girl will *die* because she lay with me?" He reached out and touched my arm, "You will die?"

I nodded, surprised by the goblin's reaction, his obvious distress. He jerked to his feet, striding across the copse with none of his previous grace. Then he came back, throwing himself down onto his knees in front of me, "Mortal-beloved, please believe me. I did not know!"

Stunned, I nodded again. "I... believe you."

He curled himself into a small ball, his head resting on my knees, "We think of you as... fruit to be plucked. I came with the others because I am old enough to mate now. I would have taken your essence, and I would have gone to the mating fields of my home. I would have shared what I have taken from you and from the others with one that I desired, and if they found me worthy, they would have mated with me. No one told me that harvesting from you would mean your death." He raised his head, and I could see sorrow and regret, "I did not know it would hurt you. I did not know you were intelligent. I did not know that you knew love." He shook his head and stood, holding his hand out to me. "Come with me, mortal," he commanded.

"Where?"

"We will make the cure for your golden girl. And we will make a cure for you. Are you sure of this?"

I shook my head, "No."

He nodded, "Then we will try. And if it does not work... then we will find another way."

I followed the goblin, my head spinning, trying to understand what he had told me. "But, what about you?"

"So long as I return to my home before dawn, I will be fine," he said. "Come and sit with me." He sat down with his back to a tree, and I knelt down next to him. He smiled at me, and said sadly, "I wish you had not told me. I will not be able to bring myself to come again."

"I'm sorry." It seemed like a silly thing to say, but I was sorry that I'd caused this compassionate creature pain. He reached out and patted my leg.

"It is not your fault. Do you have something to carry the seed in?" I jumped up and ran back to my clothes, taking an empty bottle from my satchel and bringing it back. The goblin took it and set it aside, then looked at me and held out his arms, "Come and sit with me, mortal. Touch me and help me to save your life."

I moved into his embrace, resting my cheek against the soft fur of his chest. He guided me, telling me where to touch him and how, until I knew what gave him pleasure and could do it without coaching. So I coaxed him to fullness again, and lay across him to lick his cock until he cried out and spilled his seed into his own hands. When he poured it into the bottle, the straw-colored liquid barely filled a quarter of the bottle.

"Will it be enough?" he murmured.

"For one, I think," I answered. "I'll bring it to Bess. Then..."

"Then you will come back. I will be ready for you when you return," the goblin said as he slid his arm around me. "I will not let you die. But you must be back here before dawn. If I do not return home, the way between your world and mine will be sealed, and the goblin market will never again come to this place." Gently, he pushed me away, "There is not much time."

I scrambled into my clothes, taking the bottle in my hand and turning to leave the willows; I stopped, looking back to see the goblin looking at me. Quickly, I went over to him, leaned down, and kissed him. "Thank you," I said quickly. Then I turned and ran.

I ran all the way back to Grady's house, the precious bottle clutched in my fist, feeling the goblin seed burning in my blood. I was gasping for breath as I reached the kitchen door, which opened immediately. Panting like a dog, I pushed past a shocked Moira and nearly collapsed onto the long table. She grabbed me and pushed me into a chair, then bustled away, returning with a cup that she shoved under my nose.

"Drink it," she commanded. I nodded, drinking and tasting brandy. The taste reminded me of the goblin's kiss, and I pushed the glass away with shaking hands.

"Moira, I have it," I said, holding up the bottle. She took it from me, looking at the liquid inside.

"What is it?" she asked.

"It... it's the cure." I got to my feet, painfully aware of Moira's curious look, not wanting to tell her just what was in the bottle, or how I had gotten it. I held my hand out and said, "There isn't much time."

Moira nodded, handing the bottle back to me. I stood up and wove an unsteady path to the stairs and up to Bess' room. I let myself in and closed the door behind me, then turned to see Bess watching me, hunger plain on her face.

"I've brought it for you, Bess," I said, crossing to sit on the edge of the bed. I held the bottle to her lips and let her drink, fighting to keep my hands steady. She gulped the liquid greedily, draining the bottle and then licking her lips; she shivered violently, whimpered once, then wailed, her body going stiff and jerking hard against her bonds. I jumped back, dropping the bottle, and then grabbed at the ropes, fumbling with the knots until she was free, laying limp in the middle of the bed. For a moment, I was afraid that the goblin had tricked me, until Bess moaned softly and opened her eyes. She looked up at me and smiled, "Conn."

Dizzy with relief, I pulled Bess into my arms, hugging her tightly, breathing in her scent. And it was her scent, my awareness of her as a woman, and my own growing need that pushed my restraint to the breaking point; I pushed her back down onto the bed, claiming her mouth in a possessive kiss and running my hands down her sides. She gasped in surprise, then giggled against my mouth and ran her hands up underneath my shirt.

Behind us, I heard the door crash open, then someone grabbed me by the back of the neck and dragged me from the bed. I heard Bess scream, then something came crashing down on the back of my head and I knew nothing else.

Chapter 2
The Fruit Forbidden

*"Hug me, kiss me, suck my juices
Squeezed from goblin fruits for you"*

I clawed my way out of a darkness that seemed to be filled with screaming, pain and need, and found myself on the floor of a strange room. I was alone and naked, with ropes digging into my wrists and ankles, and a foul tasting rag shoved in my mouth and tied there. I had no idea how I had gotten here, or what had happened; all I knew was that my head was pounding, and I ached with need, my cock hard and throbbing. The light slanting through the windows told me that I'd been unconscious for quite some time—it had still been dark when I reached Grady's house, with barely a glimmer of sunrise on the horizon. The shadows on the floor told me it was past midday, and any hope for me was long gone. The goblin would have returned to his world by now, and I would never see him or the market again.

I heard footsteps, and the two men who entered the room were two of Grady's rowdies: Fergus Durkin and his son, Hugh. I shivered when I saw Hugh, fear briefly overriding lust. I despised Hugh—he was a bully who fancied himself irresistible to either sex, and who abused his rank at every turn. He'd tried to coerce me into his bed once, and when I'd refused him, had haunted our gate for weeks, until my mother had threatened to turn him into a toad.

The older Durkin came over and grabbed my arm, hauling me to a sitting position.

"Nice of you to join us, bastard," he said. "I was starting to wonder if you'd ever wake up." I glared at him, and Durkin laughed. "We won't keep you for long, bastard. We're keeping you safe and sound and hidden away until Grady's girl is wedded and bedded. Tomorrow midday, you'll get your clothes back and you'll be free to go."

Hugh came over and leered down at me, and the cause of my shivering changed from fear to something else. "Grady said we could have a little fun with you while we waited, bastard. Looks like you need it." He rested his hand on his belt buckle, and I whimpered. No, not him... yes. Yes, please....

"I told you no, Hugh," Durkin snapped as he stood up. "The boy is a witch, like his ma. I won't have him cursing me and mine, so you leave him alone." Ignoring my muffled protests — let him stay! — Durkin herded his son out the door, and slammed it behind them. I heard the bolt shoot home, and then silence.

The hours passed in a kind of delirium of need and pain. In my madness, I dreamed of freeing myself from the gag, calling Hugh back into the room, inviting his touch. I dreamed of encouraging him to take me, if only so that I might find some ease for the pressure growing inside me. Desperate for some relief, unable even to touch myself, I struggled and fought against the ropes until my aching arms went numb, and I was screaming into the gag in frustration. Around me, the shadows grew longer and the room grew darker. When it was finally too dark to see, and I was too tired to move, I just lay where my struggles had left me, on my stomach in the middle of the floor.

It was there that Hugh found me. He came into the room with a lantern, walking on stocking feet to make no noise. He stood over me and laughed as I blinked in the sudden light.

"You wouldn't curse me for giving you what you want, now would you?" he asked, using one foot to flip me over onto my back. He prodded my cock with his toes, and I whimpered, making him laugh. "And you want this, don't you, bastard?"

There was a small part of me that wanted to refuse, but it was drowned out by the overwhelming waves of lust; I nodded, thrusting my hips up, moaning through the gag.

Hugh smirked down at me. "I knew it. You're a slut, just like your ma." He didn't bother to loosen the ropes that bound me, hauling me roughly over a bolster that he took from the bed. I squirmed against the cool satin of the bolster, hearing Hugh as he knelt behind me, kneading my ass with rough hands and laughing at my muffled whimpers of encouragement.

"Pretty boy," he whispered. "Been wanting this since we brought you up here, pretty boy." I heard him moving behind me, heard the door open. I expected and almost dreaded that I would hear Durkin's voice, chasing Hugh off before I'd found some kind of relief. Instead, there was a surprised gasp from Hugh; he collapsed over my legs and didn't move. I twisted, straining until I could see the door, and the figure standing there. Tall, taller than any man, and he had to stoop to get through the door. But there was no way he could be here....

The goblin glided across the floor and dropped to his knees next to me so that he could push Hugh off my legs, then tugged me off of the bolster and into a sitting position. Gently, the goblin pushed my head to the side and untied the gag, then held me tightly as I was taken with a coughing fit.

"Are you unhurt, beloved?" the goblin asked, leaning close so that he could look into my eyes.

I nodded, rubbing my cheek against his soft fur, "...touch me. Please...."

The goblin reached out to rest his long hand over my heart, "Mortal-beloved, I am here. I will make you well again."

His touch set fire to my skin, and I moaned, straining against the ropes, "It hurts...."

He leaned me back against the bolster and stood, raising his hands; I felt myself rising, moving through the air until I came to rest on the bed. My head hung over the edge, and I watched through half-lidded eyes as he removed his loincloth and came to stand at my head. He ran long fingers over my cheek and through my hair, "Open your mouth, beloved. Take what you need."

He slowly pressed his cock into my mouth, resting one hand on my chest and holding me in place. He wrapped his other hand around my cock, leaning forward to lay over me and take me into his mouth. Still bound, pinned under his weight, driven near-mad by his fur on my skin and the roughness of his tongue, I sucked and moaned and screamed under him, reaching the heights of pleasure time and time again. Finally I could take no more; I fell into darkness with the sounds of his moans ringing in my ears and the taste of honey and brandy on my tongue.

I woke with soft fur under my cheek, and opened my eyes to see the goblin smiling at me. I jumped, and his arms around me tightened.

"All is well. You are safe. I have kept watch. It is nearly dawn, and there is no one stirring," he said quietly. "Are you all right, mortal-beloved?"

I looked at my wrist and the livid rope-burns there, considered the question, "I ache all over, and I'm starving. But I think I'm all right. Do you think we can find any food?"

The goblin smiled, "We will find something. If necessary, I will hunt for you."

When I stood, I was so unsteady on my feet that the goblin had to carry me down the stairs; I looked around curiously. "Where are we?" I asked.

"The golden girl told me that this is Durkin's house," he answered.

"And Durkin?"

"Is fast asleep and will remain so," the goblin answered. "I can hold both men asleep until past dawn. We can eat, you can find clothing, and we can be away long before they wake."

He sat me down at the table in the kitchen and rummaged through the pantry, finding the remains of a good dinner. I fell to with good appetite, while the goblin nibbled at a piece of bread and then pushed it aside.

"Beloved, Conn," he said. "I... the golden girl, she is the one who sent me here."

I stopped eating, looking at him, "Bess sent you? Goblin, where is she?"

He looked down at the tabletop, "She... is not here. Conn... she is going away."

I frowned, "I don't understand. Gone where?"

The goblin wouldn't look at me, "She has gone to be married. I spoke to her last night, and she left just after dawn today. She will be married in the morning."

"Married?" I repeated, stunned. "She... but she didn't want to marry Lord Faraday! That was why she went to the market to begin with!"

"I know. She gave me something for you." He stood and disappeared up the stairs, returning a few moments later with his loincloth and a pouch. From the pouch he took a folded piece of parchment. "I do not know what it says," the goblin said, sounding apologetic. "I cannot read your writing."

I took the letter and opened it, seeing Bess' fine handwriting. She thanked me for being her friend, for caring for her. She wished me well, and would think of me fondly. She asked me to do the same. Not a word of love, or any mention of the goblin market.

I set the letter down and looked at the goblin, "I don't understand. I... thought she loved me. She told me she loved me."

He shook his head, "I asked her that. I told her that you loved her. And she said that you were children together, and that children must grow up. That children have fancies, and that you were hers. She said she was sorry that you did not understand that there was truly nothing between you." He stood up and came around the table, kneeling next to my chair. "Conn, I am sorry. I think, perhaps, that she is no longer the girl who came to the goblin market. She has been frightened, and badly. Now, she wants to forget. And she wants safety. This marriage gives her that." He shook his head. "All the same, I do not know how she cannot love you. She is a fool."

I let out a bark of laughter, "No. She's right. I'm the fool, for thinking that someone like her would be happy with a bastard like me." I turned, tossed the letter into the fireplace, and looked back at the goblin. "I need clothes. We'll have to hurry if we're to get you back to the goblin market before dawn."

Silence. The goblin stood up and walked over to a window, his back to me; he sighed and said sadly, "The goblin market is gone."

I frowned, and then remembered why that one statement was so important... and so horrifying. I jumped to my feet. "You were supposed to go home!"

He turned to me and answered quietly, "I did. When you did not return, I went home, and I confronted my sire. I demanded to know why he did not tell me that what we did killed your kind. He laughed at me, called me a sentimental fool." He sighed. "He told me I was too young, and that..." he paused for a moment, then sighed again, " ...that I should not play with my food. He was going to ban me from coming back to the market. He said that I had proved I was not mature enough. But I begged, and he relented. I came back, because I was hoping you would try to find me. And when midnight came, and you did not appear, I went to look for you. I followed your scent to your home, and you were not there. I searched until I despaired of ever finding you. Then I thought of going to your Bess. She told me where you were. I did not return home, I stayed, and I hid myself here, and watched. When it was just the two men, I came for you."

I nodded, "And now you found me, and we're safe. For now. We can still get you back to the market."

"We cannot. There is not enough time to get there before dawn. The market will vanish and will never more come to this place."

"Then we need to get you out of here. Out of Hunter's Dell, before anyone sees you. They'll know what you are, and they won't let you live if they find you." I sat back down and leaned back in my chair. "We can go to my hut. I have food and clothes there, and a bit of money put by. We can leave through the forest so you're not seen. Then ... I don't know. Maybe ... maybe we can find the goblin market again, get you home."

"No. I will not return to the goblin market."

"Why not?" I asked. "Your home...."

The goblin came back to the table, knelt down next to me. "I could not have you, if I went home. You would not be welcome there," the goblin said. "You belong in this place no more than I. There is more of my kind than theirs in you, Conn. So come with me. I want to be with you. I know the way to other places, other worlds, where we might live and be happy. If you will come with me?"

I blinked, not sure I'd heard him properly, "You... you want me to come with you? But...."

He was quiet for a moment, then reached out and took my hand. "I want you to be with me, my mortal-beloved."

I blinked, "But, I'm a bastard!"

"I do not know what that means. But truly, does it matter?" he asked. "You love, you think, you are dear to me. Is that not enough?"

My head was spinning, "I...."

"Conn," he said my name and made it sound like a caress. "I will not refuse you. I will not turn my back on you. I will not leave you.

When one of my kind mates, it forms a bond that will not be severed, will not break. When my kind mates, it is for life." He stood and tugged me to my feet. "I can show you, beloved. Join with me."

I let him lead me, and was surprised when we returned to the bedroom where I'd been held captive. "I don't understand."

"Love me. Let me love you."

I looked at him curiously. "What were we doing, then?"

The goblin laughed. "Among my people, what we have done are the games of children old enough to understand the mating process, but not old enough to mate. It is only with one's mate that one would offer their entire body." He held his arms out to me. "I am offering, Conn. If you will have me."

I looked up into his eyes, listened to my heart, and walked into his embrace. As he made to lead me to bed, I stopped him. "I don't even know your name."

He smiled, and trilled something. Then he laughed. "I doubt you could say it. We will decide later what you will call me."

I let him lay me down, and when he lay down with me, I rolled onto my side and reached out to stroke his fur. He purred like a cat, and I smiled. "What do we do?" I asked.

In answer, he rolled me over onto my stomach, moving to cover me with his body. "Trust me, my beloved. I will not hurt you."

I nodded. "I trust you."

He kissed the back of my neck, and I felt his hands slip between my legs and start playing with my balls; I moaned, and he laughed. "Relax, Conn. Let me play."

Play he did, toying with me until I was nearly as aroused as I'd been under the spell of the goblin market. He teased me with his fingers and tongue, then told me to spread my legs and slowly slid one finger into my ass. One finger became two, and two became three, doing arcane things inside of me until I was frantic with desire. I was near to howling when he took his fingers away; he drew me to my knees and I felt the head of his cock move to take the place of his fingers.

"I love you, Conn," he whispered, slowly pressing his way into my body. It was hard at first, and it hurt; but he stopped, touching me gently, whispering and trilling until I calmed and relaxed and let him try again, until at last he was inside, and I was stretched full and gasping in pleasure. He started to move, pumping slowly, working his way almost entirely out of me, and then sliding back in, letting me move with him, push back against him, demand more and more until neither of us could say a word for the gasping and moaning. I spent first, losing my balance and sprawling out on the bed. He fell on top of me, still pumping, wailing as his seed filled me. Afterwards, we lay curled around each other, my head on his chest, and I found myself feeling more at home than I ever had before. He was right. I didn't belong in Hunter's Dell. I never had. I had only been waiting for someone to show me the truth.

After a while, he raised his head and looked at me, "You have not answered me. Is it not enough that I love you?"

I smiled at him, raised myself up so that I might kiss him, reveling in the heady taste of his lips, "Yes. It's enough. More than enough. I love you, too."

By the time the sun had risen, we had left Hunter's Dell, taking forest paths that I had never before seen, following my golden-eyed lover wherever he would lead me. There were times when I wondered what they thought, back in Hunter's Dell, if they ever wondered where Conn the witch had gone, or what had happened to the goblin market. I wondered if Lady Faraday ever thought about me. Then my goblin would smile at me, or run his fingers through my hair, and none of it would matter. He loved me, and I loved him. That was all that mattered.

And we lived happily ever after.

If you enjoyed this story, you can discuss it with other readers and the author at the *To Market* story page at http://forbiddenfiction.com/library/story/ES1-1.000035

The Snake and the Lyre

Annabeth Leong

Annabeth Leong found relief in erotica. Reading others' stories opened up a world of freedom and exploration. Writing it increased the thrill. Since her first published story in 2009, she has written for anthologies by Cleis Press, Ravenous Romance, Coming Together, and Circlet. Her work has appeared online at Every Night Erotica and Oysters and Chocolate. She is pleased to participate in Forbidden Fiction's Special Collections. Besides freedom of speech, Annabeth loves shoes, stockings, cooking, and attending concerts—probably in that order. She lives in Providence, Rhode Island.

The Snake and the Lyre

Eurydice rested her cheek against Orpheus's thigh. His rich voice tingled in her ears, its timbre sweet as a persimmon. His foot tapped slowly as he plucked his lyre, rocking Eurydice's head with the ancient rhythm of the ocean.

The strings of the lyre—they trembled and thrilled beneath his fingertips. They exulted and crooned. Eurydice would have responded just that way had he thought to draw his music from her body rather than the instrument.

She didn't mind the rocks on the hill where they sat, and yet she recrossed her ankles under her body, fidgeting. Her heel pressed between her legs, sinking slightly into her cunt. Safely hidden by her skirt, Eurydice rocked on it in time with Orpheus's song.

She closed her eyes and pretended that the notes slipping into the wind around them were his hands slipping into her clothes. Her inner thighs shivered. His tongue could leave wet trails there. He could find his way to the juncture of her legs and sing only to her, his full lips and white teeth forming private poetry. Eurydice imagined his eyes, the shade of grapes in the vineyard, gazing up along her belly and between the peaks of her breasts. She would grip hunks of his black hair and pull his face tight to her. She would lock her ankles at the base of his spine and refuse to let go until she tired of finding release against his beautiful mouth.

"My love?" Orpheus's song had ended. He stroked her hair—too gently. "Eurydice, my love? What did you think of that Hypophrygian setting? I might compose in that mode for our wedding. It speaks so delicately, expressing the yearning of youth joined with the peaceable accord of family life."

Eurydice made the effort to smile. She kissed the top of his thigh through his tunic. "Your music would make the gods ache. It will be lovely." She inhaled his sharp, male scent, lifted from his body by the heat of the day. She pressed her lips to his leg again, a little higher up.

Orpheus frowned, adjusting his grip on his lyre. "The Lydian mode might be more traditionally appropriate. Simple happiness — that's a good atmosphere for a wedding." He scratched absently behind Eurydice's ear. "I think I can transpose this, so you can hear them one after the other."

She sighed and touched his ankle, just above the strap of his sandal. She angled her body to emphasize the swell of her breasts and lifted her eyes to his through the veil of her curling dark hair. "Orpheus...."

"Yes, love?"

"Perhaps you could lay aside the lyre for a little while?" Eurydice moved her hand up past the hem of his tunic. The muscles of his thigh twitched as she approached his cock.

Orpheus's indulgent smile dashed her hopes against the rocks of his perfect cheekbones. He retrieved her hand from beneath his clothes and returned it to her. "The wedding will come before you know it, my dear. We'll spend all night making love and singing to the stars."

Eurydice folded her hands in her lap, unable to resist pressing them against her crotch. "Of course," she said. "You want to try the Lydian mode, you said?"

"Go down and bathe in the spring below the juniper tree," whispered Eurydice's friend Apollonia on the day of the wedding. "Invite the Naiads to come and dance to your betrothed's lyre."

Eurydice giggled. "Does he need more recognition? The sun stands still in the sky to listen to him."

"You'll be the only woman in Thrace to have Naiads honor your wedding."

"Aren't they dangerous?"

"Playful," Apollonia said. "Beautiful. Sensual. People will talk about your wedding for years. It will be worth it."

Light splashed onto the hills like the water of the clearest stream. Apollonia grinned and waggled her eyebrows. Drunk on the promise of the day, Eurydice allowed her friend to coax her out of her clothes and point her toward the juniper.

Warm mud caressed her bare feet and tickled her naked calves. Eurydice ran her hands down the sides of her body. Now, the breeze teased her nipples. Tonight, it would be handsome Orpheus, her husband at last.

Eurydice dipped a foot into the sun-warm spring. "Sweet ladies of the water," she called. "Would you like to dance at my wedding? Silver-tongued Orpheus will play and sing for his esteemed guests."

"Or-phe-us," the water sighed, its surface rippling. The silt at the bottom bubbled. A pale arm emerged, as strong and slender as a young tree.

"Yes, Orpheus! He will be my husband!" Eurydice dove eagerly into the water and took hold of the hand, helping the Naiad out of the sucking sand.

The nymph clasped the offered hand and crawled up Eurydice, her skin cold and slippery. She darted between Eurydice's legs, her moss-green hair tickling her thighs. She wrapped her arms around the young woman's stomach and surged up to break the surface, her pebbled nipples scraping Eurydice's.

Eurydice gasped, her lungs suddenly tight.

"The wife of Orpheus," the Naiad purred. "We have heard him sing. Is his tongue worth the silver of its sound?" She winked. A clever hand darted between Eurydice's legs, parted her folds.

Eurydice jumped back, covering her cunt protectively. The nymph laughed, the water of the spring quivering with her merriment. "So shy." She placed a hand on Eurydice's waist and idly dragged a lily pad toward them. "Tell me, how does he play his instrument?"

The Naiad's lips nuzzled the young woman's ear. "Does godlike Orpheus know where to place his hands along the neck to draw the loveliest tunes?"

Eurydice realized with a shock that the Naiad's fingers followed her words, caressing up and down her throat. She knew she should make her excuses and escape the spring, but the thought of Orpheus's hands doing the same held her in place. The calluses from playing the lyre would feel rough against her skin. He could reach into her cunt and strum to his heart's content.

The Naiad pressed her slick lips to the base of Eurydice's throat. The young woman moaned. "Does Apollo's favorite musician know which touches produce which notes?" She nipped the same spot with her teeth, eliciting a shriek, then licked with her rough tongue, making Eurydice sigh.

"I long to know," the Naiad whispered. "Does our handsome player prefer his rhythms fast or slow?" Her hand returned to Eurydice's cunt, and this time the woman did not resist or pull away. The nymph's finger wriggled inside. Eurydice unconsciously spread her legs wider to accommodate the invasion. The finger stroked lazily at first, then accelerated to a pounding crescendo that made the young woman lose her feet and fall into the water, still wound around the nymph.

They floated there, Eurydice staring nervously into eyes the pale gray of river stones. "Speak, girl," the nymph demanded.

"Orpheus," she began, then trailed off and cleared her throat. Her pulse pounded everywhere the Naiad had touched her, but most strongly between her legs. She tried to disguise her longing. "Orpheus plays on his instrument, not his betrothed."

"Ah. Not a very giving lover, then, if he's left you virgin."

Eurydice bit her lip. She didn't wish to speak ill of her future husband. "He wants to share his love with me when the time is right. He says it's worth waiting for the perfect night."

"And what do you say?" The Naiad cupped Eurydice's breast, rolling her nipple between her long fingers. "Do you cherish a little girl's romantic dreams? Or a woman's desires?" At this last, she pulled Eurydice onto her thigh, driving hard against the center of her need. "I think you need more than Orpheus can offer you," said the nymph.

A whimper escaped Eurydice. She rode the nymph's leg helplessly, their hands tightly clasped together. The Naiad guided Eurydice's arms back so that her breasts thrust forward. She lifted her head from the water and flicked her tongue up and down on Eurydice's nipples.

Orpheus's bride-to-be arched into the nymph's mouth, her hips rocking in the water. She strained and reached for the pleasure that seemed just a breath away, thinking still of Orpheus's strong jaw and knowing fingers. She paid no attention to the water lapping first at her armpits, then just below her chin.

Eyes squeezed shut, Eurydice came against the Naiad's leg, the name of her betrothed on her lips. The word trailed off in a gurgle, triggering a panicked attempt to breathe.

Eurydice thrashed in the water, but the nymph's grip had tightened like a noose. She could not lift her head to the air above.

Through the wavering depths of the Naiad's spring, Eurydice saw a collection of water snakes swimming toward them, their bodies writhing and twisting. Her attempt to scream filled her lungs with water. The Naiad smiled and made a pacifying gesture.

The first snake coiled around Eurydice's ankle, weighing her down even more, holding her to the bottom of the spring. She struggled to shake it off, but before she could make headway, another twined itself around her breast. Its body squeezed the sensitive flesh, and then its head drew back. Eurydice watched in horror as its mouth opened wide enough to span a man's thigh. It's thin, sharp fangs embedded themselves in her breast, above and below the nipple.

The nymph held Eurydice in place, stroking the viper's head affectionately. The bite hurt less than Eurydice expected. Ecstatic warmth spread through her body, starting at her nipple but quickly rushing down to her cunt and up to her head.

Looking down her body, Eurydice saw another viper wending its way up her thigh. Its head probed between her legs. She would have panted if she'd been able to breathe. The snake penetrated her just as another bit her neck where it joined her shoulder.

Eurydice's body shuddered, tensing and relaxing while blackness bubbled in her mind. Would her husband have felt like this inside her? "Orpheus," she whispered, slipping entirely into the vipers' underwater nest.

Vipers wrapped Eurydice's neck and filled her mouth, smooth muscles pressing against the insides of her cheeks. Aching pressure between her legs revealed their presence there as well. Snakes around her ankles held her legs apart. Others stroked her nether lips with their bodies as they squirmed into her cunt, traveled deep inside, then out again.

Sensual heat enveloped her, sliding over, around, above, and below her. She lay comfortably, her body held and supported. Silky scales rasped gently over her skin, leaving her shivering in their wake.

Eurydice trembled. The water had gone. Instead, she and the snakes occupied a dark room, its features difficult to determine. She could not have guessed how long she had lain that way, her body being plundered by the snakes. She slid her hands carefully down her body, avoiding contact with the vipers.

Sticky residue covered her inner thighs. It felt like her own dried juices. How many times had she come? Eurydice tried to get to her feet, but the snakes resisted, suddenly binding where they had caressed.

They held her in place at dozens of points — her neck, her shoulders, her elbows, her wrists, her waist, her knees, her ankles. From the press of them, one viper rose, its body twice as thick as any of the others. Eurydice whimpered into the mass of snakes that filled her mouth.

A snake slithered out of her cunt, followed by another and then another. She wondered how many had been inside her. The massive viper found her opening and easily slid its head inside. It struggled to get in deeper, its muscles whipping its body back and forth between her thighs.

The snakes must have broken through her hymen while she'd lain unconscious. Her body slowly stretched open to allow the enormous viper room within her. The pressure of the snake's diamond-shaped head against the walls of her cunt matched a building inner tension.

Another viper, still slick with the juices of her cunt, worked its way between the cheeks of her buttocks and prodded at her other hole. Eurydice shook and poured herself into muffled screaming.

She didn't think she could come. Her body felt too full to ripple and spasm. And yet, as the thin viper pushed tentatively into her ass,

Eurydice's cunt clenched almost unbearably around the thick snake inside it. Sweat trickled between her breasts. Her hips worked uncontrollably. Her tongue worked against the vipers in her mouth.

She could have remained in that blissful oblivion forever except that familiar tones came faintly to her ears, echoing strangely as if traveling a great distance. That cursed Hypophrygian mode—she heard it clearly. *Orpheus?* Now frantic, Eurydice struggled against the vipers, shame replacing her pleasure.

A heavy foot trod outside the room where she lay. She could already envision the disappointment and contempt in Orpheus's violet eyes when he looked upon her, writhing and spreading herself like a whore. Her face and neck burned.

But the man who appeared in the doorway seemed neither surprised nor disdainful. His thick, black eyebrows knitted as he studied her. He had a broad face, as ominous as storm clouds. "Eurydice," he said slowly. "Your husband is here for you."

The man clearly expected a reply. The vipers seemed to understand. They removed themselves from her mouth. Her distended cheeks relaxed. Eurydice sighed with animal relief before she could summon words for the man. When she did, her voice did not sound like her own. "Who are you? Where am I?"

"I am Hades," he replied. "You are in my domain."

Eurydice shuddered. Dead on her wedding day, bitten by a viper while held in a Naiad's embrace. What must Orpheus think of her? "Please don't let him see me," she whispered. She smelled her sex heavy on the air.

"He has convinced me to release you to the land of the living. I came to bring you out to him."

A viper slid over her belly, and Eurydice could not suppress a moan. Could she truly return to Orpheus? Would he want her if she did? Her body now seemed a mockery to his love of beauty, his perfect intentions. She hesitated.

Hades smiled kindly, holding out a hand. Eurydice managed to stand and go to him, her knees still weak from her long stretch of rapture. "Child, don't look so fearful," said the Lord of the Underworld. "This place differs from the land under the sun. We do not flinch from our desires here, but we keep our secrets with the most sacred respect."

He tugged her to the door. When Eurydice still resisted, he sighed. "If Demeter saw the forms her daughter Persephone takes with me in this place, she would blight the earth in eternal cold fury. What you have found here will await your return, and no living soul shall learn of it."

Eurydice swallowed. "Please, Lord. Swear that Orpheus will not see me until we return to the world above."

Orpheus and his ever-present lyre walked ten steps before Eurydice. She sighed with longing. Every line of his body spoke of perfection. She admired his powerful calves, tight buttocks, strong shoulders. She wished she could see his face, but she still stumbled naked and shamed through the halls of the Underworld. Eurydice could not bear the thought of meeting his gaze while in this place, the truth of her desires crusted on her thighs for all to see.

What other man would brave the Underworld and drag his love from the grip of Lord Hades himself? Eurydice's breath caught at the romance of it all.

"My love, are you still behind me?" Orpheus said, his voice low and anxious.

"I'm here, my Lord," Eurydice replied. Creatures of the Underworld lined the passage where they walked on either side, their forms grotesque and suggestive. She tore her eyes from a woman with a face between her legs, and then from a man who opened his mouth to reveal three flicking tongues.

"How do I know you are not an apparition of my Eurydice, meant to deceive me into leaving this place without my wife?"

Eurydice swallowed. "Test me, my Lord." A snake dropped from the stone ceiling of the passageway. She jumped to avoid it, but could not help wondering if this was one of the snakes that had been inside her.

"Sing me our wedding song in the Aeolian mode."

"The mode of mourning, my Lord?"

"Indeed, this is the way I sang it when I found my love had

drowned in the spring at the base of the juniper."

Eurydice thought hard. He had made her listen to this composition in so many different forms, indifferent all the while to her panting after his body. Hesitantly, Eurydice sang the first notes.

Before she found her footing in the melody, Orpheus took over, accompanying himself with his lyre and improvising dramatic variations that made her lose her place in the song. Eurydice frowned, struggling to pass her test while also keeping up the pace through the passageway.

A man with a thick horn in the middle of his forehead threw a handful of snakes at her. One landed in her hair, slithered down her throat, and fastened its fangs around her still-bare nipple, suckling at her like a babe. Eurydice gasped at the sexual surge that passed through her body, faltering.

"Eurydice?" Orpheus asked, halting his steps. "Are you quite well?"

"Yes, my Lord." Another viper copied the first, so that a snake hung from each of her nipples. Eurydice ached between her legs, their poison making her limbs languorous and slow.

"Please continue the song. I need to know you're still following me."

Eurydice closed her eyes. She felt feverish. She struggled to force notes past her thickening tongue. Vipers crawled over the stone floor toward her in an undulating wave. They wound over her feet and worked their way up her body.

A snake with the thickest body she'd seen lifted its patterned coral head, separating itself from the others on the floor. Eurydice's body remembered the ache of the vipers' insertion and longed for it. She wanted to pierce herself on that hard, triangular head.

"My love? Will you sing?"

Eurydice managed a few half-hearted notes, but desire for the viper dominated her attention. Up ahead, Orpheus sighed and stopped walking.

"Eurydice, please."

She stole toward the snake. It knew what she wanted, arching its body up to her and shaping itself into the most pleasing curve. Eurydice stood above it, her legs spread wide. She tugged on the snakes at her breasts, her cunt clenching tightly in response to the sharp sensation. She leaned down and stroked the snake's head, then guided it toward her trembling cunt.

"My love? Did I lose you?"

The viper's forked tongue flicked over her cunt, raking over her bud just before it buried its head inside her. Eurydice sucked her breath in through her teeth and plunged onto it. The flood of vipers wrapped her and pulled her flat on the floor, but she felt held, not restrained. Eurydice worked her hips wildly, trying to force the thick viper deeper inside her. She groaned in a voice not her own.

"Eurydice? What have they done to you?"

Too late, she realized what would happen, but she could not extricate herself from the vipers before Orpheus turned. They engulfed her flailing body, but the ecstatic motion of her fingers against her cunt left no doubt of her feelings about the situation.

Orpheus's handsome face contorted with disgust and horror. "Eurydice? No! It can't be!"

She wanted to respond to him, to explain herself, but when she opened her mouth, a mess of snakes slipped in. She closed her eyes, another orgasm beginning to take her over.

Orpheus's wails shattered the passageway, but the vipers covered Eurydice's ears as they dragged her back into their underground nest forever.

If you enjoyed this story, you can discuss it with other readers and the author at *The Snake and the Lyre* **story page** at http://forbiddenfiction.com/library/story/AL1-1.000052.

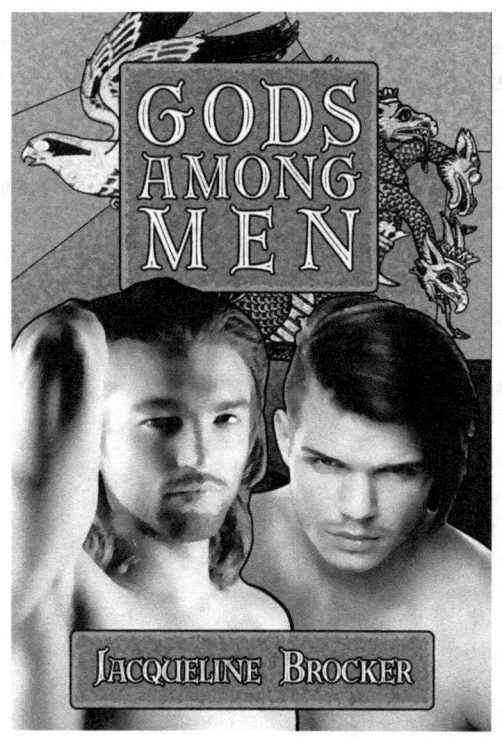

Gods Among Men

Jacqueline Brocker

Jacqueline Brocker lives and writes in Cambridge, England. Her short erotic fiction has appeared in anthologies such as *Smut Alfresco* (House of Erotica), *Under Her Thumb* and *Best Bondage Erotica 2014* (both from Cleis Press). Her novella *Body & Bow* and short story *Oasis Beckoning.* have been published by Forbidden Fiction. Originally from Australia, when not writing she is a Scottish Country Dancer, a recent convert to Lindy Hop, and dabbles in foreign language (current dabblings being German and Korean).

Chapter 1

Rain

Nikolai

Nikolai leaned languidly against the frame of the window of his second-floor study and watched the bay below, and beyond. The water shimmered with the afternoon sun. Yachts and fishing boats bobbed at the docks, and in the distance windsurfers sped along the Adriatic. Vendors sold cold lemonade along the boardwalk while mothers and fathers pushed prams and held dripping ice-cream cones for their capering toddlers. Three old men sat on a bench: one stared vacant out over the harbour while the others contemplated a chessboard. A pair of teenagers kissed and giggled as they sat on the low wall above the water. Other groups played in the water or sunned themselves on the beach. Nikolai smiled; this was summer at its most perfect, for the day was pleasantly hot, and peaceful.

That was, until Ilya charged along the harbour road in his bright red American Mustang. He parked the car, slammed the door and stomped up the boardwalk. Straight towards Nikolai's house.

Nikolai narrowed his eyes, glaring down at Ilya. Although he'd been expecting a visit, he ground his teeth together.

There he was: Ilya Gromovnik. The same nick-name as his father, also the namesake of St Ilya. All of them—saint, father, and son—called Gromovnik; that is to say, Thunderer. Ilya Gromovnik, owner of the furniture factory, the largest employer in town, president of the chamber of commerce. So well-respected by everyone in the town for his capacity to employ many people, to be good to them in return for their complete loyalty; for his generous donations to public works (the painting of the town hall, the play parks for children, the new local museum); for his gorgeous, buxom wife Dobrana and that brood of children. How many did the man have now? Six? Nikolai had lost count.

His striking looks aided him too. Ilya was a tall man, his chest square and broad. As he charged along the boardwalk, the sun caught glints of his close-cropped coppery hair and long, neatly kept beard. His features — handsome and with a hawk-like nose — were creased in anger and he walked as if he owned everything that lay before him.

Nikolai supposed in many ways he did. Not only did he have his factory, but he also had his house on the hill that overlooked the town with pompous pride. It was high enough that anyone in the market square could gaze up over the rooftops and see Ilya's home, watching over them all. Like a beloved god.

Beloved. Nikolai snorted. *Feared is the better word.* For who would dare to cross a man who could make drug cartels scurry away to neighbouring towns with a single phone call, an action the police could not take? Who would fight with a man who, when riff-raff sailors made trouble when they came ashore, would ensure said sailors would be found floating in the harbour the next day? And those who failed to give him proper respect or decided to try and run the town or their business a little differently had felt Ilya's wrath, and found themselves friendless or destitute.

Lord and protector. In a town where councillors were weak-willed and the police ineffectual, who needed a mayor when they had Ilya Gromovnik?

Nikolai sighed. He was well aware of the power of Ilya's rage. Well aware, too, that everyone in town knew that he and Ilya despised each other. Even now in the bay below, the teenage girl turned her head. Likewise, a father pushing a pram saw Ilya's progress; stopped to grasp his wife's shoulders and whisper something into her ear. The man who'd been staring dumbfounded out to sea started as Ilya passed him, and a child's ice-cream tumbled to the ground as the kid froze to gaze at Ilya. As Ilya closed the distance, Nikolai could feel and hear — even through the glass — Ilya's thundering purpose and the hush that fell over the bay. Only the gulls continued to chatter.

They were not business rivals; Nikolai ran a shipping business. He, too, was a member of the chamber of commerce. Longer than Ilya at that — he suspected that Ilya would have blocked his application had Ilya been a member first. However, he kept a number of smaller operations running that the upright and self-righteous Ilya would have loved to have seen abolished. His dance club, for instance, which on paper was perfectly legal, but where Nikolai well knew all kinds of licentious and illicit behaviour took place. His patrons — mostly tourists, male and there for other men — as far as he was concerned, were dancing and embracing the joys of life. Nikolai turned a smirking blind eye to what else besides dancing went on there.

Someone at the chamber told Nikolai he was surprised that Ilya hadn't run him out of town yet. Nikolai had only grinned. Ilya probably would have if not for Nikolai's generosity: people in need of loans found themselves with a discreet envelope slipped through the door. Builders would arrive at a storm-damaged house and do the repair work, refusing payment and shrugging when asked why they had come. No trumpeting, no fanfare, but Nikolai was aware that his name was mentioned. He'd have preferred otherwise, but secrets were a near impossibility to keep.

The only kept secrets he knew were the ones between himself and Ilya.

People left in Ilya's wake, quickly packing their bags and rushing up the beach. On the horizon, dark clouds began to gather, the signs of a sea-born storm, bringing with it a suffocating heat.

Nikolai sighed, rolled his shoulders back, and stood up straight. For all his irritation and hatred of Ilya, this meeting was unavoidable. *Inevitable.* The wheel that had been set in motion since they were children was now rolling towards a climax that neither of them could ignore.

Ilya

Ilya's mind was set with determination, and he was governed by red rage. He let his emotions reign freely on his face. The path cleared before him. People raced to their cars and motorbikes. He heard the whispers of 'Ilya' and 'Gromovnik' and 'Nikolai' in the air.

Good, he thought. *Let them all know that I will no longer tolerate Nikolai's scheming.*

More importantly, he would not give in to what had been drilling through his mind and body this past month.

These past years, you mean, a quieter voice said in his mind. Ilya ignored it.

Soon, Ilya stood before Nikolai's house: it was a fortress of glass and steel, crouching back into a rocky outcrop. So modern and fashionable, possessing none of the traditional values that Ilya held so dear. This home was not suitable for children; Ilya would never have let his near this place. The house may have seemed transparent, but it was another facade for Nikolai's wretched subterfuges. It was no surprise that Nikolai lived here, right at the end of the bay. He'd want to keep his activities well out of sight from the public. A pity that Ilya could see it from his own house on the hill!

Fortress it may have been, but Ilya could have kicked it over with his rage.

Instead, he tested the glass door in front of him, discovered it was locked, and so smashed the glass pane nearest to the handle to let himself in.

That's when he discovered that it wasn't a house; it was a jungle.

Lush green hangings fell from the walls. Potted plants loomed tall, and the furniture was upholstered in a deep, velvety dark green. It was open-plan living, with a mezzanine towards the back — over which a vine grew, thick with broad leaves — and a dining area to one side.

A man built like an ox and wearing a tight t-shirt sat at the dining table. Bodyguard or boyfriend? Maybe both: he carried a side-arm. Ilya didn't know or care, but when the ox saw Ilya he leapt to his feet. He was nearly beside Ilya, hand at his weapon when a smooth voice spoke from from above.

"Risto, that's not necessary. Leave him."

Ilya's eyes shot upwards. Nikolai was standing on the mezzanine, one hand leaning on the balcony. His black hair was slicked back with hair gel, and his pointy features were filled with mocking arrogance. He wore a dark silk shirt, as green as the surroundings and his eyes, with a snakeskin belt holding up his tight black jeans. A gold scarf was draped around his neck. He was dressed as if for a nightclub. Ilya doubted if he'd ever worn proper clothes, like the shirt sleeves and plain slacks Ilya wore then, or if he had any sensible jewellery. Ilya's watch and gold ring were as far as he'd ever go.

Risto's hand hovered a moment, his gaze trailing slowly between Ilya and Nikolai. Ilya watched the gun, ready to duck if Risto should grab it.

Nikolai said, "Leave us, Risto. I can defend myself against Ilya should he prove troublesome."

Risto looked sceptical. *As he should,* Ilya thought. Nikolai had long arms and legs, but was slender, with little muscle, while Ilya could have broken Nikolai into pieces. As he might well do, with or without Risto there.

A wave of Nikolai's hand, though, and Risto obeyed, moving up the staircase, passed Nikolai into the upper level of the house.

When he was gone, Nikolai chuckled. "He is new. How is he to know of our old friendship?"

Ilya scoffed. "That is not what we are."

Nikolai feigned surprise, but soon his mouth curled into a languid smile, teasing, taunting even.

"I suppose I should fetch some champagne. This is an occasion to celebrate; in all these years, you have never been in my home before." A pause as he cocked his head; all pretence. "Nor have I been to yours, have I, Ilya?"

Ilya only glared.

Nikolai smirked, then descended the stairs, steps like a slinking cat. He slid onto the couch, hand out in an inviting gesture.

"Please, Ilya. Take a seat."

Ilya crossed his arms and remained standing. Childish perhaps, but he'd not give in to any of Nikolai's suggestions. Not today of all days.

"Suit yourself."

Nikolai began to toy with that ridiculous gold scarf. It was made of material like a harem veil, opaque and alluring.

"Are you here to simply glower at me? Come on, Ilya, talk."

Words were not Ilya's strength, so he went straight to the point. "You are taking bribes from Mishka to support the application for his club."

Nikolai twirled the scarf, cocked his head to one side, trying to convey the picture of innocence. Ilya held himself steady, keeping his arms over his chest as if that could contain his bubbling anger, and glared at Nikolai.

At last, Nikolai sighed.

"I suppose it is no surprise that you have found out. You have your informants after all. Yes, it is true. Me, and a number of other members of the chamber, as I'm sure you know. But what concern is it of yours?"

It took Ilya great control not to splutter. "It is illegal."

"I think you'll find it is a legally grey area, my dear Ilya."

The words came at last, and they fell out of Ilya's mouth. "Do not call me your dear, and do not pretend that what you are doing is the right thing. The man wants to open a sex club. Do you really think that is appropriate for this town?"

"I think it will add a certain kind of appeal." Nikolai held the scarf below his eyes, peered at Ilya and fluttered his eyelashes. Just like a harlot. "You may even get something out of it yourself."

Ilya flexed his hand opened and closed again. He would not give in and punch Nikolai, or touch him in any way. He would do this the right way. He had to.

He spoke carefully, his voice controlled. "We are in a fortunate position with our chamber of commerce. The planning section of the council which allows us to vet applications for new businesses has served all of us well. If we start to be open to bribery, we will undermine ourselves."

Nikolai dropped the scarf. His voice was still casual when he said, "I am less open to bribery than seeing it as an added bonus. Mishka is a sordid man, and it would serve me well for him to think he has me in his pocket. He made me the offer of money without my asking, and it hardly seemed good business to say no."

You would you dirty little schemer, Ilya thought.

"Nikolai, this is serious." Ilya took a deep breath, and tried to appeal to Nikolai's goodness — assuming he had any. "He wants to open it where families will be coming for holidays, right on the promenade. Our town is for everyone, not the coarse and the sexually depraved!"

Nikolai shrugged.

"I am not the only one taking the money. Why don't you convince someone else? You only need to convince two of them to change the vote to what you want. I am sure they will respond very well to your threats."

Ilya stepped closer to the couch with the intent of looming over Nikolai. "Your refusal will send a better message. I do not want only a minority vote. Mishka needs to understand that no one will accept his money or wants his club."

"Such regard for my power. I am very flattered."

Ilya closed the distance between them, nearly hitting Nikolai's knees. He glowered down at him. "You will do this, Nikolai. You will meet with Mishka and tell him the deal is off. Then you will contact the other chamber members and tell them to do the same."

The leisurely look disappeared, and Nikolai's face went as hard as stone. "Do not order me around, Ilya."

Ilya's fists curled up. "You will do as I say, Nikolai."

Nikolai sprung to his feet, teeth bared. "Make me."

In an instant those two simple words pushed Ilya over the edge. Yes, he would make Nikolai bend to him and his demands, and he would do it the only way he knew how. As his body rushed with enraged arousal, Ilya said, "I will."

Ilya threw himself at Nikolai. He grabbed his chin, forcing Nikolai's face up to his, and snatched Nikolai's lips into a biting kiss. Nikolai tried to lean away from Ilya, but Ilya urged his bulky frame right up against Nikolai's slender body. Nikolai groaned, knotting his fingers into Ilya's beard. Nikolai's erection pressed into Ilya, and Ilya's cock responded. Ilya relished the hardness, but refused to give it attention.

Outside, thick rain began to fall, splashing into the bay and hammering against the glass. A distinct clap of thunder sounded in the distance. Inside, a moist warmth began to form between Ilya and Nikolai's bodies.

Many centuries ago...

The land remembers.

It remembers the centuries aeons before written records began, before Christ, before the one God and his saints swept away the pantheons of old. When humanity gathered in small villages and lived off the land, existing between terror and hope of the fickle ways of the gods that stalked above and amongst them. It remembers days of bronze, of forests yet unconquered by farms and cities.

In such a time, in the sky high above the world where it is airy and clear, standing proud in a golden chariot pulled by a buck goat, Perun rode across the clouds. His eagle perched on one arm and his axe was fastened to his back. Beneath the chariot lay the land: mountains and steep valleys, green forests, rich and abundant fields of wheat. Cattle and sheep grazed, and the farmers looked after their flocks and herds with patience.

It was a perfect day, busy with the activity of life. Perun stroked his long, coppery beard, and was content.

Then Veles came in the form of a dragon from beneath the ground, from the base of a great oak tree. He shot into the air like a giant lance, his body green-scaled and terrible, his fangs long, his eyes golden with greed, and his wings like a giant bat's, veiny and leathery. He, too, surveyed the lands, flapping his great wings just above the treetops. He saw the tender flesh of the waiting cattle. He licked his lips. With a sudden swoop, he snatched a cow up in his jaws and tore it to shreds in the air, devouring it in his flight. The farmer below wailed in horror. Hot blood gushed down Veles's throat. His stomach was sated, and he smiled.

Perun, watching the whole scene from above, angry at the dragon-god's mischief, shouted out to Veles. Veles turned, hovering in the air like an awful cloud. He winked at Perun.

"Greetings, Perun, God of the Sky and the Thunder. Why do you scream at me in such rage?"

"Oh Veles, God of the Underworld. You are meant to protect the cattle! And now you have caused a poor farmer much grief."

Veles laughed, low and rumbling. "I, too, must eat."

"Then you are nothing but a thief."

Veles sneered, lips curling around his fangs. "And you are a stubborn overlord who frightens the people to your will, Perun Gromovnik, with your fury and your lightning that kills with a single strike. You dare to presume you are better than me."

The eagle at Perun's arm shrieked, flapping its wings. Its eyes and Perun's bore down at Veles, ferocious, enraged. Again Veles only laughed. The sound filled Perun with greater anger. He urged his chariot downwards, like a bolt from the blue, towards the mighty dragon Veles. Veles beat his wings and dove towards the earth. His body was filled with the vitality of the meal he had consumed. He would give Perun a merry chase, across the four corners if he had to.

As they had always done and always would.

Croatia – eighteen years ago

Nikolai

At the end of the day, the gymnasium was usually empty. Even the staff would have gone home. So Nikolai would go to the punching bag and practice alone. Boxing was his favourite of the sports at the gym, and despite his slightness, he was among the best. It was a status he could not maintain without practice, however: he did not wish the others to see just how hard he worked at it, or learn his techniques. So this time of the day was the best.

That evening, Nikolai hopped and darted around the punching bag, hitting it with teasing taps and thudding blows. The first hits designed to foster confusion in his opponents, followed by direct hits that would leave them dazzled. He was on form, and — though he sweated and his heart raced — he smiled.

It was the largest gymnasium in town. It was an old building and held a space for weights, a boxing ring and wrestling mats. The changing rooms were a little grubby, but it was a place of activity and community for all the young men. While no sign indicated that women were not welcome, most didn't enter, or if they did they did not linger: such was the scent of maleness in the air. Outside an old elm tree stood, too close to the building in the minds of some; they feared it falling and destroying the gym. But there it remained, for people loved it.

For Nikolai it was more than just a place for exercise and sports: it was the battle ground on which Nikolai and Ilya fought for the minds of men.

Nikolai smirked as he thought on that, and pictured Ilya's face as he landed a triple punch on the bag.

It was an old rivalry, a war that had begun when they were still children. Nikolai remembered being only five years old and looking across the classroom to see the solid boy with the proud face whom everyone wanted to love. His own scrawny body had failed to inspire such devotion, but he traded marbles for sweets, was generous with his friends and so found his own place. But in that instant, in that first look, Nikolai knew Ilya hated him and that he hated Ilya. He could not explain why; he only knew that their hatred was mutual and that was that.

Of course the children flocked to Ilya's side, his father being the richest man in town, and Ilya destined to take over the factory from him. Ilya's father was benevolent, but he was a proud man who was not easily crossed. Everybody knew when he was angry. They called him Gromovnik.

And Ilya became him as he grew, Nikolai thought, taking another punch at the imaginary Ilya.

Nikolai did not mind the attentions Ilya received. He had his friends and he also had his place. As he grew up he swapped marbles and sweets for sexy magazines and videos (the teenagers he traded with knew not to ask questions about their providence). He found himself giving away the money he began to accrue. Though quietly. There was no need to puff out his chest and brag about it.

In the year before he was due to graduate, Nikolai began selling hashish. A risk, but worth it for the proceeds he made. He knew Ilya watched him with piercing eyes, waiting to catch him off-guard. He was careful, but the day came when—on Ilya's evidence—Nikolai was expelled with no diploma to take into the world. His father had been angry, but when he saw Nikolai's self-accumulated wealth, he'd shaken his head in amazement and urged Nikolai to go into business school.

Nikolai knew he wouldn't need that. He started a small business in the docks, keeping smaller and more shadowy businesses on the side.

Ilya, meanwhile, finished school with good marks and joined his father's factory, and began courting the loveliest girl in town, Dobrana. Theirs was a relationship from a Hollywood film, as much for everyone else to enjoy as it was theirs, replete with public displays of chaste affection. Nikolai found it sickeningly amusing. His own interests lay with older men who he sought out in darkened pubs and one ill-lit park on the outskirts of town. He learned that he liked the fierce grip of another man's hand on his cock, and how to best use his tongue on theirs.

Nikolai slowed his punches down, practicing his technique over his speed. He considered where he and Ilya stood now; each kept their distance from the other and that suited them both fine. The gymnasium was another matter. They might be out of school, but the same battles for their favours continued to play out there.

Most still wanted the attention and favour of Ilya. They regarded him with solemn respect, and stood aside for him when he walked. Not grovelling, for it was understood Ilya liked confidence, pride in oneself. But they would never stand in Ilya's way if he had his mind set on some goal.

Nikolai snorted. Only a fool would stand in front of a charging bull. And indeed some tried. They found themselves shunned by others, not always for reasons they could fathom. And because it is a man's duty to survive and to show he could fend for a family when the time came to have one, they turned instead to the shadows, where Nikolai operated. What good operatives he had, too, for Nikolai found the gymnasium the perfect place for his latest scheme: selling steroids to the attendees.

How easy men were to convince that they needed to enhance their strength and virility.

Nikolai swung at the bag one last time, landing his punch with a grunt. It flung back with juddering force and Nikolai smiled, satisfied.

Sweat dripped from him. He picked up his towel and bottle of water, and was drying his face when something caught his eye.

Ilya was leaning against the wall. He'd clearly been watching Nikolai. Watching and waiting.

Nikolai's blood ran hot. He ran his knuckles across his still girlish chin, conscious of how Ilya's short and sharp beard made him appear so much more like a man. But he did not bare his teeth at his old enemy. He stood nonchalant, with his arms folded. Ilya could speak first.

Ilya took his time, but at last he said, "You punch well, but I wonder how you would fare on the wrestling mats."

Nikolai filled his mouth with water, swishing it around before swallowing. "I am told it is not your size that counts, but the way you move."

Ilya raised an eyebrow. "So you've been told? Well... why don't we see if that's the case?"

"Now?"

"Yes."

Nikolai chuckled, and his already hot blood began to boil.

Chapter 2
Lightning

Croatia – eighteen years ago

Ilya

Ilya took his place on the mat. Nikolai went through some absurd routine of wiping himself down, drinking more water. As if it might help him win. Soon enough he would know Ilya's will and wrath.

Ilya thought himself a tolerant person. As much as he hated the devious little man, as much as they had their factions in the gymnasium, Ilya was content to leave Nikolai alone. But something had changed that Ilya could not abide.

Drugs had begun to circulate at the gymnasium. The kind that would allow a user to become stronger, faster, better than the others. At first, no one knew where they came from. It didn't take long for Ilya to suspect their source. Nikolai would spring and bounce across the boxing ring, seeming a waif but with a sneaky punch. He never took the drugs himself (as far as Ilya could tell), or kept them on his person; even after Ilya sent his men to raid Nikolai's locker, they found nothing.

But Ilya knew. And he wanted it to stop.

Nikolai bent forward, kicking his legs up as if about to start a race. His face showed that he thought this was all a game. Ilya's lip curled up in a sneer. Everything was a game to that man — apart from his little business in the docks, everything else he did was all about hedonistic pleasure, about giving to people what sated their basest needs. No sense of civic duty or pride, just fun and games and consequence be damned. Like the hashish, like the steroids.

Like the men he was rumoured to be fucking. A vision of Niko-lai in congress with another man flashed before Ilya. He stopped the thought before it could... grow.

Ilya had been with two girls his own age, but was now keeping himself for Dobrana, who wanted a long engagement for the best pos-sible wedding. That was the right thing to do. Nikolai wouldn't know the right thing to do if it reared up and struck him.

So, Ilya reasoned, it was his job to do the striking.

Across the mat, shirtless, only in shorts—Nikolai's tight and fitting, Ilya's hanging loose— the two men circled each other, pad-ding the mat like panthers, eyes hooded like hawks. Nikolai some-times slapped his thighs, and he wore his damnable grin, the one the seemed as if he was keeping a secret that only he had the pleasure of knowing. Ilya, meanwhile, was still, quiet: he felt no need for sudden sounds. Patience and watchfulness, he knew, were how you won at wrestling, not with darting games. And nothing would distract him from his task.

Nikolai lunged first. It made Ilya smile. That was his first mistake. He caught Nikolai, stumbled backwards, and Nikolai briefly grinned in triumph, only to find himself on his side, Ilya's shoulder pressing his down. He heard Nikolai gasp and saw his panicked eyes. Ilya chuckled, but Nikolai locked his legs around his own and twisted un-til Ilya too was on the ground, Nikolai half on top of him.

Nikolai bent in, close to Ilya's face. "See, I told you—"

Ilya pushed back at Nikolai's shoulder and once more Nikolai was on his back. Nikolai tried to squirm away, but Ilya held him firm in his grasp.

"Now that you cannot get away, I want to—shit!"

Nikolai had bit Ilya's hand: a sharp and decisive bite. Ilya wrenched back and Nikolai rolled away.

Ilya shot a furious look at Nikolai.

"That's against the rules."

Nikolai shrugged. "But it worked."

Ilya snarled, got on his haunches. *Two can play at that game,* he thought. He launched himself at Nikolai who deftly moved out of the way and caught Ilya's legs, lifting them just enough to throw him back onto the mat. Ilya winced and cursed when Nikolai fell on top of him, trying to press his small weight against Ilya's body. Nikolai managed to twine himself enough around Ilya so Ilya couldn't move.

"So, I am here, you said you wanted to... what?"

Ilya jerked, but he was quite subdued. He could only move one hand and that hand was very close to Nikolai's... crotch.

The cotton stretched over Nikolai's cock and balls, making them appear soft and vulnerable. The scent of salty sweat rose from his body. His skin, Ilya knew, would be sensitive to touch, and his cock and balls even more so.

Ilya began to reach forward, inch by inch. "I want to talk."

"Well then, talk." Nikolai smirked as if he'd won already.

"No. I mean, I talk," Ilya grabbed Nikolai's cock through his shorts, "and you listen."

Nikolai yelped, his arms going limp around Ilya. Ilya, not letting go, threw Nikolai back. Nikolai landed on his side, whimpering. Ilya tightened his grip.

Nikolai beat the mat with his fist. "Not... fair..."

Ilya hooked his fingers through Nikolai's hair, and forced his face onto the gym mat. "Says the man who bit me."

The sight of Nikolai trembling, of his face twisted in pain, sent a shot of arousal to Ilya's own cock. It shocked him. But Nikolai was so close, their bodies locked together, it was almost as if they were one. Ilya stroked the cock he already held. A more tender hold, but still firm, and he realised that Nikolai was growing hard, too.

Nikolai tried to lash back, but Ilya's grip was too much. Ilya had to grin at the feeling of total power over Nikolai, his nerves crackling. With Nikolai's hardening cock in his hand, Ilya knew exactly what he needed to do to teach Nikolai his lesson.

Swiftly, Ilya grabbed Nikolai's shorts and pulled them off his body, leaving Nikolai naked on the mat with Ilya looming over him.

"Ilya!"

Nikolai's voice held a warning, but Ilya's hand rubbed his cock, then splayed to stroke down its length, to catch his balls and rub the whole of his sack and cock at once. Nikolai swore, but he thrust his hips into Ilya's hand.

Of course he would.

Ilya lifted Nikolai's buttocks off the mat, spreading his legs. He rubbed harder. Nikolai gasped, and Ilya delighted in knowing he liked it despite himself.

Ilya leaned down to speak straight into Nikolai's ear. "I thought size didn't matter... little Nikolai."

A snigger. "It still doesn't. What do you have that's better?"

Ilya's hand left Nikolai's cock and pulled his own shorts down, revealing his erection. Nikolai swallowed. Ilya smiled: he knew his cock was huge, red and hard. It wanted attention. He was not betraying Dobrana, for this was not sex; this was necessary education.

So Ilya flipped Nikolai onto his knees, and spread his legs once more. Nikolai reached to pull away, but Ilya's grip on his hips was too strong.

Ilya spat into his hand; for his comfort, not for Nikolai's. He smeared the spit on the blade of his hand, divided the cheeks of Nikolai's arse, pushing momentarily at the puckered hole.

Nikolai beat the mat again.

"Don't you fucking dare!"

Ilya paid no heed. He took his cock in hand, angled it to Nikolai's hole, and shoved it inside with a grunt.

Nikolai shouted like a loud and sudden bell. "Fuck!"

Ilya threw his body over Nikolai's back, grabbed Nikolai's wrists to hold them down, and drove his cock in deeper. "Yes! Until you say yes, I'll fuck you."

Ilya began to rock his hips, his cock sliding in and out of Nikolai. It was as though he could tear Nikolai in half, and Nikolai's grunting sounds gave credence to that thought. Ilya relished the motion of his body, the total power he had over Nikolai in this moment. And oh, how Nikolai was tight, tighter than any woman's cunt — and there was something almost better about this. Pleasure seared through Ilya, though he told himself it was necessary, a duty, to subdue the arrogant little shit.

Ilya paused, half inside Nikolai. "Now you will listen to me!"

"Fuck you!"

Three times Ilya slammed against Nikolai, leaving Nikolai whimpering, barely able to hold himself up. But Ilya knew his spirit was not yet subdued, even if his body was. It would take more than that with Nikolai.

Ilya spoke again, murmuring into Nikolai's ear. "The steroids? You will stop selling them. Do you hear me?"

Nikolai made no response.

Ilya dropped his voice and pressed his lips right to Nikolai's skin. "I said... do you hear me?"

Only a nod.

Ilya continued to pound into Nikolai until Nikolai's voice came up, taunting, "I hear you... but I will not stop."

"You will stop."

"Why should I?"

"Because..."

Ilya drove his cock all the way into Nikolai and held it there while he kept speaking.

"If you do not, I will find you, and once again..."

He drew back, leaving only the head inside Nikolai.

"I will fuck you."

Nikolai hissed, his head twisting around to glare at Ilya with hate. A hatred, Ilya saw, streaked with need for Ilya's cock.

Ilya began thrusting again, harder and faster than before. Nikolai tried to stretch away from Ilya only to be dragged back for more. Ilya watched as Nikolai bit his lip, a moan barely suppressed under it. Ilya pounded again and Nikolai expelled a tortured sound.

A small victory.

Keeping Nikolai to him was like trying to contain a bundle of coiled springs. Ilya had to grapple with him to stop him from scrambling away. He would make Nikolai take this, take all of Ilya's cock. His cock could have burst with the incredible intensity as Nikolai's tight channel contracted around it again and again. Then Nikolai moaned like a whore, flooding Ilya with the desire to come.

Ilya spoke again, his vicious thrusts punctuated with his words. Each of them jabbing Nikolai with pain and rippling pleasure.

"You. Will. Stop. Selling. Steer. Oids. Do. You. Un. Der. Stand!"

Nikolai screamed, "Yes!" His body shuddered as he came.

Despite himself, Ilya was impressed, for neither his hand, nor Nikolai's, had so much as brushed Nikolai's cock since Ilya had penetrated him. Yet Nikolai shot his load all over the mat, his come splashing against Ilya's knees. His whole body shuddered, and he squeezed the orgasm out of Ilya's cock. Ilya coated

Nikolai's insides, and thrust until the last wave of it fell.

Ilya pulled Nikolai's head up by the hair, forcing Nikolai to meet his eyes.

He smiled, showing all his teeth.

"I'm glad we understand each other."

He dropped Nikolai back on the mat. With a sharp tug he withdrew his cock and was filled with a pure satisfaction.

Ilya stood, keeping a close eye on Nikolai who still lay on the mat, exhaling slowly. He looked like a gym towel rung out after being used to wipe away sweat. Ilya smirked. *Serves him right.* Ilya waited until Nikolai caught his breath, crawled away and left the gymnasium.

Ilya found some towels and began to clean up their sweat and cum, invigorated with purpose. He hummed, proud that he had done the right thing and taught Nikolai a lesson. Then a sudden, sharp crack echoed through the gymnasium. Ilya started, gasping. The sound had come from outside. He left the towels and moved slowly through the gymnasium towards the front door.

The elm tree was on fire. Ilya scanned the sky, saw the thick wooly clouds hanging there above the pelting rain. It must have been lightning. Ilya's eye went wide at the sight of the beautiful tree burning. A branch snapped off and fell onto the roof. Ilya cried out, and raced to call the fire brigade.

When the firemen arrived, they immediately set to work with their hoses and water.

"Anyone inside? Anyone with you?" one of them asked Ilya.

Ilya shook his head. "I was alone."

Nikolai

Nikolai's body shook as he pulled his clothes on, gingerly packed his bag and hobbled out of the gymnasium.

As he hauled himself home, rain began pelting down. He wrapped his arms around himself and hunched his shoulders. Nothing could ease the ache inside him. He winced with each step. When he heard the sirens, he turned to watch their progress, and saw above the tops of the houses, the roof of the gymnasium and the elm tree alight. Nikolai began to smile, before his mouth spread into a devilish grin.

Centuries ago...

The chase was on.

Perun pursued Veles through the skies and over the hills, down low valleys and rollicking over houses, urging his buck goat forward. Veles swam through the air, glancing over his shoulder, his laughter mocking. He breathed noisy fire to distract Perun.

Then Perun brought out his stone arrows. He threw them at Veles. The dragon only writhed out of their range.

The arrow struck a great elm tree standing by a field of corn. It split directly in half. A young girl in the field cried out, seeing the arrow as lightning from the heavens. Her lips trembled as she cast her eyes nervously to the sky.

"Great Veles flies, and Great Perun is angry."

She ran from the field to her father's house, declaring that they had to make a sacrifice of a bull soon. The thunder was coming again.

In the sky above, Veles laughed, a hissing bellow.

"You will have to aim better than that, Perun!"

And he dove straight into a dark forest.

Perun screamed in fury. He grabbed another arrow, aiming into the forest. It would surely strike close this time, and indeed, it struck the tallest oak. The oak crashed through the trees, a leafy, fluttery wave of destruction as it fell and smacked against the other trees. Foxes, squirrels, wild boar, deer and a lone wolf all scattered in a terrible panic.

This time when Veles emerged, wings still beating hard, he bore a large scratch on his shoulders. He craned his head over his shoulder, lips curling in a sneer. Perun smiled, feeling his triumph imminent, and aimed another arrow.

Veles shot straight over the cornfield, towards the barn. Perun cursed as the dragon vanished through its doors.

The girl and her family ran from the house and headed toward the town. The other people needed to know that the gods were doing battle; a sacrifice had to be made and they had to find a suitable ox. Perun aimed towards the barn and hurled his arrow once more.

The lightning struck the barn with such force and heat that the wood, the straw and the leftover grain caught fire. Soon the whole barn was ablaze and Veles, screaming at his wretched luck, took to the air once more.

As the farm blazed below Perun stood with his hand on his hip. "Give up your flight, Veles! You cannot outrun my arrows."

Perun's eagle laughed as well, its head flinging back cawing.

Veles felt sorry that the barn was alight; the barn had given him shelter. He twirled away from Perun, dashing to get away as fast as he could, though as he departed, he threw a bag of coins through the window of the farmers' house; a recompense for the damage done.

He glared at the thunder god still pursuing him. How dare he suggest Veles was no more than a thief? Well. This thief was going to make Perun's task the hardest it could possibly be.

And still, the chase was on.

Croatia - ten years ago

Ilya

Summer was approaching an end. At an outdoor cafe on the town promenade by the bay, Ilya and his wife Dobrana sat with their three children. Two children occupied themselves with a quiet game — they were well-behaved — while Dobrana fed the toddler in a highchair, cradling her pregnant belly and smiling as she did.

Ilya, however, seethed. In his line of sight, Nikolai draped himself over a bulky, muscular man and turned sporadically to wink at Ilya.

Eight years ago the fire hadn't spread through the gymnasium. No one ever did learn about what passed between him and Nikolai. But ever after people associated Ilya's quick call to the fire department—

thus saving the gymnasium — with the end of the steroid trade.

Ilya married Dobrana soon after. They named their first child Ilya, keeping with the family tradition. Ilya continued to work at his father's factory, and now that his father was considerably ill, he took over most of the duties of running it.

Nikolai did not marry. Ilya doubted he ever would. His shipping business expanded, as did his shady deals. He'd kept his word: he had stopped the steroids at the gymnasium long ago. But his side business branched into other areas very quickly. No one could ever track anything back to him, he was so cunning.

Ilya grabbed his coffee and gulped it down hard as Nikolai nudged the muscle man's knee and then skirted away, looking coy and innocent when the man glanced at him. How was it that Nikolai already sat on the chamber of commerce, while Ilya did not?

He knew the real answer: although his father had given most of the power of the factory over to Ilya, his father still attended the chamber meetings. It was still, as far as his father was concerned, his factory, and therefore his position to maintain. Ilya did not wish his father dead. But he hated watching Nikolai pass him on his motorbike, heading for the meetings, giving Ilya a quick wave as he went.

Nikolai giggled and squeezed the muscle man's bicep. The man himself seemed bemused but tolerant of the attention. Ilya had to stop himself from snarling. Nikolai could smile and disarm anyone with it, with his hips rocking with a seductive grace as he walked and those deceptively shy eyes. Shouldn't a man like the one he was fawning over be repulsed? Shouldn't he hit Nikolai? Hadn't Nikolai learned he was vulnerable after Ilya's punishment in the gymnasium? Ilya despised his knowing grin, the sly look that said Nikolai had a secret that he was not going to tell anyone, but he just might if you knew how much to pay. His blood raged to think that he'd fucked another man and the man still had not learned. Ilya still thought on that night and his cock would become half-hard. There was order that must be maintained in the world. Order. And Nikolai brought chaos.

Ilya had been ignoring his anger. It would not do to repeat the events of that night in the gymnasium. Then Nikolai had begun to breathe words into the ears of the workers at the furniture factory. Tempting offers of greater pay, with side benefits that Ilya could only dream of giving them. When five men and two women left the factory, murmurs that became rumblings passed from house to house, eventually reaching Ilya's ears. From his house on the hill, he glared down at the docks, wishing his own hands could bring down lightning to strike at Nikolai's office.

Nikolai glanced over at Ilya and gave him a cheeky wink. *Almost flaunting how he undermines me, the bastard!* Ilya thought.

Ilya finished his coffee, and called the waiter over. He asked for a pen and pad of paper. He wrote a furious note on it, marched over to Nikolai and thrust it in his face without a word. Nikolai took it and began to read.

Ilya waited with his arms crossed for a response. Nikolai read the note, and folded it. He leered up at Ilya.

"Tomorrow," he said.

Ilya nodded, and left Nikolai to his muscle man.

Chapter 3

Thunder

Croatia - ten years ago

Nikolai

Nikolai rode his motorbike along the coast road, smirking beneath his helmet. He'd bought the bike to celebrate his first year of success in business. He loved it. Furthermore, it enabled him to ride out of town to the larger cities and find deliciously built men who would fuck him hard and rough.

No one had matched Ilya's brutality. Nikolai had ached for days after the fight in the gymnasium, sore and tender, flinching from everyone. When he'd emerged into the world again he'd vowed to make Ilya's life hell.

In the years since then, he found other deals to thread through the town, to keep his business afloat and keep life interesting. Mostly he was amused by Ilya's puffing and posturing, by his sense of assurance he was doing so much right in this town. Though sometimes he would seethe when Ilya treated Nikolai like he wasn't worthy of address, like something beneath his shoe. He would not acknowledge Nikolai on the street, though Nikolai always offered him a cocky wave, a sway of his hips, if only to see Ilya barrel his chest and storm away — people scattering out of his stride — back to his wife to prove that he was unaffected by Nikolai's presence.

Nikolai knew the best way to keep people happy was by generosity and kindness. He hadn't really meant to steal workers from Ilya. Of course, when a man named Goran had come to him with a broken arm and a tale of woe about Ilya's treatment of him, Nikolai's heart had been quietly moved. To him when a poorer man borrows money and is late on repayment there were other ways to deal with it than breaking his arm. A job in Nikolai's business seemed most fitting.

So now, pleased with his busy docks and his eager new workers, Nikolai would look up from the boardwalk on his morning stroll to that towering house on the hill and smile smugly.

Thus he was not wholly surprised when Ilya had handed him the written note in the cafe with a request that Nikolai meet Ilya in in a hotel room in a town some miles south, where they would not be recognised, and where they could talk.

Ilya was already there when Nikolai arrived. Nikolai wore tight fitting clothes, the kind he knew that Ilya would stare at and curse him for. Ilya, in his open shirt and rolled up sleeves, shook his head as his gaze passed over Nikolai. Nikolai suppressed his smirk, raked his eyes over Ilya, but said nothing. There was a small bottle of oil in his pocket. Unnecessary perhaps, but Nikolai suspected not. Outside there was a roll of distant thunder.

Ilya offered Nikolai a bottle of beer; Nikolai knew well that it was a pretence of civility.

Nikolai hesitated before taking it.

"I wonder that it is not poisoned."

Ilya snorted, and leaned back on the wall as Nikolai sat in the armchair. Nikolai put the beer bottle to his mouth and sucked, eyes suggestive, mouth laving the top and neck. Ilya shifted to cross his legs; Nikolai wondered what stirred between them.

There was no need for ceremony or preamble. Ilya said, "I know why my workers have left. I have heard what you promised them. I've lost a good group of people because of your pernicious words."

Nikolai blinked, deliberately coquettish. "Pernicious? I'd hardly call a better offer pernicious."

Ilya's face creased. Frustration, Nikolai had no doubt. Nikolai always had the advantage with words — small as he was, he had had to learn — while Ilya's reliance on strength meant that speaking left him tongue-tied.

Delighting in Ilya's discomfort, Nikolai lay back in his chair, opened his arms behind him, and parted his legs. His cock was growing in his trousers, pressing against the material. Ilya saw it, his eyes unmistakeable on Nikolai's groin. He folded his arms, his expression disgusted, but Nikolai suspected that his balls were hanging heavier, filling with seed.

Nikolai grinned. "It is not my fault you cannot do better."

Ilya's arms tightened, his teeth clenched. He threw his bottle at Nikolai. Nikolai ducked. The bottle struck the wall behind his head, not shattering but spilling beer everywhere. Lightning flashed outside.

Nikolai glowered back at Ilya.

"Always with violence. That is your way, isn't it, Ilya? You know Goran? The man who borrowed money from his ever so benevolent boss? What about his broken arm? Perhaps it is your own ways you need to check, not mine."

Grabbing Nikolai by his shirt collar, Ilya hauled him to his feet. "You stop what you are doing."

Nikolai was so close he could have spat at Ilya. Instead, he leaned forward, and began to caress Ilya's mouth with his lips and tongue. He pressed his body against Ilya, who stood frozen, his mouth hardly moving under Nikolai's attention. Then Nikolai pulled back and whispered,

"Make me."

The thunder rolled again. Nikolai's chest heaved. Ilya's blue eyes became electric, and he began to pull off Nikolai's clothes. Nikolai felt liberated from their confines, enthralled as he did the same to Ilya, revealing his powerful body. Their clothes fell to the floor — there was a clunk as the little bottle of oil hit the carpet — and Ilya's mouth was all over Nikolai's neck.

Ilya shoved Nikolai onto the bed and leapt on top of him. He ground their hips together. His large cock rubbed against Nikolai's slender one, a hot friction that made Nikolai's body tense, for he would not lose himself under Ilya, would not give in, but the sensation was incredible.

"Make me," Nikolai repeated, craning up, rolling his hips as he did so.

Ilya pushed him down again. Nikolai laughed, more turned on by Ilya's forcefulness than he'd realised as Ilya glared at him. Ilya stood and turned away. Nikolai frowned, wondering what Ilya was up to, until he saw Ilya bend to the floor and rise again holding both the beer bottle and the bottle of oil.

Then Ilya emptied the beer bottle, and Nikolai knew his intention.

Nikolai began to dart away. But Ilya only had to press his chest down and trap his thighs with his own to stop him. Ilya placed the bottle next to them and spread Nikolai's legs. He lifted Nikolai's rear up, propping it on his knees, making Nikolai lock his legs around Ilya's waist.

Ilya opened the bottle of oil, poured it onto his fingers. He smeared the oil onto Nikolai's hole for only a few seconds, before inserting two long, fat fingers.

There was less pain than the last time, but only just.

Nikolai flung his head back, moaning. Ilya savagely crooked his fingers around. He quickly found a tender place and rubbed it without mercy.

Nikolai whimpered; he saw Ilya's huge cock growing. He wanted to beg, oh he wanted to, but he wouldn't. He'd wait for all of Ilya's punishment. He could hear, under his the nonsensical murmurings, the desire to beg for more, to want to be punished for his actions. And he knew Ilya would punish him with everything he had.

Nikolai tried to take hold of his own cock, but Ilya smacked his hands away at every attempt. Nikolai swore and tried to fight so he could just give himself some relief, but Ilya made it impossible. And when he wouldn't stop fighting, Ilya withdrew his fingers, picked up the bottle, and slid the neck all the way into Nikolai before Nikolai could even protest.

"You bastard," Nikolai said, teeth clenched, but Ilya cranked the bottle upwards so the rim hit that perfect spot. Nikolai gasped. Thunder struck again, closer than before, and another flash of lightning filled the room with brief, stark brilliance.

The bottle was cool, the glass unyielding. It took all of Nikolai's strength not to try and slide along its length, to feel more of it; he would not show Ilya he found it at all arousing.

Ilya worked his hand like a lever, as if he were pumping water. Each press made Nikolai pant, and he wanted more, his body twitching with each probe.

Above him, Ilya smiled. "You will stop stealing my workers?"

Nikolai wouldn't say yes. Not yet. He gave Ilya a hazy look, and only growled quietly.

Ilya jammed the bottle in as deep as he could. Nikolai winced, and Ilya said in a vicious whisper, "Have it your way."

He yanked the bottle out and threw it to the ground. Ilya grabbed Nikolai's body and hauled him onto his knees. Nikolai almost bounced on the mattress. He tried to drag himself away, but Ilya encircled his waist with one powerful arm.

As much as the bottle had stretched him, Nikolai had forgotten how huge Ilya was. Ilya, chuckling darkly, dripped more oil against Nikolai, then took his time as he urged the head of his cock against Nikolai's hole. And slowly, aching movement by aching movement, Ilya pushed his cock all the way into Nikolai.

Nikolai mewled, feeling full, spread apart by Ilya's cock. Ilya wrapped his body around Nikolai, trapping him. He took Nikolai's cock and balls entirely in his hand, not pumping, just squeezing, holding. Ensnared in Ilya's grasp, completely in his power, Nikolai succumbed to washes of pleasure. With Ilya hunched over him, hips thrusting his cock into Nikolai, it was as if his whole body was swollen, throbbing, like a giant cock himself, meant for nothing but fucking and harsh strokes, or fierce bites and slaps.

Nikolai felt Ilya's grip change. His arms left Nikolai's stomach and instead he grabbed his shoulders. Rather than thrusting himself, he began to pull Nikolai against him. Nikolai felt like a rag doll, flopping back and forth on Ilya, letting himself be impaled over and over again.

Ilya's clutch grew hard, almost bruising. Nikolai hissed, and went to swat the hands away, loosen the grip... when he saw a pair of talons digging into each shoulder. Clawing into his skin like a hawk. Nikolai would have shuddered if his body was not being pummelled. He tried to pull away, but the talons tore like nails, pinning him to the spot. This new pain was excruciating, and as Ilya thrust deeper and harder, the claws began to cut. Nikolai screamed as his skin broke; he saw his blood drip down onto the bed.

Did Ilya not *see*? Maybe not, for Ilya grunted and came. He withdrew sharply and let his seed splatter against Nikolai's hole and buttocks. Beneath Ilya, Nikolai whimpered. How could Ilya not see this? Ilya was violent but never so cruel... what the hell *was* he? And all the while, as Nikolai desperately tried to ignore the pain, he bit back his desire to beg for release. He didn't need to come, he told himself.

Until Ilya reached around, and took the stiff cock and balls in his hand again. It was a hand, not talons, but Nikolai still jerked to the touch.

"You will stop stealing my workers?" Ilya asked.

Nikolai gritted his teeth.

But with one squeeze from Ilya, and a clutch from the talons, Nikolai screamed, "Yes!"

Ilya, only taking a couple of hard pumps, made Nikolai spurt all he had into Ilya's hand. Nikolai's tortured body rocked with the orgasm, his vision swam, and he tumbled to the bed when Ilya dropped him without care. He shivered as the talons left his shoulders.

Ilya smeared the mixture of their spunk over Nikolai's stomach, chest and face. Nikolai tensed, but saw to his amazement that there was no blood on Ilya's hands, though his shoulders still stung from the tearing. Ilya dressed quickly and left, closing the door with a slam. At the same time, a loud clap of thunder shook the windows.

Nikolai tentatively brushed his shoulders. To his shock and relief there were no open wounds, though it felt as if his skin had been ripped. No blood on the sheets, either.

Nikolai lay on the bed, pulling the sheets around him. As the thunder outside swept into the distance, he felt small, quite alone as the rain began a gentle patter. He tried not to think about those terrible talons and what they had meant. For he had felt them in his skin as sure as he had felt Ilya's cock inside him.

Ilya

Ilya stroked his beard as he drove back to town, back to his house on the hill. He was satisfied with the outcome of their meeting, but would it be the last time he would have to punish Nikolai? It gave him pause, as he locked the door of his Mustang in the garage; a tiny thrill ran through him to consider the possibility. The way Nikolai's body had drawn out his orgasm... it was unlike anything else he experienced. Even with Dobrana he had never felt such a surge. The power that ran through him, almost all-consuming... he was sure there were moments that he was not himself. Like he became some kind of ravaging beast. Ilya knew well his own temper, the red rushes of rage that sometimes flooded his being. Yet he'd never forgotten himself, lost himself in the moment. With Nikolai... he shuddered, and left the garage.

Inside, Dobrana was on the floor with the youngest child playing with building blocks, while the other two were on the couch, reading like good children. Unnoticed at first, Ilya smiled on the scene. His perfect brood, and another to join them later that year. Dobrana had said she would give him many children. Ilya was glad for that, and glad to for the many proofs of his virility. They were a well-matched couple.

Dobrana looked up from the floor and beamed at him. Ilya nodded, but he did not go to her for a kiss. Instead, he went to the bathroom to wash away the scent of Nikolai.

As he showered, he thought how he made love to Dobrana, the gentleness of it, how easy it was. Not the sharp fucking he'd given Nikolai. Not the digging of his fingers into Nikolai's shoulders...

Ilya's hands froze on his body. He drew them out to look at them, to see his fingers and nails. In the midst of it, he'd felt something else. The power of rearing up over Nikolai, of having him in his control: yes, that was present, but something more too.

An image flashed through his mind. His hands as talons? No. He must have only dreamed that, imagined it. What kind of imagining was it, though?

He looked again. There was no blood under his nails. Only the lingering sense that Nikolai had been under his command.

Ilya shook himself and turned off the water. This was ridiculous to even consider. He was a man of reason and the modern world: superstition was for the weak-minded and backward looking. Beast and giant talons. How preposterous.

Centuries ago...

Veles continued his frantic flight, ducking and weaving through streets and towns. Every so often he would pause at a hiding place, but Perun's eyes were sharp and always found him. Perun flung down his stone arrows. Lightning blazed where those arrows struck.

"Gromovnik!" the people cried, for though his form was not visible to them, they knew his anger and his power.

"The great dragon..." others whispered, knowing that where each bolt fell, Veles had been.

There was a moment's relief for Veles as he hid behind a hedge. He heard Perun's chariot above him, but Perun had not yet seen Veles. Veles leered, content for a time.

Until he overheard a young man speak.

"He chases Veles... have we displeased them both?" the young man asked, his voice frightened.

Veles peered his head above the hedge, enough to see the young man with his arm around a old woman's hunched back, guiding her, trying to run to be out of the storm. But they could not move fast for her back and her hobbled legs. Rain drenched their clothes and matted their hair to their faces.

"The gods are always fickle," the old woman said, her face hardened by the harsh lashes of living. "And we are at their mercy."

On hearing this, Veles curled behind his hedge, stung and moved by their words. This merry chase was bringing destruction, and it was leaving the people desperate.

Veles wondered how much longer he could run.

He eyed Perun in the sky, who had not yet spotted him. Veles made his choice and reared up. He shot back into the air, turning to face Perun.

"Come get me."

And he flew before the next bolt could strike him.

Chapter 4
Cloud

Croatia - one month ago

Ilya

As he drank a glass of cool cherry nectar, Ilya was content. There was a gentle shower of rain falling, just enough to cool the town's sweltering heat. He stood on his large covered balcony, casting his eyes across the town.

He was wearing shorts. He had been on a long run, the kind he only took when Dobrana and the children — all seven of them — were away. They were with his wife's sister and his only duty was to his work and to himself. He had not quite escaped the heavy drops of water before getting indoors. He wore no shirt, and the light rain had mingled with his sweat and begun making droplets in his beard. His body was filled with the satisfying ache of exertion, both tired and energised.

Ilya took another sip of the nectar. This was *his* town: after all he had done for it, he had earned the right to call it that. Since his father had died seven years ago — and after he had grieved — he had at last become president of the chamber of commerce. The factory was entirely his. He also inherited his father's nickname, so he was now the true Thunderer. Not the one only in waiting, creating his small storms, but able to cast his power where it was needed. From where he stood he felt as if he could scoop the whole town up in his arms and embrace it.

The rain began to fall harder. Steady at first, then faster and faster.

It was a beating rhythm, a quickening pace, and it created a stirring in Ilya's belly. His loins began to tense and tingle. Without any prompting from his hand — or from images floating from his own mind, as the rain beat heavier and faster — Ilya's cock hardened.

Ilya dropped his glass. It shattered as Ilya gripped the railing in front of him, as he breathed deeply, trying to will his cock soft again. Why this, why now? But the rain did not cease and his arousal intensified.

Ilya grabbed the underside of his balls. They were like two stones, his cock like the trunk of a tree. He squeezed the whole lot, wanting it covered and free all at once, but the friction of the material and his hand gave no pleasure. Even when he slipped his hand under his shorts, skin to skin, his cock felt numb. Ilya could have roared in frustration. He wanted to stroke himself to climax now. Not later in the bath, nor in bed, but now. Even Dobrana had she been there would not have been able to satisfy this feeling. His body insisted on it, demanded it, wanted it as much as the hot summer earth must have begged for the pouring rain.

His body knew — even as his mind fought it and he cursed himself — exactly how to fix it.

Ilya pulled on sweat pants and a t-shirt and charged out to his Mustang. The wheels spun hard, water splashing the side of the car as Ilya sped into town, into the docks, and strode into Nikolai's office building. He was forced to push employees aside, one man doubling over, before he kicked open the door to Nikolai's office.

Soaking, he stood before Nikolai, who looked up from his work as if Ilya's entrance was expected. A pulse beat through Ilya's cock. He clamped his jaw, hoping to quell it. Nikolai's eyes cast down to his groin and a lascivious smile crossed his face. *Oh, how typical!* Ilya thought, yet without that smile he may have turned and left. He could not ignore that he wanted this from Nikolai, and Nikolai wanted it from him.

God, is this really what I am? Ilya remembered the thrill of Nikolai bent to his will, Nikolai on his knees, Nikolai's cock hard under his clutching hand. Another flush through his groin. *Yes*, he thought, his stomach sinking. *This is what I am.*

Nikolai stood. He sauntered out from behind his desk, twirling the gold chain at his neck around his fingers.

"You have not come to lecture me on my business practices, I see."

Nikolai moved too slowly; Ilya charged at him, grabbed Nikolai's shoulders, and forced him onto his knees. He tugged down his sweat pants just enough, and pressed his cock to Nikolai's face.

"Take it," he said.

Nikolai peered up at Ilya, and said in the sweetest, stickiest voice, "Make me."

Blood rushed down Ilya's cock. The head leaked with a drop of pre-come, and Ilya grabbed a fist-full of Nikolai's hair and shoved him again.

"Suck!"

Nikolai laughed, but he complied, taking Ilya's cock with an obliging yet cheeky wink.

Nikolai's hot, wet mouth was a blessed relief. Ilya groaned, his fingers almost tenderly brushing Nikolai's cheek as Nikolai sucked and sucked. Nikolai's head bobbed up and down on Ilya's cock. Ilya groaned as his cock brushed against the back of Nikolai's throat. Ilya wanted to shove it all the way down his neck, deep into Nikolai, wanted him to take everything he had, swallow him fully. He rolled his hips, urging his cock down more and more.

Nikolai drew back, spittle lingering like string on his lips and the head of Ilya's cock. Ilya clutched Nikolai's hair, jerking his head back so he had to look up at Ilya.

Ilya gritted his teeth. "I didn't say stop."

A dark smile played on Nikolai's lips. He puckered them, kissing the head of Ilya's cock once. Ilya sighed at the gentleness he knew wouldn't last. Outside thunder clapped, accompanied with a lightning flash. Suddenly, the lights in the office went out. The workers cried out in surprise, the sound ringing through the walls. Ilya gasped, eyes out scanning the window as Nikolai licked his still rock-hard dick. Another flash of lightning, another lick. Ilya's eyes cast down and he froze.

Nikolai's tongue was now forked and slender. It flickered along Ilya's shaft, underneath to his balls. His teeth too, before Ilya's eyes, began to grow, until a pair of fangs rested on either side of his cock.

Panic grew in Ilya's chest. Another thunder clap sounded. It shook the building. More gasps from the workers, and this time from Ilya too. The creature that Nikolai was becoming... Ilya should have run, should have thrown Nikolai away, or even killed him. But the moving tongue and the gliding of the fangs rooted Ilya to the spot.

Nikolai drew back from Ilya's cock and laughed. Ilya felt like a hunted animal succumbing to its predator. As if reading his fears, Nikolai grasped Ilya's hips and pushed him on his back. Ilya stared into Nikolai's now glowing golden eyes, paralysed as Nikolai reared up over him, cobra-like, tongue flicking out, almost hissing.

Then Nikolai threw himself over Ilya's body and attacked him with his hands and mouth.

Ilya could do nothing but lie in frozen horror as Nikolai ravaged him, tearing his t-shirt and sweat pants. Nikolai licked his muscles, bit Ilya's nipples hard. He suckled his balls, and roamed all over with his fangs and nails. Ilya wanted to scream as Nikolai found each part of him that reacted either with pleasure or pain, but the sounds were trapped in his throat like an eagle caught in jesses. Nikolai pinned Ilya down — as if terror was not enough to bind Ilya — winding around his arms and legs. It was the undulating coils and squeezes of a snake; fang-like bites appeared on his body. He quavered in and out of the lightning — sometimes it was him, sometimes it was green scales and long, throttling grasps. The snake that Nikolai had become laughed, and that terrible head shot down to Ilya's cock, taking all of it in that hideous mouth. Ilya's felt his stomach turn, even as his cock was sucked with a brutal wetness.

Ilya came, his orgasm dragged from him as if he was tied to a speeding car. Nikolai swallowed most of it, but pulled back at the last, some of it splashing on his chin. He met Ilya's eyes. Again, he chuckled. Ilya stared back, horrified and still aroused all at once.

A flash of lightning, another thunder clap and Ilya found his strength. He pushed away from Nikolai and slammed the door behind him. The end of the storm beat down on him as he sped home, but was a light drizzle when he stumbled into his house.

He locked himself in the bathroom. His body felt as if it had been torn to pieces. But when he looked in the mirror, he only saw his body. No marks. No blood.

Ilya shuddered, brushing his fingers on the perceived wounds. He thought of the fangs, the forked tongue, Nikolai's glowing eyes. What had Nikolai, in that moment, become? Had Ilya simply imagined it? As he'd imagined...

His eyes dropped to his nails. He thought about the hotel room ten years ago, about Nikolai screaming under his hands, his... talons. And now he had been under a striking mouth and a long body that had threatened to suffocate him. Nikolai would not have hesitated to do so.

Ilya's knees gave in, and he slid down the tiled wall to the bathroom floor. What kind of... thing... was he? And if Ilya was that, then what in all of heaven was Nikolai?

Nikolai

In his office, Nikolai guided his hand on his cock, smiling and licking his lips.

Oh that surge of power! He could still taste it; it hung on his tongue like the taste of Ilya's cock. It had tasted like rain and fresh cut grass. It had filled his mouth entirely. Nikolai must have made a perfect 'O' with his lips it was so large. Ilya's cock was like the perfect hunk of meat: tasty, succulent, it created a craving akin to a deep hunger in Nikolai's stomach. The thought of swallowing Ilya whole, consuming him entirely starting with his delicious big cock, had made Nikolai suck with a ferocious wildness. He would have all of Ilya, every last inch of him. He'd grazed his teeth a little along the length, earning a gasp from Ilya. Oh yes, Nikolai had had him perfectly. He'd taken Ilya's balls in hand and ground them together like boulders.

The moment he'd sensed his tongue was something else, he'd almost panicked, gulping hard. But the terrified brightness of Ilya's eyes had said it all: Ilya was more frightened than he. That had tasted better than any cock in his mouth.

Stroking himself, Nikolai thought on how he'd ridden the power, turned and twisted with its rolling force. The sensation of his teeth growing, his features smoothing back. Controlled it, though, for to give in to it would not do; he had to watch Ilya's fear beneath him, had to wound him. Such vengeance it was, the years since Ilya had — almost — torn him to shreds.

Now cupping his balls, Nikolai recalled what he'd done to Ilya's body, how he'd enjoyed hearing his expression of agony entwined with pleasure. Nikolai stroked and squeezed, picturing the man beneath him like a terrified goat. *Yes*, he'd thought, *you can suffer as I have under you.* A thought as delicious as Ilya's hot come that he'd milked with glee.

His own orgasm was not far off. Hearing the sounds of the warehouse, workers talking, the whir of forklifts and moving trucks, Nikolai stalled, sinking his teeth into his lower lip, noting that they were his own once more. His own, as if before he was becoming someone — or something — else. A frightening prospect, but Ilya he knew, so conventional in his thinking, would be more frightened than him.

Whoever, whatever he and Ilya were did not matter. Nikolai increased his rhythm, driving himself to the brink. What mattered was that on most days Ilya could use his size, his pomposity, his brute force to win. But not today. Today, Nikolai knew with lightning clarity as he came, the victory had been his.

Centuries ago...

Perun threw another bolt. He almost shouted with victory, but the lightning only singed the tail of the dragon. Veles kept the same straight track through the sky, but each time Perun came closer to him, Veles would be just out of reach.

Perun snarled. The buck goat pulling his chariot looked back at him, as if to say he could work no harder than he already was. Perun saw that his chariot was cumbersome. He would not catch Veles in it, no matter how keen or how much he drove the goat.

His eagle nipped his ear. Perun turned to it. The eagle ruffled its feathers up and rose on one foot, an itching eagerness, only held back by Perun's will.

"Yes," he said, stroking the eagle. "Of course."

Perun removed his axe and held his gloved hand aloft. The eagle took flight, wings spreading wide and mighty. Then Perun leapt off his chariot, up towards the eagle, before he began to fall. The air flapped on his cloak as he plunged to the earth. The eagle dove, like aiming for prey, and with a shriek pierced Perun's chest. Perun screamed. The eagle burrowed into his body, merging with it, becoming him... and Perun ceased falling. Now he could grasp the air, move with it, be part of it. His arms were now wings, and he beat them wildly, and once again began his pursuit of Veles.

Veles turned once, smiling. But Perun saw the sinewy reptilian lips quiver, and Veles's eyes grow wider, attempting to suggest combat but really serving as a mark of growing fear. Perun saw a smile that was hesitant, trying to mask fear. And Perun gained his distance on him. They kept flying and diving, weaving around mountaintops, through clouds, until they were over a lake. Perun was right on Veles' tail. Veles cried out and ducked away, but Perun curved his wings to match him. They were flying in tandem now.

It was time. Perun reached for Veles, talons almost breaking with the strain. He was almost within his grasp. Only a little further...

Croatia - three days ago

One would think, Ilya seethed, *that a half open shirt was not appropriate for a meeting of the chamber of commerce.* Nikolai clearly disagreed, practically inviting gazes as he brushed his fingers down his chest that was boyishly slim and girlishly enticing.

Could no one else see what a reptile he was? Could they not see the fangs in his mouth, that beneath that smooth chest were green, slippery scales? No. No one saw anything but Nikolai the cunning businessman with some eccentricities and a taste for stocky men. The fools!

But Ilya had no strength to point this out. Since their last — encounter — Ilya had wandered through work and home and town with a listless step, unfocussed, as if a fog drenched in sleeping draughts had fallen over him. Dobrana had demanded to know what was wrong, threatening to take the children away if he failed to give them and her the attention they deserved. Worse though, a quiet rumour had spread that he and Nikolai had fought, that their rivalry had come to physical blows and Nikolai had won.

Ilya was only grateful that the true nature of their battle had remained secret. All the rest being true, however, made him feel lower than he'd ever been.

Normally he'd chair these meetings, but today he'd waved everything to the secretary, a fastidious middle-aged man with the kind of attention to detail Ilya did not possess. It was a good working relationship in that regard.

The secretary cleared his throat. "We have before us applications for new businesses in town. As usual the town council has allowed us to vet the applications, and we shall consider each of them in turn. This meeting shall be used to discuss them, and we will vote at the next one."

They went through the applications. Ilya flipped the pages over. The other members offered their opinions, then eyed him for guidance, but he found himself murmuring things like, "Your view is quite correct," or, "That sounds reasonable." He had little energy to do otherwise. He paid no heed to the uncertain glances the men exchanged — and especially not to Nikolai's smirking. They could surely make decisions without his views from time to time.

When they came to the last one, he started to nod, when the secretary said,

"Um... Ilya, have you read this one carefully?"

Ilya looked at his secretary askance for questioning his capacity to read. The secretary though seemed genuinely concerned.

Ilya sighed. "Which one?"

"The one from Mishka Samovic? For his club?"

Ilya held the paper up, peering at it, the words not registering. "What is the nature of the club?"

The secretary coughed. "It is, ah... a sex club, Ilya."

Chapter 5
Storm

The black ink suddenly burned on the page, bright as suns. Clarity came to Ilya like a flash of lightning. No. No, this would not do in his town at all. And this Mishka wanted it on the promenade? Right where everyone could see it! Ilya would not let this happen.

A low chuckle came from Ilya's left. He swerved his eyes to Nikolai, who leaned back in his chair, flicking his pen around his fingers.

"And what is your opinion of this club, Nikolai?"

"Oh, I'm all in favour of it."

Ilya stared at Nikolai. "It would compete with your own night-club."

"I welcome a battle. It makes one stronger." Nikolai licked his lower lip, and Ilya suspected had they been alone he would have winked too.

Ilya straightened his back, the vigour returning after its month-long absence. "Well, I'm sure that no one else agrees with you." He turned to the rest of the chamber. "Am I right?"

The secretary and two others nodded emphatically. Four more, on the other hand, shifted in their seats or began to play with their papers. Ilya glared at the one closest to him.

"Am I right?" he repeated.

The man shrugged. "Well, Ilya… I can see the merits in such a club. We do get all kinds of visitors here, and our tourism industry is growing rapidly."

"Yes," one said. "I agree. It… fills a gap, so to speak."

"Is it not filled by Nikolai's club?" Ilya said through his teeth.

The third piped up. "I believe this one will cater to more specific interests..." His voice trailed off as Ilya glared, not wishing to hear anything about those 'specific interests.'

"I agree that we need to concentrate on the tourist industry," Ilya said. "But are we looking to attract perverts!"

All eyes shifted to Nikolai, who only grinned as if pervert was a compliment.

"There is money to be made from sex," Nikolai said. "There always has been."

If Ilya could have, he'd have launched himself across the table and slapped Nikolai across the face.

They argued for sometime. Or rather, Ilya and his supporters made their emphatic case, while the others slipped and slid, bleating about money and attracting more people. *Have they lost the point about principles!* Ilya thought. With a vote of five to four, the application would be accepted. He expected this from Nikolai, but not the others.

Ilya smacked his fist on the table. "This is getting us nowhere. We are not voting today, so this will give all of us," he cast his eyes across those who supported the application, "time to reconsider our positions."

The members of the chamber glanced at each other, but there was, as far as Ilya could see, no shift in them at all.

The meeting continued, and when it was done the members packed up and started to leave. Nikolai paused at the door to chat with one of his fellow supporters. He occasionally glanced back at Ilya with an expression of assured victory.

Ilya beckoned the secretary down so to speak to him in a low whisper. "Find out what's going on. Those men would not defy me but for very good reason."

The secretary nodded. "Of course."

Ilya met Nikolai's eyes again. Nikolai ran his tongue over his teeth and slinked away. Ilya suppressed a flinch, but for the first time in a month, his anger had begun to boil again.

Croatia - present day...

Nikolai

When Nikolai had hired Risto, it was as much for his body, taut with muscle, as it was for his ability to protect Nikolai. That he wasn't averse to fucking Nikolai on occasion was a rather tasty bonus.

But the sex was never like it had been with Ilya. Because unlike the others to whom he'd happily given himself over to be dominated, he wanted to beat Ilya at this game. He had once, and he was determined that he would again.

Ilya had broken into Nikolai's house in his threatening way, flung his accusations at Nikolai about the bribes. Of course they had been true and Nikolai did not feel the slightest guilt. Besides, he had mostly accepted them in order to see how Ilya would react. And Ilya had reacted beautifully, looking hilarious standing on his moral high ground, trying to coax Nikolai every way he knew. Nikolai had goaded, teased, flirted, watching Ilya's fury grow. The last straw had come when Ilya demanded that Nikolai obey him. How dare he?

Nikolai leapt to his feet. "Make me."

Ilya's face darkened. Nikolai saw in it his rage and desire, so different and yet one and the same.

Then Ilya breathed, "I will."

Their bodies smashed together like the claps of thunder outside.

Ilya clasped Nikolai's buttocks, digging his fingers in deeply. Nikolai moaned, and tugged down on Ilya's beard until he screamed.

Ilya pulled back just an inch from Nikolai.

"Stop taking the money from Mishka," he whispered against Nikolai's mouth.

Nikolai rolled his hips, his cock rubbing against Ilya's thighs. He sniggered, and whispered back,

"No."

Ilya pushed Nikolai to the floor. Nikolai winced as lightning flashed through the room.

Ilya towered above him. "Why do you keep disobeying me?"

"I am not yours to control."

"You will hurt the town if you continue with your ways."

Nikolai narrowed his eyes, glaring up at Ilya. "This is not to protect the town. This is for your pride!"

Ilya roared, and thunder shook the house. He grabbed Nikolai's collar, hauled him off his feet, bringing them nose-to-nose.

"Nikolai, you will make me do this?"

Nikolai spat in Ilya's face. The gob hit Ilya's cheek, sat like a wet blob.

"Do your worst."

Lightning filled the room. Ilya reached between Nikolai's legs, and twisted...

...While above the lake, Perun made his final stretch, and at last, he snagged Veles' scales.

Nikolai cried out, beat back at Ilya, the pain pure and intense... *and Veles screamed as Perun's talons tore as his scales.*

Ilya latched his mouth onto Nikolai's throat. Nikolai trembled, the searing hot mouth demanding. His engorged erection grew in Ilya's hand.

Ilya muttered against his neck, "You've always been a slut."

Perun twisted Veles to face him. "You will not escape me."

With Ilya's hand clawing at him, Nikolai remembered being helpless beneath Ilya's talons. A pulse of fear transmuted to ferocious rage, and he recalled his reptilian self. This time, when the power ran through him, he welcomed it and let it do as it will.

Nikolai hissed, and the change began.

Ilya... and Nikolai

Ilya gasped. Nikolai's pupils elongated, eyes glowed gold. Ilya stared into those eyes, remembering their sinister seductive gaze in the office. Now, seeing their enraged heat, all the justification of his hatred for Nikolai scorched through his body.

"Snake," Ilya said.

"Dragon," Perun said.

"Yes." Nikolai's voice was not his own.

Nikolai's body began to mould against his like molten clay. Ilya tried to keep his hold, but because of Nikolai's shifting form, his hands could not hold the scales that were sliding away from him...

Veles reeled his body, turning this way and that, but Perun dug his claws in deeper. Then Veles, seeing Perun's sleek feathers, shot upwards, and began...

...to coil around him.

Nikolai saw the horror in Ilya's face, knowing he was being crushed in Nikolai's grip. Nikolai arched around to lick Ilya's cheek, mockingly. The bastard would not win this time. Not this time!

Ilya stood paralysed, fearing for a moment that his life would be crushed out of him. Something though boiled in his chest, and he knew. There had always been a monster waiting beneath his skin. He had long denied it, even fought it. Now, as Nikolai threatened to squeeze him to death, incandescent rage overtook him. An ancient rage he could not ignore, and he knew to defeat Nikolai he must embrace it.

Ilya's beard receded. Coppery feathers ruffled down his chest. His mouth and nose merged and extend, and a giant beak formed as eagle eyes blinked into existence.

And Perun beat his wings as Veles the dragon tried to ensnare him in a hold. He dug his claws in harder...

...and Ilya's hands became talons. They turned on Nikolai, hooking into his scales. Nikolai threw his head back with a loud hissing cry. He curled his neck back and struck Ilya's feathery chest, sinking his fangs in. But as he did so he loosened his grip and Ilya's newly formed wings beat, forcing Nikolai to unfurl from him.

Thunder rocked the whole house, and with the next burst of lightning, the roof opened up. Rain poured into the green room, covering both of them as they both struck at each other, the assault beginning anew.

With his enormous claws, Ilya grabbed for Nikolai. They caught the snake, and Ilya lifted his wings, carrying them both into the air. Nikolai hissed and thrashed against Ilya, fangs glinting in the lightning. Ilya now began to peck, and Nikolai twisted and rolled, each strike sending a sharp pain through his whole body. There was no pleasure now: only the battle, only the fight.

Nikolai retaliated...

Veles sunk his fangs into Perun's flesh...

...and Ilya shrieked. The snake was latched onto him, using his body as leverage to once again try and coil around him. Ilya beat his wings and avoided Nikolai.

They drew higher in the air, closer to the roaring thunder and the lightning infected clouds. As did Perun and Veles. Beneath them, the town, the land, all that lay in their domain and power bore the brunt of the beating rain and rocking thunder, the lightning strikes and the howling winds. In the turbulent air they fought and turned and rolled. Ilya and Nikolai, Perun and Veles.

At last Perun and Ilya delivered a final mighty blow to the dragon and the snake's head. Nikolai and Veles screamed, and they fell, coiling and twirling through the thunderous sky. Veles hit the water with a mighty splash, and with a heavy thump Nikolai landed onto his carpet.

The roof closed in again. Ilya, now himself once more, stood over Nikolai's body. Their shirts were torn. Both of them were soaked with rain, as was the whole jungle of a room. Nikolai's eyes were open, but he wasn't moving, except for a small rise and fall of his chest.

"Perun..." he breathed.

Ilya swallowed. "Veles."

The words, their true names, hung heavy in the wet air.

Nikolai spoke again with a low croak but steady certainty. "This is what we always have been."

Ilya trembled, but only for a moment. He shook it off and said, "Yes. Always."

Nikolai grinned. "You accept it at last."

Nikolai tried to lift himself up, but collapsed back down. No, he'd wait a little longer. He'd had dragon's wings once and he would find them again. He remembered the fields and the sea below him, riding the air as the windsurfers did the waves. And he remembered the dark place, his home in the underworld in the roots of a great tree.

"How fitting," he said, and smiled.

Ilya frowned. "You always knew?"

"Not everything... but there was always more to us than you ever wanted to know, Perun."

Ilya crouched, flexing his fingers that were no longer talons, recalling how they felt reaching and straining for the dragon-snake, the sensation of lightning in his hands, the thunder— actual thunder—

boiling in the sky behind him. This was him, this ancient god. A rare sensation of humility settled over him. He'd always known he had a duty to fill in this world, and there was none heavier than this.

But he was no longer riding a chariot in the clouds. Nikolai lying before him was a man, not a dragon.

He bent down to Nikolai's ear. "Cease your mischief, and refuse Mishka's money."

Ilya stood and started to leave, when Nikolai said,

"You have not won, Perun... Ilya..."

Or whatever we should call ourselves now.

Ilya turned back, meeting Nikolai's eyes. "But I have, Nikolai... Veles... as I always will."

Nikolai laughed, then winced, for laughter hurt his chest. "So you say, Gromovnik. So you say."

Ilya left Nikolai on the floor. He walked slowly back to his Mustang, holding himself like royal china: fragile but filled with dignity. Outside, the thunderstorm had rocked the harbour. There was no one around, but now — with only the lightest of rains — the town was quiet, peaceful even.

Nikolai eventually stood with a shaky step. He went to check on Risto and to find Mishka's phone number.

Meanwhile, Veles burrowed into the earth beneath the lake. He slunk through the soil, past the dirt and the worms, until once again he was back at his the oak tree. The roots shifted a little, and Veles knew that Perun was perching on the branches above.

Perun puffed up his feathers, proud that at last his task was accomplished, and bellowed in a grand voice, "You go to the earth and you stay there!"

Veles sniggered. He coiled around himself, around the roots of the great tree. His wounds gaped with each breath. It would take some time for the bites and the cuts to heal, for his spent essence to grow inside him once more. How long before he emerged again he did not know, but surely he would.

And the fight would begin anew.

As it always had. As it always would.

Even when gods die, they are reborn in many ways. When the disciples of Christ spread the word into the Slavic lands, the old gods fractured, splintered into forms so they bore new names and old habits. With the end of the worship of Perun, the dragon-slayer St George took on his role, but more strikingly the chariot-riding St Elijah (Ilya), became the new Gromovnik, the Thunderer. Meanwhile, Veles, with his many facets and roles as a god, morphed into the Devil (so often dragon-like in modern day perception), St Blaise, and also St Nicholas (Nicolai), a gift-giving and sometimes trickster saint, whose rivalry with St Elijah still appears in Slavic folktales today.

If you enjoyed this story, you can discuss it with other readers
and the author at the *Gods Among Men* story page
at http://forbiddenfiction.com/library/story/JB1-1.000192.

The Fair, Laudanum, and Passion

Madeleine Swann

Madeleine Swann has had short stories published in *The Big Book of Bizarro*, Analogpress.net and ForbiddenFiction.com and writes in various forms from her home in deepest, darkest Essex, England. She has also had articles published in various magazines including *Bizarre*, ranging in topic from church restorations to the toe wrestling championships, and performs as part of comedy group Braintree Ways.

The Fair, Laudanum, and Passion

Gabe pulled her through the crowds past tall, brightly lit booths, each sign at the entrance proclaiming a lurid horror within.

"Abraham the Half-Man," roared one of the moustachioed barkers, his eyes wide with frenzy as he beckoned his customers inside, "the eighth wonder of the world!"

Ettie saw the carnival poster on Blackfriars Road in London. "Wiley's World of Wonders," it screamed, "New Year's Day of 1880, one day only." She hopped up and down despite the weight of her bustle, but one glance at Gabe's arched black eyebrow sank her excitement. A familiar half smile crossed his thin face. He leaned his tall frame over her small one and smoothed the ends of her light brown hair.

"As a new partner at Bradford's, I'm expected to keep up appearances," he chided gently. "As my wife, you will be expected to purchase ball gowns and hold parlour soirees. We simply haven't the time or expense for such frivolity." Ettie followed him meekly, but after a few steps he replied. "Look at your pout; it's as if a child was told she could no longer play with a doll. Perhaps it would do us good to be seen enjoying ourselves. Very well my dear, we shall go. Now, to the boutique for my new waistcoat."

And go they did. Clowns made balloon animals and contortionists stretched on a plinth while the sideshow tents lurked from the borders of the melee. Ettie pursed her lips against the roughness of her husband's grip, smiling forcedly when he shot her a shrewd look; she could almost hear him denounce the funfair's claims of terror. As he said often, he was a travelled man about town while Ettie's parents had been furiously protective after her bout of cholera.

She glanced nervously at signs for two-headed calves and dog-faced boys, the bellows from their terrible wardens and the squeals from the crowds pervading the air.

"You will soon see, my dear, these folk are nothing but liars and thieves," said Gabe. "Stay close to me; this is no place for a woman alone."

Ettie paused to watch fire-breathers in Indian dress spouting flames higher and higher, while others spun figures of eight against the darkening sky with long burning sticks. A small crowd gathered to watch a young girl as she lay on her front on the miniature stage, contorting her legs from behind and placing her feet beside her head. The ladies squealed in delighted outrage when she tipped them a lascivious wink.

"They live for this," said Gabe derisively, "a flash of colour and sulphur in their magnolia tea-room existences. They'll go home and tell their friends how awful it is, over and over as they savour the details." Ettie sighed heavily, wishing they could enjoy themselves for once.

"Come see the world-famous Great Ra-mi, Sword Swallower extraordinaire. You will not believe your own eyes!" boomed the nearest barker. Ettie turned to Gabe, who elaborately checked the time on his gold chain pocket watch. Ettie wanted to scream, to weep with frustration, but she dutifully waited for him to place it neatly back in his frock coat.

"Very well, my dear," he said ponderously, "we shall go inside and see what chicanery awaits us." Ettie breathed in as they were ushered into the tent, filling herself with excitement.

The cheap grease lamps cast everything in a smoky red glow and they were ushered to the back to join a small crowd. A lady in a fussy lilac dress told all who listened about the best flowers to plant in London, her voice a touch too shrill for relaxed chatter.

"Of course, roses look best against one of Charles Frederick Worth's dresses; he truly is a master," she simpered until a movement forced her into silence. The smartly dressed man appearing from the back of the tent was of slender, wiry build, his brown moustache jauntily upturned in the corners. His dark eyes glinted with promises of mischief.

"Ladies and gentlemen, boys and girls," announced the barker, "for you the Great Ra-mi shall perform this act so dangerous, so ter-rifying, I must ask you to leave if you are at all faint of heart." Despite ripples of concern, everyone stayed put.

"And now, in front of your very eyes, The Great Ra-mi will at-tempt to swallow this very sword!"

Ettie's lilac-gloved hand flew to her mouth in shock; she heard a dismissive snort from Gabe.

"These people have been rehearsing and performing such acts for many years. The likelihood of his death is rather minimal," he mut-tered.

The Great Ra-mi pulled an apple from his pocket, offering it to the crowd to touch.

"As you can see," he said with a warm smile, "this is a regular apple." With that he placed it onto the floor and sliced downwards, chopping it in two. The crowd gasped. He raised the sword above his head, sharpened tip pointing downwards. Silence spread through the crowd and even Gabe was transfixed. The Great Ra-mi opened his gullet and allowed the thick steel to slide down into his gullet.

"Oh my," wailed the chattering lady. The crowd was mesmerised. Down and down it went and was removed with a flourish, his eyes barely watering. Ettie applauded with the others, a strange sensation tickling her hardening nipples and the secret crevices between her legs. The oddness of him, the contrast between him and Gabe's staid pompousness intrigued her.

To her dismay The Great Ra-mi didn't pay Ettie any special at-tention, and as they filed out she tried to ignore the disappointment weighing on her chest.

"Well, that was better than expected," Gabe said. "Now, please can we make our way out of this place?"

"Yes, Gabe," said Ettie.

They wandered towards the exit only to be confronted with a clown selling candy floss, his eyes black crosses and his mouth a hu-mourless grin.

"Right," muttered Gabe, his mouth pinched and eyebrows rigid. Ettie was silent as they tried another way, no street signs visible.

"Why do we not ask somebody?" Ettie suggested gently as they almost knocked into a man thrusting swords into a tiny box.

"I come to London every day. I have no need to ask for directions like some fresh-faced apprentice."

"Yes, I am aware," soothed Ettie, "but it is quite impossible for us to know where we are amongst this mayhem."

"Of course it is difficult," Gabe smiled reassuringly, "my little muffin barely knows what's at the end of the road. Take my arm; we can't have you getting frightened." Ettie reached out as a large family crashed between them. She wandered past them, hoping to reach the end of their group and re-join her husband. When she arrived at the expected spot, however, he wasn't there.

Raising her hand to her throat Ettie tried to quieten her jittering heartbeat. She described Gabe to various people and was met with the same blank look. She crashed through families and chaperoned sweethearts, their voices reaching a furious pitch until she knew she had to hide from the loudness around her. She needed a few minutes to be calm, she told herself, before she found her husband. If Gabe knew she was having one of her hysterical moments he would be furious. She couldn't bear the doctor's disapproving appraisals or his courses of phosphates. The bitter liquid made her feel as though she were in a different room to everyone else.

Patches of sweat soaked her gloves when she reached a wooden, green painted building, almost tripping on a board leaning against the door. She kicked it out of the way and threw herself into the quiet safety inside. She tiptoed up the stairs, her chest tightening again when the steps slanted madly to the left. Gripping tightly onto the rail, she reached a long hallway where rows of mirrors hung from dusty, attic-scented walls. The screams and laughter faded as she wandered down the darkening corridor, the tapping of her shoes echoing loudly.

Her reflection in the mirror beside her stretched upwards to impossible heights, and in the next her body was compressed into a squat troll. Her heart skipped again, but instead of screaming and wailing for help she began to giggle. She placed a hand over her mouth to regain composure but couldn't stop, and when she saw herself with great long legs and a tiny body she cackled like an old maid until her eyes watered.

Shuffling on she noticed a door slightly ajar and pushed it, finding herself standing in a sparse room containing five threadbare armchairs. Seated in one was a woman she'd seen handling snakes. Her flowing blue dress was almost thin enough to be scandalous and barely covered her toothpick legs, and knots made a bird's nest of her thick black hair. Next to her the strongman casually filled a pipe. His eastern outfit sparkled while his muscles and bald head glowed under the flickering light of a candle lantern. In another chair sat the Great Ra-mi, frock coat draped on the seat behind him and white shirt untucked. The mischief had gone from his brown eyes; he lightly tugged the end of his moustache in what seemed an action of habit. Ettie realised at once she wasn't supposed to be in there and her corset seemed to tighten.

"Hello?" said the strongman, as all eyes turned to her.

"I am terribly sorry, I must have – well, I shall be off," she said, turning back to the corridor.

"Is anybody with you?" asked The Great Ra-mi sharply.

"N-no," she replied, immediately wishing she had lied.

"Then there is no need for you to go," he said, rising from his seat. "We put a sign outside closing the Funhouse after a lady twisted her ankle, but no harm has been done," he smiled easily.

Dust rose when Ettie sat in the armchair, specks floating in front of her. She felt she ought to speak but had no conversation for the circumstance.

"Did you truly swallow that sword, Great Ra-mi?" asked Ettie eventually, and the snake-girl snorted with laughter.

"His name's Art," she said in a coarse East End voice.

"Pleased to meet you," Art took her hand. Ettie noticed a long metal nail and hammer on a table beside him. "Oh," he gestured vaguely, "I shall be hammering that into my nostril later. It's quite safe," he assured hurriedly, "it merely enters the nasal cavity here," he said, pointing to a spot near the bridge of his nose.

"Oh, I see," said Ettie, at once repelled and fascinated.

"Why not have some brandy with us?" he offered eagerly, seemingly concerned she was frightened.

"Good idea," said the snake-girl, "I've got a bottle of Laudanum in my bag. We should add some." The strongman cheered.

"Heathens," joked Art. "You can just have straight brandy if you would prefer," he said, turning to Ettie.

"No," she replied, drawing a shocked glance. "I shall have some. A small glass," she corrected herself hurriedly. Her words filled her with a delirious freedom, the like of which she had never experienced. It felt like the most outrageous thing anybody had ever done. She reasoned the hours spent lighting the gas-lamps against the dark, waiting for Gabe to shuffle indoors with the reek of bordellos and opium dens oozing from his coat, had earned her the right to taste his world.

"Here you are," said the snake-girl after slopping the contents of a bottle into glasses of amber liquid. "My name's Penny."

The liquid burned, and Ettie's eyes watered for the second time that day. Art shrugged and accepted a glass himself, and for a time they chatted amiably. As the strongman, Gus, explained that the weights were not as heavy as some were led to believe, Ettie noticed the beautiful way the dust floated in the candlelight. A silence followed.

"I have always wanted," said Gus eventually, his voice soft and thoughtful, "to be a voyeur, or to instigate a group situation."

Ettie almost choked, too shocked to speak.

Penny laughed, "This again. You should stop talking about it and just do it."

Ettie glanced at Art, who shifted uncomfortably in his seat.

"Perhaps I will," said Gus petulantly.

"Very well, then do so," replied Penny provokingly.

Gus lowered himself to the ground in front of Penny. Ettie's mouth opened in horror when she realised what he was going to do. She had seen it in the pictures in Gabe's secret books but had never thought of it as something people truly did. Penny giggled self-consciously and opened her legs for him. Ettie realised her own breath was quickening as Gus lifted Penny's skirts to remove her undergarments. She helped him, sighing deeply when his lips made contact with her private ones. The embarrassment seemed to leave her as she opened her legs wider, making soft appreciative noises. She pulled her arms free of her dress, exposing her breasts and hard nipples. Ettie hoped her sharp intake of breath was inaudible, realising she was hot and wet between her legs.

She glanced at Art as Penny bucked against Gus's face, her moaning increasing. Ettie experienced another surge of heat and confusion when she saw the bulge straining against Art's trousers, his knuckles turning white as he gripped the arms of his chair. She knew she should be running from them in horror, shrieking for her husband, but she didn't want to move. Her heart tightened when Penny turned her brown eyes to her, rising from the chair and discarding her dress completely. Her body, though small, was an acre of exposed flesh to Ettie; a vast expanse of nudity glowing white under the candlelight.

"You should join me," she whispered.

Ettie opened her mouth to refuse, to tell them she was leaving, and found herself unbuttoning her blouse. Her hands shook with excitement and she flung the gloves as far as she could throw. Penny slowly untied her corset and Ettie took a great breath in, dizzy with weightlessness. When Penny helped her step free of her skirts and long underwear she saw her thighs were slick with wetness. All three pairs of eyes flicked over her appreciatively.

Ettie was uncertain of her next move, her arms hanging limply at her sides, when Penny leaned in to kiss her, her hair smelling of sandalwood. Ettie thought kissing a girl felt much less insistent than kissing a man, the lips softer and gentler. The quick motion of Gus stroking himself caught her eye and instinctively she placed a hand near her private lips. Penny turned her attentions to Art, kneeling to the floor and pulling at his trousers until he was free. His erection sprang forward and she took the shaft into her mouth, a soft moan escaping his lips.

Ettie had never done such a thing for Gabe, but now Penny was motioning for her to take charge. Nervously, Ettie sank down next to Penny and tried to copy her, the eagerness plain in Art's face. The scent of his soap was laced with sweat, and his blood pulsed as she gently licked around the head. His hand gripped her shoulder as she sucked downwards, taking in as much as she was able. Before rising she flicked her tongue upwards, proud of the satisfaction she was giving him.

As she gently rubbed her hand along his shaft she glimpsed Penny guide Gus to the floor, laying him on his back and lowering herself onto him. Gus gave a great gasp and reached for her hips, pulling her up and down.

Her pupils dilated and cheeks red with pleasure, Penny beckoned to Ettie. When she crawled nearer Penny took her hand and placed it over her breast, which Ettie gripped gently with wonder and tweaked the hard brown nipples. Growing in confidence, she traced her fingertips down to Penny's private lips as they rose and fell over Gus. Wondering if Penny had the same spot between her legs that felt good when rubbed, Ettie tickled her wetness, her question answered when the other girl bit her lip and sighed. As Ettie circled the hardening nodule, Penny's breathing quickened and her hips bucked against her fingertip as Gus gripped her tightly.

"Is that good?" Ettie asked her.

"Yes," Penny sighed.

Art stroked his shaft as Penny cried out, her face reddening and body shuddering. Gus pumped hard inside her and Penny leaned down to him, her hair covering their faces.

Ettie turned back to Art, her own private lips aching for attention. Too shy to speak, she opened her legs as a hint. He kneeled to the ground, his lips apart and pupils large, their eyes catching each other self-consciously. His fingers sought her private lips and she moaned with relief, goose-bumps rising over her skin. She looped her hands behind his neck and wrapped her legs around him, pressing herself against his hot bare skin and sliding onto his erection. "Oh," she moaned, needles of sensation flooding her body. Looking directly into his face she saw his red flush and furrowed brow, his excitement inducing fresh waves of pleasure in her. The sounds of Penny and Gus's moaning enveloped her as Art's length stroked her from inside, and she dug her teeth and nails into his shoulders to keep him there, keep him a part of her.

All shyness gone, Ettie freed herself from him and turned away, meeting the eyes of Penny as she writhed on top of Gus. Ettie leaned forwards, the floorboards hard against her hands and knees, waiting and praying she hadn't gone too far, that she hadn't shocked him. With relief she felt him wrap one arm around her waist as he fumbled to guide himself in, gasping as he pushed himself deep. His tip stroked her innermost point, her furthest hidden reaches. Penny's eyes were on her as Ettie grabbed Art's hand and led it to her private lips, circling the nodule with his finger until he understood. She rocked against him as the heat and the wetness built higher and higher, his shaft growing more and more insistent. She kept her eyes on Penny as Gus's hands slid from her hips to her breasts, and in turn Penny watched them.

Ettie's nipples tightened and the fire spread from her groin upwards, and at the same time Penny's moans deepened. Ettie knew the other girl was reaching her peak and she tried to hold hers, to hang on until they could reach it together. Penny's brow furrowed and Ettie knew she couldn't hold back the release, and soon it spread from her groin throughout her body and flooding her brain as she stiffened and cried out. When she was still, Art pushed against her harder than before, her body more pleasantly sensitive to him, until he moaned his last and loudest.

His seed tickled her inside and she felt him pulse until his body became a heavy weight. They lay down together on the wooden floor, the scent of the old chairs and their sex mixing with the dust. She half expected Art to cast her aside like the women in the cautionary books she had read, but instead he ran his fingers gently over her skin. Already she began to form the words of her farewell letter to Gabe. She felt a small twinge, reminding herself the man she thought she married never truly existed.

The following year, the tents were up by dusk when the first curious locals drifted in. A few performers were changing their clothes and rehearsing as Ettie sighed contentedly by the ticket booths.

"You'd better stay wake if you're to sell those," said Art, his voice making her jump.

"I was lost in my own world," she laughed, embracing him. His skin still smelled of soap.

"The clowns will have a difficult time tonight; Markus' ankle hasn't healed," said Art pensively.

"Oh dear," said Ettie, "tell him to put it in a pail of ice." Art nodded and turned to leave. "Oh," called Ettie, "remind Penny she's to teach me more of the snake-dancing tomorrow." Art nodded.

"Oh, and Art," she called again, a smile forming at the corner of her lips, "tell her we shall see her later." As she watched him tip his hat and saunter away, she hummed a merry tune.

If you enjoyed this story, you can discuss it with other readers and the author at the *The Fair, Laudanum, and Passion* story page at http://forbiddenfiction.com/library/story/MS1-1.000061.

About the Publisher

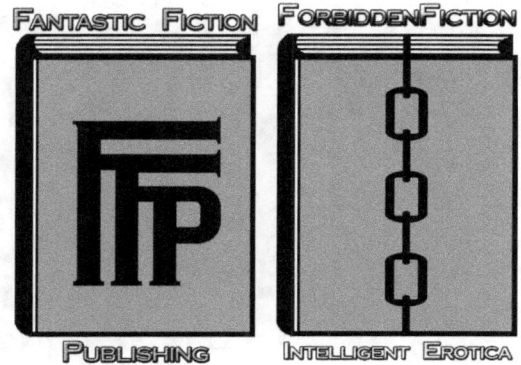

ForbiddenFiction.com is a publisher devoted to writing that breaks the boundaries of original erotic fiction. Our stories combine intense sexuality with quality writing. Stories at ForbiddenFiction.com not only arouse readers through sensations, but also engage them emotionally and mentally through storytelling as well-crafted as the sex is hot.

ForbiddenFiction.com is also designed to be a social reading environment. You'll have fun even if just reading the latest post each day, yet you will have the chance for so much more. Readers and authors can be part of ongoing discussions of specific works and individual authors as well as more general topics.

Sign up for a FREE Membership today at ForbiddenFiction.com

www.ingramcontent.com/pod-product-compliance
Lightning Source LLC
Chambersburg PA
CBHW070120260626
47160CB00004B/1560